"Something funny?"

he asked coldly.

Her lips quirked and the laughter won. At the dark look in his eyes, she controlled her mirth hastily, however, and shook her head. "I'm only glad to know my arrival isn't interfering with your love life, that's all," she said in a voice that quavered with enjoyment.

"Don't worry about that," Matt snapped. "That'll never happen, I assure you. You may have fifty-one percent of my business, but you'll never have even one percent of my personal life."

Her amusement vanished. "You're so bad tempered, I wouldn't want it," she countered. "I'm only a bit surprised to hear you making a date."

Matt sneered at her. "Why? Am I so unattractive you think I can't get a date?"

"Oh, now, come *on*," she shot back. "If that's a hint for me to stroke your ego, forget it. I'm sure you're very well aware of your effect on women.

Dear Reader,

Spellbinders! That's what we're striving for. The editors at Silhouette are determined to capture your imagination and win your heart with every single book we publish. Each month, six Special Editions are chosen with *you* in mind.

Our authors are our inspiration. Writers such as Nora Roberts, Tracy Sinclair, Kathleen Eagle, Carole Halston and Linda Howard—to name but a few—are masters at creating endearing characters and heart-rending love stories. Their characters are everyday people—just like you and me—whose lives have been touched by love, whose dream and desire suddenly comes true!

So find a cozy, quiet place to read, and create your own special moment with a Silhouette Special Edition.

Sincerely,

Rosalind Noonan
Senior Editor
SILHOUETTE BOOKS

SONDRA STANFORD
Equal Shares

Silhouette Special Edition

Published by Silhouette Books New York

America's Publisher of Contemporary Romance

SILHOUETTE BOOKS
300 East 42nd St., New York, N.Y. 10017

ISBN: 0-373-09326-8

First Silhouette Books printing August 1986

America's Publisher of Contemporary Romance

Printed in the U.S.A.

Books by Sondra Stanford

Silhouette Romance

Golden Tide #6
Shadow of Love #25
Storm's End #35
No Trespassing #46
Long Winter's Night #58
And Then Came Dawn #88
Yesterday's Shadow #100
Whisper Wind #112
Tarnished Vows #131

Silhouette Special Edition

Silver Mist #7
Magnolia Moon #37
Sun Lover #55
Love's Gentle Chains #91
The Heart Knows Best #161
For All Time #187
A Corner of Heaven #210
Cupid's Task #248
Bird in Flight #292
Equal Shares #326

SONDRA STANFORD

wrote advertising copy before trying her hand at romance fiction. Also an artist, she enjoys attending arts-and-crafts shows and browsing at flea markets. Sondra and her husband live happily with their two children in Corpus Christi, Texas.

Chapter One

The summer house looked the same as ever, bringing back memories of childhood vacations—of damp bathing suits, berry-brown skin, seashells and sand caught between her toes. How cruelly deceptive it had all been, lulling a little girl into the mistaken expectation that life would always be so kind, so love filled, so comfortable and so secure.

The young woman who stepped out of the car knew better. She had long since lost her innocent faith in happiness. She had also outgrown pleasant holidays on the south Texas coast. This time she had not come for the rest and recreation, but because the hard, incomprehensible obstinacy of one man had left her no alternative. He was obviously a crook and a scoundrel, trying to take advantage of her, and she was here to see that he didn't get away with it.

Golden-brown eyes behind dark sunglasses took in the gray-weathered cedar house on stilts, the dark-brown storm shutters at the windows, the sweeping lawn with gnarled, twisted live oak trees and the thick borders of white and pink oleander bushes. Beneath the shelter of the house was her father's motorboat, shrouded by protective canvas, and beyond the house, the sparkling blue waters of Copano Bay. Although it had been nine years since she'd last been here, nothing seemed changed. Even the crookedly lettered, wood-burned sign reading Main Hideaway, which she'd made herself at age twelve for Father's Day, was still tacked on the wall beside the outside staircase.

Shannon Edwards's throat constricted with grief. The recent loss of her father was still so fresh, the wound so raw. Today she felt the void he'd left more keenly than ever. This had been the place he'd loved so much. It seemed almost a sacrilege for her to be here without him.

She had never known her mother, who had died when she'd been an infant. As a result, Shannon and her father had been exceptionally close. In all of her twenty-six years he'd always been her bulwark, there to lean on when she'd needed him, as she had so desperately a few years ago. Without him now, she felt abandoned, cut adrift. It still seemed impossible that Charlie Main, who'd seemed the picture of health, should have died so unexpectedly after an invigorating game of tennis.

Shannon sighed and became aware of the warm spring sunshine beating down upon her head and shoulders, of the sea breeze whipping her honey-blond hair into tangles. She welcomed the balmy weather because it was such a delightful change from the bone-chilling rain she'd left in Denver three days ago.

Though she was exhausted, she allowed herself no time to bask in the tempting rays of the sun. She still had much to do. There were her bags to carry up the stairs and unpack, groceries yet to buy.

As for her real business in being in Texas, that unpleasant task would have to wait until tomorrow when she felt rested enough to cope with it.

She had just unlocked the trunk of the car, when an old pickup truck pulled into the oyster-shell driveway. A man of about seventy, lean and leather-skinned from years at open sea, got out and came toward her.

Sam Bole was a retired shrimper who kept busy doing odd jobs. For years he'd taken care of Main Hideaway for Shannon's father, and when she'd decided to come, she'd called and asked Sam to make sure everything was in good order.

Deliberately she'd told no one else she was coming.

His ruddy face creased into a welcoming smile. "It's good to see you, Shannon. It's been a long time."

"Yes. It has." Shannon smiled back with genuine plea-sure, unaware that it miraculously transformed her face from standard beauty into breathtaking loveliness. She ex-tended her hand and clasped his firmly. "How are you, Sam? And Nellie?"

"Can't complain." He shook his head in wonder as he looked at her. "You've grown up so since the last time I saw you, I almost didn't recognize you. Back then, you and Caroline Daniels were scooting around town all summer in that little car of hers with half the local boys in hot pur-suit!"

Shannon laughed. "Gosh, that was a long time ago, wasn't it?" It seemed like a hundred years since she'd been so young and carefree. Now Caroline Daniels was Caroline Avery, wife of an attorney, the busy mother of two while she… Quickly Shannon thrust the remainder of the thought away as Sam spoke again.

"You been here long?"

"I just arrived. I haven't even had a chance to go inside yet."

Sam nodded. "I'll help carry up your bags, then. I checked the house yesterday and everything seems to be in good working order, but I found a couple of loose steps on the stairway. I didn't have my tools with me, so I came back to fix them today."

"That's fine. I appreciate it. The lawn looks nice, Sam. You must have mowed it yesterday."

"Yeah, I did." Sam's pleasant face sombered. "I sure was sorry about Charlie. He was a fine man and I thought a lot of him."

"He thought a lot of you, too."

"I know it must be hard for you without your dad."

Tears moistened Shannon's eyes and she was grateful that her sunglasses concealed her weakness. "Yes," she said softly. "I miss him a lot."

"I understand you had another hard knock a few years back," Sam went on.

Shannon nodded and a lump swelled in her throat. In the past three and a half years the whims of fate had spared her little.

"Sometimes it's not easy figuring out why things happen the way they do." Sam shook his head and looked uneasy discussing such a topic. He cleared his throat and said briskly, "Here, let me help you carry those bags."

Together they unloaded the luggage from the car, and as they climbed the stairs, Sam said wistfully, "I guess you've come to see about putting the house up for sale, haven't you?"

"I probably will," Shannon admitted, "but not right away. I may stay a little while."

"One last summer fling at the old place, hmmm?"

"Sort of," Shannon said vaguely. She kept silent about the real reason for her visit.

Inside the living room, Sam turned on the window air conditioner, while Shannon stood still, gazing around her. Deep sadness filled her, for nothing seemed to have changed in here, either. Every item, from the brown-and-beige sofa to the sailfish mounted on the wall to the marine books on the pine shelves, were vivid reminders of her father.

While Sam went back outside to secure the loose steps, Shannon carried her bags into her old bedroom. The room looked untouched since she'd left it at seventeen. She hadn't realized then that that summer would be her last lazy, happy one here, but college and later still, the life she'd established for herself, had kept her too busy to come. Now the cheery yellow bedspread and curtains greeted her like old friends, and in spite of her low spirits, she smiled at the dusty display of shells she'd collected throughout her childhood.

Leaving the unpacking, Shannon went into the bathroom, where she splashed cold water on her face, brushed her hair and applied fresh lipstick. The blouse and slacks she wore, though slightly creased from long hours behind the wheel, would have to do. She knew if she stopped long enough to shower and change she would never be able to force herself out of the house. A bath would relax her too much and all she'd want to do would be to collapse on the bed or, better yet, in a lounge chair on the sun deck.

She went back to the bedroom, grabbed her handbag and left the house. "I'm going into town to pick up a few groceries, Sam," she said as she inched past where he was working on the stairs. "See you later."

"Okay. If you run into any problems or find something's not working, let me know."

"Thanks, Sam." Shannon ran lightly down the stairs and got into the car. She knew that Anchor Development Company's newest project, a resort complex of homes and a condominium, called Spinnaker's Run, was going up not too far from the house. Her business partner might very likely be found there now. As she left the driveway and turned onto the road, she was strongly tempted to locate the site and pay an impromptu visit, but she restrained the impulse. She was tired and her wits were probably not as sharp as they needed to be to deal with an adversary. After a good night's rest she'd be better equipped.

It was a shame, though, that she didn't even dare telephone her friend Caro. They'd been great pals as girls and had kept in touch by mail and telephone through all the years since. There'd been a period a few years ago when Caroline had called Shannon daily to help her through the bleakest period of her life, and Shannon would never forget it.

During the past couple of months, whenever she'd spoken by phone with Caro's husband, Mike, he'd seemed as baffled by Shannon's business partner's behavior as she, and sympathetic to her frustrations. But the fact still remained he was the attorney used by Anchor Development Company. She couldn't risk letting him know she was here, because he might warn her partner, so getting in touch with Caro would have to wait. Tomorrow she aimed for the element of surprise on all fronts.

As the car sped along the outskirts of the community of Fulton, Shannon noted with interest that the highway was crowded with businesses and shopping centers. Most were new since she'd last been here. Back then much of the area had been thick brushland.

A few minutes later she entered Rockport. To the left lay Aransas Bay, and then came the bowl-shaped harbor. Bait stands and piers edged the water and shrimp and pleasure boats were moored at the docks. Fishing nets flapped in the stiff Gulf breeze, drying in the late-afternoon sun.

Shannon found a parking space at the supermarket and went inside. She hadn't taken time to write a list, and that plus the fact that she was unfamiliar with the layout of the store made the going slow. Of necessity she took her time moving through the aisles as her eyes searched the contents of the shelves.

She became preoccupied as she compiled a mental list and started loading her basket accordingly... bacon, eggs, butter, milk, bread... She was searching for her favorite brand of coffee, when disaster struck.

Without warning her grocery cart was thrust backward. Abrupt, violent momentum hurled it against her right hipbone. Shannon's fingers clutched frantically at the coffee cans before her, but this only succeeded in bringing several of them tumbling with her to the floor.

She fell with a thud, and the polished tile floor did nothing to cushion the impact. Bruising pain reverberated through her like thunder, and Shannon moaned softly and closed her eyes. She was dazed, disoriented, too stunned even to question what had happened, much less to move.

She heard hasty footsteps and then a man's urgent voice. "Are you hurt?" When there was no immediate response, he demanded more sharply, "Open your eyes and look at me! Tell me where you hurt!"

Slowly Shannon's senses were returning. She realized she was lying on her left side, that her shoulder felt sore, that her legs were stretched out at strange angles. She was also acutely aware that she was sprawled in the middle of a supermarket aisle and that her situation was eliciting unwelcome attention.

It was humiliating, and forcing herself to open her eyes as the voice commanded took a lot of effort, yet she had no choice. It wasn't likely that she'd be spirited away, though she wished such an event would occur.

Her eyelashes swept up and the man swam into view. He was kneeling beside her and his face was close to hers. Anxiety glowed in his deep brown gaze. Tiny lines furrowed his forehead, and thick, unruly eyebrows knit together in a worried frown. His skin was like burnished gold, smooth and glowing with healthy, male vitality. In a stern voice he repeated his question, "Are you hurt?"

"I'm...I'm not sure," Shannon murmured. She brushed her hand across her face and then tried to sit up.

Instantly the man was helping her. One hand clasped hers, while his other arm slid beneath her, supporting her weight. His touch was firm, yet somehow gentle. "Take it easy now," he said kindly. "That was a nasty fall. Are you dizzy? Do you feel pain anywhere?"

Her left shoulder was sore and throbbing, but Shannon was too embarrassed to admit it. Reluctantly she finally tilted her head and met his gaze. He was peering at her intensely, only out of concern, of course, but his gaze triggered something within her. She was jolted by the sheer male appeal of him. Deep grooves marked the area on either side of hard, yet curiously sensual lips, and Shannon knew instinctively that whenever he smiled and those grooves softened into arches, the effect would be dynamite.

Appalled by the bizarre direction her thoughts were taking, she hastened to free her hand from his. "No," she said, answering his question. "I'm fine, really. Please don't trouble yourself any more about me."

She made a second move to get up, but the man forestalled her. "We'd better make sure nothing is broken before you try to stand," he said. "At the very least, you may have sprained an ankle."

Shannon was paralysed with embarrassment as he reached down and gently began to probe first one ankle, then the other. Her skin was suddenly on fire where he touched her, and she could only be grateful that at least she was modestly dressed in slacks.

While he examined her ankles, her gaze was fixed on the back of his well-shaped head. His dark, almost black hair curled slightly at the ends, and the gray shirt he wore hugged his wide shoulders, emphasizing their strength. Shannon was mesmerized by this close-up, almost intimate view of a man she didn't even know.

A moment later he drew back and said, "There's no sign of bruising or swelling, so I think you'll be okay."

"Are you a doctor?"

He tossed back his head and laughed heartily, and his laughter was one of the most pleasant sounds Shannon had heard in a long time, deep and full and rich, as though it came right from the heart. He continued to smile, and when his eyes made contact with hers again, she saw that her instinct had been correct. The effect of his smile *was* devastating—no question about it. She caught her breath beneath its powerful impact. His teeth were dazzlingly white against his dark gold tan and the way the skin crinkled at the corners of his mouth was most engaging.

"Far from it," he said, chuckling. "But growing up, I had my share of bruises and sprains and broken bones, so I guess that makes me a semiexpert on the subject."

Shannon smiled back. "I guess it would at that. Well, now that you've pronounced me all in one piece, I suppose I'd better stop cluttering up the floor."

"You'd better let me help you up, just to be sure everything's intact."

Before she could dissent, his arm slid around her once more and he clasped her hand tightly in his. Then his long legs unwound and he rose, bringing Shannon up with him. She was pressed close to him, and the enticing male scent of him, as well as the unfamiliar sensation of leaning against a strong male chest, sent tingles shivering along her nerve ends.

He didn't seem in any great hurry to release her once they were standing. Shannon's face warmed, and she was exceptionally conscious of his proximity. Something caught in her throat, rendering speech difficult, but finally she was able to summon an uncertain smile.

"I'm really okay now. Thank you for your help." She glanced down quickly to avoid the intensity of his gaze, and withdrew her hand from his.

Since she seemed fine, Matthew Tyson didn't understand the reluctance he felt as he dropped his other hand from her waist. There was no further reason to touch her. Yet he found himself wanting to go on holding the enchanting young woman who stood before him. Even though there was now a small distance between them, he could still catch a faint drift of her perfume.

She was lovely, of course, and that was part of her appeal. Long waves of wheat-gold hair swelled and billowed across her shoulders, and even her light-brown eyes were flecked with gold. Her face was delicately shaped and her skin was creamy, with a hint of apricot at her cheeks. Her lips were enticingly shaped, generous and soft. She wore a simple sea-green summer blouse with white slacks, and his gaze was drawn again and again to the superb figure they covered. Matt was somewhat bemused by his attraction toward her. It wasn't like him to be easily bowled over by any woman.

But he knew it was more than mere physical magnetism, strong as that was. There was something gentle and vulnerable in the depths of her gaze that captivated him. He wished she were someone he could get to know. But that was impossible—he had just noticed the wedding rings on her left hand. Matt well knew he had a multitude of faults, but poaching on another man's preserve wasn't one of his sins.

A movement at his left caught Matt's attention. He turned his head, motioned with his hand and said, "Come here, Jason, and tell the lady you're sorry for crashing into her." He looked at the woman again and explained, "I'm afraid he's a reckless grocery-cart driver. I'll have to revoke his license."

Shannon watched as the little boy approached. He appeared to be about four years old and he had a cottontop head and round blue eyes. Just now his eyes held frank terror and his right forefinger was thrust between his lips as though for comfort.

The man clasped the little boy's shoulder in a gesture of encouragement, and the child mumbled, "I'm sorry for knocking you down."

Shannon melted instantly. She stooped to the child's level and gave him a broad smile, intent on only one thing—to ease his anxiety. "I can tell just by looking what a good boy you are. You didn't do it on purpose, did you?"

The boy shook his head and his voice quavered as he said solemnly, "It was an accident."

"I know it was, and we all make mistakes sometimes. Even grown-ups." Shannon rose to her full height again and gave him another smile. "Don't worry about it anymore, okay?"

A responding smile brightened the child's eyes, and then it reached his lips. He nodded, more confident now. "Okay."

"Well," Shannon said, noticing the cans of coffee still littering the floor. "We made quite a mess, didn't we?"

"Jason and I will pick them up," the man said quickly.

"Fine." Shannon nodded briskly, plucked one can from the shelf beside her and dropped it into her basket and added, "Goodbye, then."

She moved down the aisle, around the corner and out of sight. Matt watched until she was gone before he stooped to pick up the scattered cans of coffee. Her kindness to Jason had only further emphasized that she was the type of woman he wished he could have the opportunity to get to know. She had been gracious and charming to a careless child, and under the circumstances another person might have been snappish or abrupt. Besides being a wife to some lucky man, she probably had children of her own, as well. That would explain her sensitivity and understanding toward another child in a difficult spot.

Sighing and trying to put her out of his mind, Matt grinned at Jason. "Better let me drive the rest of the way, pal. And remind me to buy you an ice cream on the way out."

The rest of the grocery shopping was uneventful, and Matt was soon finished. On the way back to his sister's home, he started to grin. He certainly hadn't known what he was letting himself in for when he'd left his office that afternoon! He'd dropped by his sister's house, something he often did. She'd invited him to stay for dinner, which he'd accepted, and when she found she needed a couple of items from the supermarket to round out the meal, Matt had offered to go for her. Naturally his nephew had wanted to go along.

When they returned to the house Jason spotted a familiar car in the driveway and squealed, "Daddy's home!" He scampered ahead of Matt into the house.

Matt followed and found his sister and brother-in-law in the kitchen. June Madison, at twenty-nine, was two years younger than Matt, an attractive, feminine version of him. Her hair and eyes were also dark, her skin a golden tan that was the result of her love of the sun. Her husband, Harry, had blond hair and friendly blue eyes. Just now he was perched lazily on a barstool, watching his wife prepare dinner.

"Hi. How's it going?" he asked casually when he saw Matt and Jason.

June glanced over her shoulder, took one all-encompassing look at her son's ice-cream-covered face and cut her eyes menacingly toward the real culprit. "Honestly, Matt! How many times do I have to tell you not to give Jason junk food so near to mealtime? Now you've ruined his dinner!"

"Aw, go easy on him, honey," Harry said placatingly. "You just said dinner's still an hour away. He'll be hungry again by then, won't you, tiger?"

Jason could only bob his head, and not easily at that, for already his mother was scrubbing his face with a wet paper towel.

"Besides," Matt said as he extracted a head of lettuce from the grocery bag he'd placed on the counter, "what's the use of having a nephew if I can't buy him a treat now and then?"

"Humph!" June released Jason from her viselike grip. "If only it were now and then. Between Harry, his parents and you, Jason's already spoiled rotten! I'm the only one in the whole family who's trying to instill a little discipline!"

Matt and Harry both just grinned, not in the least perturbed by the outburst. It was a familiar complaint, and one that nobody took seriously, least of all June. Matt handed her the butter she'd wanted and then pulled a six-pack of beer from the paper bag.

"I hit a lady with the basket," Jason volunteered, artlessly tattling on himself. "She fell down."

June stared at him in dismay. "You knocked a lady down? My goodness! Was she hurt?" She swung around to question Matt.

"Not at all. She took it like a champ." Matt tossed a can of beer to Harry, then opened one for himself.

"She was purrty," Jason went on. "Uncle Matt was hugging her." After dropping that little bomb into the conversation, he skipped to the patio door, opened it and went into the backyard.

"'Purrty,' hmm?" June's eyes were lively with interest.

"She was good-looking, yes," Matt conceded.

"Is that why you were 'hugging her'?" June's eyes were dancing now.

"Don't be silly," Matt said more sharply than he'd intended. "I was merely helping her to her feet."

"Sure. Come on, Matt, out with the rest," his sister prodded. "What's her name and when are you taking her out?"

"You're barking up the wrong tree," Matt told her. "She's married."

"Oh."

"It's just as well," Harry said. "Matt's got enough woman troubles right now without looking for new ones."

"You said it, brother!" There was the unmistakable tinge of bitterness to Matt's voice. "It looks as though for the second time in my life a woman is going to steal my business away from me.''

"The two cases aren't similar at all," June said, attempting to soothe him. "There's no reason to assume that just because this woman is suddenly the majority stockholder of Anchor Development she'll attempt to take control away from you. Why would she be vindictive the way Vicky was? After all, this is not a divorce. Besides, since she's never been involved, she'll probably be quite happy to let you keep running the company without interference. Charlie and Bud did.''

"True, but then I was a majority stockholder," Matt pointed out. "Now she holds the big stick and she wants to exert her new power. I've resisted her demands so far, but it's just a matter of time before she backs me into a corner." He sighed heavily. "If only I'd been able to buy out Bud's shares last year when he wanted to sell, I wouldn't be in this mess!''

Harry nodded in sympathy. "Well, nobody could have foreseen Charlie's death.''

No, nobody could have foreseen that. Charlie had certainly seemed the picture of health when he'd last been in town almost a year ago. Matt had always held Charlie Main in high regard. He had been an honorable man and a congenial business partner. When Matt had needed some investment partners to start his business five years ago, Mike Avery, a local lawyer, had introduced him to Charlie, a longtime summer resident. Charlie had not only placed his trust in Matt's ability and bought a thirty-five percent interest, but he'd also brought in Bud Carr, who had bought a sixteen-percent share. That had left Matt with a forty-nine-percent controlling interest in the fledgling land-development company.

It had been a successful partnership. The trio of men had gotten on well together and had seen the fruition of a number of profitable property-development projects, from a shopping center to an office complex to the one under current construction, an exclusive residential resort community. When completed, the development, named Spinnaker's Run, would boast homes, a condominium, a marina and a clubhouse in addition to a private golf course. Matt was particularly proud of it.

His troubles had begun last year, when Bud Carr had decided he wanted out. He was moving to Arizona and wanted to take all his assets with him. Matt badly wanted to buy his shares, but he'd been overextended and couldn't manage it. In a separate deal only months before, he'd invested in a limited partnership in Houston, which had left him short on liquid funds. Only Charlie could afford to buy Bud's shares without bringing in an outsider, and neither Matt nor Charlie had wanted that. Charlie had not had any desire, either, to own controlling interest himself. Semiretired and only a summer resident of Rockport, he preferred to remain a silent partner. Except for concerning himself with loans or major expenditures, Charlie was content to leave the running of the business to Matt. It was a small company, manageable by one boss, and Matt was the real backbone of the company.

In the end Charlie had purchased Bud's interest in his daughter's name, but he had placed it in a trust. In that way the daughter drew the income, but had no actual power in the running of the company. There was also a provision in the contract that gave Matt the option to buy those shares himself within five years.

But now everything had changed and the trust no longer applied. It had ceased to exist at Charlie's death. The daughter had full voting power with the shares bought in her name, and in addition, she had inherited her father's thirty-five percent interest in the company.

It was a shocking blow to Matt. Day by day, hour by hour, he had built up the business by the sweat of his own brow. It was *his* company. Yet now an utter stranger owned fifty-one percent of Anchor Development and had controlling interest. The situation was intolerable.

That night Shannon unpacked her things. Among her clothes was a framed color photograph. She carried it into the living room and placed it on the bookshelf, then stepped back to look at it.

A handsome young man and a baby were pictured in the photograph—Shannon's late husband, Brad, and their baby son, Timothy. Although it had been over three years since she had lost them and the worst of the grief was over, there were still times her heart ached unbearably.

Like this minute.

Her thoughts drifted to the little boy in the supermarket, the one who had sent her crashing to the floor. He'd been such an appealing child. But what had struck her most about him was that he was around the same age Timmy would have been if he had lived.

Sadness washed over her. After all this time it was still difficult for her to be near children. Their sweet innocence and lively energy always seemed to remind her of the precious years of life her own child had been denied. That was why she'd been unable to go back to teaching school.

Shannon's gaze went from her baby's face to Brad Edwards's smiling image. A familiar twinge of guilt assaulted her, made even stronger tonight because of her shocking reaction to the man in the grocery store. Obviously the man must be married and the child with him his son. That knowledge alone was deterrent enough to make her wonder at herself, but looking at Brad's picture increased her sense of shame. There was no denying it, her pulse had raced at the man's touch as he'd helped her up. It was the first time she had felt such an attraction since Brad's death, and it had been a feeling she'd begun to believe she would never feel again for any man. This disturbed her, because she didn't want it to happen.

"I'm so sorry, Brad," she whispered softly. And Shannon knew she was apologizing for far more than her unexpected reactions to a stranger this afternoon.

She turned away from the photograph abruptly, flipped on the radio to distract herself from her muddled thoughts and went back to her unpacking.

By eleven she had finished, taken a hot bath and was more than ready for bed. She was so tired she could scarcely keep her eyes open, and she was certain she would fall asleep immediately.

But to her dismay, her thoughts returned to the man in the supermarket. What was it about him that had so attracted her, she wondered with annoyance. Why him in particular? Just because she was lonely and upset? Or was there something more?

Anyway, he's married, she reminded herself. *So forget him.* She tried to think of Brad, instead, but when she did, the familiar unhappiness returned. It seemed she would never be able to forgive herself for her behavior their last night together.

With an effort she thrust those memories away and concentrated on what lay ahead tomorrow. All her life Shannon had been protected and taken care of, first by her father, then by her husband, then by her father again.

But now she was on her own, and she was about to wage a major battle. She had to be combat ready.

Chapter Two

Wearing a comfortable warm-up suit, Shannon carried her cup of coffee outside and wandered across the lawn and onto the fishing pier. The morning sun was bright and already warm, and its rays cast jewel tones on the gently lapping waves of the water. The tide was out and shells littered the shoreline, while a few gulls swooped down among them, searching for their breakfast.

Pleasant images of the past flashed through her mind: dragging a net with Caro through the shallow waters; casting a fishing line from the edge of the pier at high tide while her father patiently coached her; floating near the shore on an inflated inner tube; skimming across the bay in a motorboat, her hair flying and saltwater spray in her eyes. She had so many happy memories of this place, and she regretted that she and Brad had never managed to come here together.

Shannon sighed and gazed into the distance. Someone in a small boat left a nearby dock, chugging out toward the center of the bay. He saw her standing there and waved. She waved back, then began to retrace her steps toward the house. After her business here in Rockport was resolved, she had some serious thinking to do about her future.

It was strangely frightening suddenly to be so rootless. After Brad's and Timmy's deaths, she had sold their home, moved into a small apartment and taken an office job. Recently, when her father died so unexpectedly, she had put most of her own belongings in storage and moved into her father's house so that the task of settling all his affairs would be easier. Even so, it was more complicated than she'd expected and she'd given up her job in order to spend all her time getting a grasp on his business concerns.

Once those matters were settled, she'd realized she didn't want to remain permanently in the house. It was too huge, required too much care for just herself, so she'd put it on the market. It had sold almost immediately and she'd signed the final papers only a few days ago.

Now Brad's folks were about to desert her, too. Her father-in-law would be retiring in a few more months and they intended to move to Florida. Shannon had nothing more to keep her in Denver except her stored possessions. She had come to a point where she had to decide whether she wanted to go back there to live, whether she should stay here, or sell this place, too, and perhaps start a new life someplace entirely different. It was unnerving to have so much freedom, and she wasn't at all sure what she should do with it.

But first things first. Before the future, she had to deal with the present. Shannon resisted the lure of the sunshine and went inside to the telephone. Though her partner had thus far shown her little consideration, nevertheless she would be considerate herself. Instead of just showing up at the office, as she'd first meant to do, she would call and let him know to expect her.

The same feminine voice she'd heard the other times she'd called answered the phone. "Good morning, Anchor Development Company."

"I'd like to speak with Mr. Tyson, please," Shannon said.

"I'm sorry, but he isn't in just now."

Shannon nibbled her lip in displeasure. "Can you tell me when you expect him?" she asked.

"It's hard to say. He hasn't called in this morning. May I ask who's calling?"

Shannon sighed inwardly. She was reluctant to leave her name. She'd done that on too many occasions in the past couple of months and her calls had not been returned. All the same, she answered, "This is Shannon Main Edwards."

"Oh. Yes, of course, Mrs. Edwards." The voice took on a respectful, and wary, tone. "As soon as Mr. Tyson comes in, I'll tell him you called."

"Let me give you my number," Shannon went on. "It's a local one. I'm in town right now and I'd like to set up a meeting with him for sometime today."

"I'll give him the message," the woman promised.

"Fine. I'll be expecting his call shortly." Shannon put soft, but unmistakable emphasis on the last word.

As in all the other times before, the answering call never came. As the morning wore on and still the telephone remained silent, Shannon's sense of expectation turned to impatience and finally to outrage. How dared the man treat her as though she were of no account? It had been bad enough when he'd ignored all her attempts to contact him while she was in Denver, but now that she was actually here and he knew that sooner or later he'd have to deal with her, it was beyond all comprehension!

But, then, the entire situation was bizarre and baffling. In the past when her father had spoken of Matthew Tyson, it had been obvious that he thought highly of his business partner. Yet since Charlie Main's death, Shannon could get nowhere with Tyson. She'd received business checks due her and very scaled down, nonrevealing financial statements, but that was the extent of his communications with her. Whenever she'd tried to call him, like today, he'd always been out, and not once had he ever returned any of her calls. When she'd requested, by mail, more detailed financial reports, they were not forthcoming. Several times she'd called Mike Avery, and though he'd agreed she was entitled to everything she'd requested and had promised to speak to Tyson, nothing had come of it.

Finally, in desperation, Shannon had consulted a Denver attorney. The lawyer wrote to Tyson without results and finally advised Shannon to travel to Texas and see what was going on. After the sale of her father's house in Denver, Shannon decided to make the trip.

Her decision to come to Rockport was reinforced today when it became obvious that once again Tyson was going to ignore her phone call.

At noon Shannon ate a light lunch, then changed into a tailored skirt and blouse. By a quarter past one, when she was ready to leave the house, the telephone still had not rung. Anger, and determination, heightened the natural color of her cheeks.

Though her resolve wouldn't allow her to back down, Shannon was not eager for the confrontation ahead, and she took her time driving toward Rockport, taking the Fulton waterfront road past the renovated historic Fulton Mansion, the condominiums and the homes on Key Allegro, a land-filled peninsula that jutted out into the bay. The ski basin, where she'd learned to water-ski, separated it from Rockport's public beach.

Despite her lack of haste, she arrived at the offices of Anchor Development Company all too soon. The company occupied half of a small brick building not far from the courthouse. The other half of the building housed an insurance firm. Shannon got out of the car and smoothed her hair nervously. Resolutely she lifted her chin and strode toward the entrance.

The interior was cooled by air conditioning and, though not large, was pleasantly decorated. A sofa stood against one wall with a low glass table before it. Above the sofa hung a framed painting of a fleet of fishing vessels on the sea, and a tall potted palm gave a splash of greenery in an otherwise dark corner.

On the opposite side of the room was a desk and, lining the wall behind it, several file cabinets and a communications radio. A woman who appeared to be in her middle thirties sat behind the desk. Slightly plump, she had short dark hair and a pleasant face, but the instant she saw Shannon, her eyes widened, then narrowed into a shuttered expression. In that moment, Shannon knew that the other woman realized who she was.

"Good afternoon." The woman's voice was polite, but her smile was painfully forced. "May I help you?"

Shannon smiled back, her own equally false. "Yes, you may. I'm Shannon Edwards," she said, pretending she was unaware that the woman already knew that. "You can inform Mr. Tyson that I'm here to see him."

"Oh, yes." The woman rose swiftly and extended a hand. "It's so nice to meet you, Mrs. Edwards. I'm Anne Paulson, Mr. Tyson's secretary. I was so sorry at the news of your father's death. He was a very kind man."

"Thank you." Shannon shook the secretary's hand, then returned to the subject of her visit. "Mr. Tyson?" she prompted.

"I'm sorry, but he's not in the office right now."

"I see." Shannon had expected that response. "And when will he be in?"

"I really couldn't say. He might not be in at all today." Anne Paulson looked unmistakably nervous.

So the man was still avoiding her, just as she'd thought. Shannon was suddenly filled with disdain. Matthew Tyson was too much of a coward to see her himself, so he'd given his secretary the job of fobbing her off. She had no intention, however, of being fobbed off by anyone. Not anymore.

Shannon pursed her lips in a considering manner, then said calmly, "In that case, I'll just wait in his office on the chance that he'll be stopping in sometime this afternoon." She took a step toward the inner door that obviously led to Tyson's private office, then paused and added as though in an afterthought, "As long as I'm waiting, I may as well keep busy. Bring me all the financial statements pertaining to the last quarter."

The secretary looked as though she couldn't have been more shocked if Shannon had pulled a loaded gun on her. "But you... but I... I can't possibly do that without Mr. Tyson's permission!" she gasped.

There had been months of playing cat and mouse, with Shannon in the role of mouse, and now she was very tired of the game. Softly she said, "As you know, I inherited controlling interest in Anchor Development from my father. I can appreciate your loyalty to Mr. Tyson and to the company, but if you wish to continue here, I expect the same loyalty and service."

"Yes, ma'am." Anne Paulson nodded. In a subdued voice she said, "I'll get the statements for you right away."

Shannon entered Tyson's office and glanced around her. It was clearly a working office. There were stacks of papers on the desk, and blueprints leaning against the wall and across the top of a file cabinet.

She sat down at the desk as Anne brought her several file folders and placed them before her.

"Thank you."

"Would you like a cup of coffee, Mrs. Edwards?"

"No, thanks. This will be all for now."

The secretary left the room and closed the door. Only then did Shannon let down her guard. She slumped against the back of the chair for a moment and breathed deeply. Her bravado had worked. But would it work equally well with Matthew Tyson?

Sighing, Shannon opened the first folder.

Standing beside the foreman, Matt watched gloomily while a couple of men from the crew unloaded lumber from the bed of his pickup truck. "Be sure to have everything carried back to the warehouse and locked up when you quit for the day."

The foreman, a broad, muscular man named José, grunted. "It's gonna be a real pain and a time waster, but what else can we do?" he asked rhetorically. "We can't go through this every day."

"You're telling me? We'd go broke besides, and then we'd all be out of work."

Both men fell into a morose silence. That morning when the work crew had arrived on the construction site at Spinnaker's Run, they'd discovered a stack of lumber missing. It was the third time in as many weeks that such an incident had occurred. The other times the losses had been less severe—a couple of bags of cement, some wiring. But this latest theft had made a greater dent in the budget, and clearly something had to be done.

Thus had begun a bad day. Matt reported the theft to the sheriff's department, then called Anne to let her know he wouldn't be in the office until late afternoon, if at all, since he was leaving immediately for Corpus Christi. He had to pick up a new supply of the lumber the crew so badly needed. Anne told him Charlie Main's daughter was in town, expecting his call and wanting to meet with him today. That had been the topper on an already fouled up morning. The woman's timing couldn't have been worse. When Anne had asked whether she should call her back,

Matt had told her not to bother. He'd been so infuriated that Shannon Edwards would arrive like that without warning, not to mention demanding a meeting on a day when he had no time for it, that he'd decided to let her cool her heels. She could just wait until he had time to deal with her. He was darned if he was going to meekly submit to her beck and call just because she happened to show up out of the blue!

The men had finished unloading the truck and stacking the lumber near the condominium that was going up. Matt turned to José. "I'm going to take off now and grab a bite to eat. I never had time for lunch."

José nodded. "Okay, Matt. See you tomorrow." He strode purposefully toward his men and shouted instructions at them, while Matt climbed into the cab of his truck.

Before he drove away, he decided he'd better let Anne know he was back. Matt switched on the radio speaker. "I've just dropped off the lumber and I'm leaving the development now, but I'm going to stop for something to eat before I come in," he told her. "Anything been happening?"

"Thank goodness you called!" Anne exclaimed. Her voice, though low, was anxious. "You'd better come in right away!" She burst into a barrage of words and Matt had to strain to make sense of them. But when he finally grasped the meaning of what she was saying he was incredulous.

"She's *what*?" he exploded.

"She's in your office," Anne repeated. "Looking at last quarter's statements."

"And you gave them to her?" Matt demanded in outrage.

"I had to, Mr. Tyson." Anne sounded close to tears. "She insisted, and she *is* an owner, too."

Of course. The big owner now, with her whopping fifty-one percent of the company stock. Matt was suddenly sick with dread and frustration. But he knew there was no point in taking out his frustration on his secretary. Technically

Anne was working for Shannon Edwards now, too. Legally he didn't have a leg to stand on, and he knew it. That knowledge only made him angrier.

"I'll be there in a few minutes," he said grimly.

Matt nursed his grievances while he sped toward town. He was still bitter about the threatening letter he'd received a month ago from some hotshot Denver lawyer. Angrily he'd shown it to Mike Avery, his friend and company lawyer, but Mike had only shrugged. "Well, what did you expect—a love letter?" he'd asked mildly. "You just can't keep ignoring the woman's requests, Matt. She's a partner and she has a right to full disclosure from you concerning every aspect of the business." But even now, irrational as it might be, Matt didn't see it that way. He only saw another woman ready to rob him of everything he'd worked so hard to build.

Matt's brown fingers gripped the steering wheel with uncalled for strength. Now the woman had the nerve to prance right into his office, making demands, taking over—exactly as he'd envisioned! Lord preserve him from all women except his sister!

At the office he found Anne anticipating his arrival. She inclined her head toward the closed door of his private office and said in a half whisper, "She's still in there."

He nodded and, with swift, long strides, went to the closed door. He twisted the knob, entered the room and slammed the door behind him.

His abrupt entrance startled the woman at the desk. Her head jerked up as though pulled roughly by a puppet's string, and when she saw him, the papers she held dropped from a nerveless hand. Wide, surprised golden-brown eyes met stormy dark-brown eyes.

Matt was so shocked that he halted beside the door—he was having a difficult time believing the evidence of his eyes. The person behind his desk was the same woman he'd encountered in the supermarket. There was no mistaking those lovely eyes, the honey-colored hair, the slender, shapely figure that today was clad in a neat white blouse and a navy skirt. He'd been entranced by her yesterday; his feelings were vastly different today.

She was equally taken aback at the sight of him. She shot to her feet, and the color ebbed and flowed in her cheeks.

"You!" They exclaimed in dismayed unison.

For a long time afterward they were silent, wary adversaries as they studied each other with ruthless appraisal.

Matt ended the stalemate by stepping forward. "Well, well," he drawled with heavy sarcasm. "I'd always heard that looks were deceiving. You've proved that old adage true."

"What do you mean?"

Matt pressed his lips together. "Yesterday I found you beautiful, nice, even a good sport. Today I find you're someone who enjoys barging in and throwing your weight around. You have a hell of a nerve coming in here and commandeering my office, no less!"

Angry red spots dotted her cheeks, but she didn't back down an inch. She was not easily intimidated by his gruff anger, and grudgingly Matt gave her credit for at least having courage.

"I wouldn't have needed to come here and throw my weight around if you'd been reasonable and cooperative in the first place," she flared. "So you can just stop glaring at me like that. You have no one to blame but yourself. I called this morning for an appointment, but as usual, you chose to ignore me, to shut me out! Well, I won't be shut out anymore!"

"After the veiled threat I got from your lawyer," Matt said furiously, "did you really believe I'd roll out the red carpet once I knew you were here?"

"I expected exactly what I got," Shannon replied in a hard tone. "The usual cold shoulder from you. I had no desire to come here at all, but you left me no choice, since it's obvious you have no intention of being square with me at a distance. I'm warning you, Tyson, I've come to protect my business interests and I intend to do just that—whether you like it or not!''

Matt's jaw tightened. His eyes were dark, shiny pebbles of hostility. ''Oh, I don't like it, but I can't say I'm surprised. As a matter-of-fact, I've been expecting you for some time. I knew you'd be eager to take my business away from me.''

''Take it away from you?''

Shannon stared at him blankly, so evidently shocked that for a moment Matt had serious doubts about his assessment of her. But the doubts flew when he remembered. ''Of course,'' he said in a harsh voice as he knotted and unknotted his hands at his sides. ''Through a fluke of fate, you're the big winner in the stakes with your fifty-one percent majority interest.''

There was a thoughtful expression on her face, and it softened her features. ''So that's it! The truth is, I hadn't thought about taking over anything, but—'' her eyes and voice became frosty ''—I certainly won't hesitate to do whatever is necessary if I discover that you've been cheating my father and me.''

It was Matt's turn to be surprised. ''You're crazy!'' he burst out. ''Really crazy! I've been honest right down to the last penny.''

She tossed her head. ''You'll not mind, I'm sure, if I reserve judgment on that until I've had time to go over the records? The same records, as a matter of fact, that you were not, for *some* reason, willing to send to me.''

Matt felt a dull flush creep under his skin. He had no real defense and he knew it. Mike had warned him he was playing with fire by not responding cooperatively to her requests. Now the fire was here, burning in Charlie Main's daughter's eyes, flaming in her determination to destroy him.

Shannon saw, with deep satisfaction, that she'd pierced his armor at last.

Last night she'd reacted like a foolish, smitten schoolgirl to the man who'd been so solicitous of her well-being after her fall in the supermarket. She'd thought over the tiniest detail she could recall about him...the way his hair lay across his forehead, the attractive curve of his lips, the gentle concern in his eyes, his soaring height as he'd stood beside her, his appealing lean male build. To her shame, she'd dwelled on the sparks that had burst through her veins when he'd touched her and, worse yet, had even wondered what it would be like to have his lips on hers. It was only when she'd reminded herself that he was married and a father that she'd been able to put him out of her mind and finally fall asleep.

Yet despite his unavailability, despite the knowledge now that he was actually her enemy, she found him excitingly attractive—much to her self-disgust. He wore a pale-blue golf shirt tucked into dark blue slacks. His hair was in disarray, tossed by the wind, and though his face was swarthy and filled with unmistakable anger, his demeanor rigid, there was nevertheless something magnetically appealing about him, although for the life of her she couldn't decide just what it was. He wasn't handsome; certainly he wasn't as good-looking as Brad had been. His face was a bit too square, his eyebrows too menacingly thick, his mouth perhaps a shade too wide. All the same, he exuded virility, even this minute.

Shannon was horrified with herself for even noticing these things about him. He was beneath her contempt—he'd been trying to keep her from what was rightfully hers—and it was important that she keep that thought in mind.

Abruptly he came around the desk, so that she was penned right where she stood, like a trapped rabbit. There was nowhere to go to get away from him, for behind her was the window, to her right the immovable block of file cabinets.

His manner was cold as he leaned toward her, his face intimidatingly close to hers. "How much business experience have you had?" he demanded.

Shannon felt her cheeks warm, and she swayed backward just a fraction. "That has nothing to do with—"

He leaned closer, recapturing the fraction-of-an-inch distance she'd placed between them. "I asked, how much?"

She hissed between her teeth. "All right," she conceded. "Very little."

He pulled back, drawing to his full height. "I thought so," Tyson said. "I thought I remembered Charlie saying you were a school teacher. How many business reports do you read a day in the classroom? You're not qualified to make judgments concerning this business!"

"Actually, I've been working the past couple of years in the billing department of a large department store, so you see, I *can* add and subtract!" Shannon said hotly. "I know I'm not qualified to make business judgments yet, but I'm a fast learner. If you think you're going to get by with anything underhanded just because my father is gone and I'm inexperienced, you'd better think again!"

Matt crossed his arms in front of him and tilted his head. "You're out of your depth here. How long do you really believe this company would last with you in the driver's seat? I bet you don't know one end of a hammer from another, much less how to put together an entire housing development!" She raised her left hand just then to brush back her hair—a nervous gesture—and he was jolted anew by the flash of diamonds on her finger. His mouth twisted derisively as he added, "Why don't you just go back to Denver? Don't you have a husband or something?"

The gold in her eyes disappeared entirely. They were now muddy brown, as though a storm had churned up the murky bottom of a lake.

"My personal life is none of your business!"

"Ah! Didn't work out, eh?"

The strange expression that came over her pale face told him at once that he'd gone too far. She paled and seemed to sway, as though she'd just gone through some terribly traumatic experience.

He was beginning to regret his words, but before he could even decide whether he ought to make an apology, he was stunned by her unexpected reaction.

Shannon Edwards slapped his face, hard.

Matt stared at her, too shocked for a brief instant to do more. But her action seemed to free her from the almost cowed demeanor she'd had a few moments earlier. Although she was trembling, she shoved his chest so that he was forced to step backward, out of her way, and she brushed past him as she hastily moved around the desk.

Then she whirled around to glare at him. "You're even more despicable than I'd imagined," she said huskily. "All the same, nothing you can say is going to chase me away from what is legally mine!" She paused, breathing harshly. "I honestly hadn't thought before of getting involved in the business permanently, but given your hostility, I just may. Therefore, the first thing I want is for an office to be made available to me."

Matt rubbed the angry red streak on his cheek. He was still somewhat bemused that she had actually become incensed enough to strike him. He was also extremely furious. Now he snapped, "I don't know where you think that'll be! Mine and the reception room with Anne's desk are the only rooms there are."

"In that case, we'll just have to squeeze another desk in here, won't we?"

Matt looked around at the crowded room, then back at Shannon. "Like where?" he demanded incredulously. "From the ceiling? Be reasonable, for Pete's sake!"

"I'll admit it'll be a bit of a tight squeeze, but we'll have to manage."

"You've got to be kidding! We'd be sitting in each other's laps!" He gave her a scornful look. "Look, you've made your point. You'll get your detailed statements from now on. Now why don't you go home so that I can get on with the business of making a living for both of us?"

"You still don't get it, do you?" Shannon said. "I will *not* be shunted aside. I have no intention of going away and letting you ignore me again. For the time being, I intend to stay here and take an active interest in this company, *my* company as well as yours. If you continue to thwart me, I'll see you in court."

Chapter Three

The barmaid brought their drinks. Mike Avery reached for his wallet, but Matt shook his head. "I've got them," he said firmly. He tossed his money onto the tray and added to the woman, "Keep the change."

"Thanks."

When she walked away, Mike stirred his whiskey and soda and said, "I hate to be an I-told-you-so, Matt, but I told you so."

"I know," Matt answered. He took a long draw at his beer. "The thing is . . . now what do I do?"

Mike grinned. "Well, you could try to salvage everything by turning on your charm."

"What charm?" Matt growled.

The two men had met when Matt had visited his sister and her husband after his divorce had become final. When Matt decided to leave Pennsylvania for good and start a new business in Rockport, Mike had been most helpful, introducing him to potential investors and drawing up all the necessary legal papers. They had become fast friends and often enjoyed tennis or fishing together.

At thirty-two, Mike was a year older than Matt, and while no one could accuse him of being good-looking, his personality always overshadowed the fact that he wasn't quite as tall as his wife or that his ears slightly protruded and detracted from his one great feature, his gray eyes rimmed by long, thick eyelashes. He also had a kind heart, and when Matt had telephoned and asked to meet him, Mike had agreed without hesitation because Matt had sounded upset and quite unlike himself.

"Look, you want it straight?" Mike asked. When Matt nodded, he continued, "You've been flying in the face of the law by not giving her access to all the records she's requested and had a right to, let alone not consulting her about major decisions. Now you're only reaping the harvest."

"Okay, okay," Matt said irritably. "I brought it on myself. But could this really turn into a court battle?"

"I'd say it's dead certain unless you open the books to her and start trying to get along. She's not just some minor irritant like a mosquito bite that's going to go away if you ignore it. Face it, whether you like it or not, the fact remains that she's the majority stockholder in the firm now. She deserves to be treated with honesty and respect, and if you refuse to give her that, you're going to wind up in court. And speaking as your attorney, I have to tell you I think you'd both come out losers. A legal battle would only drain off company profits, not to mention probably bringing work to a complete standstill. The company's just not big enough to survive that."

"I know that," Matt said in a subdued voice.

Mike sipped at his drink, then set down the glass. His gray eyes leveled on Matt's face. "What I don't understand and never did," he said thoughtfully, "was why you behaved the way you did in the first place. You were never belligerent or overbearing with Charlie or Bud. For the life of me, I can't figure out why you've been behaving like such a jerk toward Charlie's daughter."

Matt shrugged. "It was stupid, I know."

"Very stupid," Mike agreed. "And foolhardy. Now you've got her hackles up good and proper, and for what? I'd really like to know."

Matt shrugged again and his mouth twisted into a bitter smile. "A legacy from my dear, sweet wife, I guess. You know the story, Mike. She took me to the cleaners when we got divorced. She got just about everything, including my business. *That's* what a good lawyer can do for you, whether you deserve it or not! And now she and that creep of a second husband of hers are enjoying the fruits of my labor!"

"I'll admit you got took on that one," Mike agreed, "and, as your friend, I'll ignore your blanket condemnation of lawyers. All the same, you're just asking for the whole thing to happen again if you don't cool off and cooperate with Shannon Edwards." He glanced at his watch, gulped down the last of his drink and added, "I hate to drink and run, but it's Mom's birthday tonight and Caro will kill me if I don't show up."

"Sure," Matt said with a vague wave of goodbye. "Sure. See you, Mike."

Mike came around the table and patted Mike's shoulder. "Don't take it so hard. Things will work out. At least they can," he amended, "if you're willing to be sensible and meet her halfway."

After Mike left, Matt ordered a second beer and wished he could be as optimistic. He was still livid with Shannon Edwards, but he was also just as furious with himself. All along, ever since Mike himself had begun receiving letters and phone calls from her, the lawyer had tried to tell Matt that he was courting disaster by not responding to her, but Matt had been too hostile to listen to reason. He'd been so outraged that he hadn't thought things out. He hadn't thought period. That was the root of the matter. He'd merely reacted, and now look what a mess he'd made of things! She was ready to haul him into court!

Before Charlie's death, his daughter had never shown any interest in Anchor Development. True, her share had been in a trust and she hadn't had any voting power, but not once had she telephoned or written the office about anything. So it had been easy for Matt to assume—wrongly, as it turned out—that she still wouldn't be really interested in anything that was going on. He'd thought he could get by sending her dividend checks and brief, quarterly statements. The last thing he'd wanted was for her to start meddling in internal business affairs, and he'd thought that by ignoring her, she'd probably soon lose interest. Instead he'd incited her to do the very thing he'd hoped to prevent. Now she was here to wrest control of the company he'd worked so hard to establish.

It wasn't fair, he thought savagely. In Pennsylvania, when he'd been married, he'd begun a small construction company, and just when it had started to really pay off, the marriage had fallen apart. Vicky's lawyer had stolen it from him for her. Now he had to face the possibility of the whole nightmare being repeated.

What made this even worse, in a way, was his unwilling attraction to Shannon. By the time his ex-wife had gained control over his company, the last shred of any tenderer emotion for her had long since gone. But despite his dislike for Shannon Edwards his undesirable business partner, Shannon Edwards the woman was something else. He couldn't shake from his mind the image of her exquisite hair, her delicate face, her magnificent body. Her skin was dewy soft, making him long to touch it and her lips—

Matt caught himself and chewed at his lower lip. *Damn!* Here he was daydreaming over a woman who, like Vicky, was out to kill him!

He was in an even fouler mood by the next morning. He'd lain awake far too long worrying about what Shannon Edwards's next move would be and how best to try to appease her, much as it went against the grain. He was also very concerned about the lagging sales closings at the development his company was working on and about the recent thefts going on there.

Sometimes he wondered why he even bothered. Maybe he should simply throw up his hands, chuck the whole thing and hire on as a deckhand on a shrimp boat. Matt flattened his lips against his teeth as he glared at his face in the bathroom mirror, then slapped on shaving cream, picked up his razor and grimly set to work.

Despite all his problems, and they were plenty enough, the real reason Matt was in such a rotten mood was that Shannon Edwards had even invaded his dreams last night, just as she'd invaded his business. She'd been all burrowed up close to him, kitten soft and just as warm, desiring him as much as he'd desired her. Awakening, Matt hated himself for the dream, for the aching need that throbbed through him. He didn't want to desire her. Besides all the other reasons, she was also a married woman.

Now he rinsed the shaving cream from his face, patted it dry with a towel and wondered what Shannon's husband was like. Maybe he was the male equivalent of his ex-wife, the cheating Vicky, since his barb yesterday in the office about her marriage had brought about that violent reaction. In an automatic reflex at the memory, Matt's long fingers went up to touch his cheek where she had slapped him. He eyed himself in the mirror and thought that if his conjecture was true, he'd deserved that slap.

As was his habit each morning, Matt drove first to the development, Spinnaker's Run. He always liked to know that everything was under control there before he got to the office and delved into paperwork. And lately, what with the thefts going on, it was a matter of serious concern. He hoped to high heavens that today he wasn't going to be greeted by any more bad news.

Instead, it was worse. Or so it seemed to Matt.

At first he was unaware of anything unusual. The work crew was still in the process of arriving, and a few who were already there were standing around, drinking coffee and laughing.

Matt didn't see José, so he joined the knot of men near the idle bulldozer. "Anybody seen José?"

Grinning broadly, one man pointed toward the building going up. "Somewhere in there."

Matt automatically looked in the direction the man pointed, and just as he did, he saw a figure emerging from the interior frames and step out onto the scaffolding. José's husky form followed, and it was obvious that he was pointing out something to the other person.

Matt's heart lurched. He recognized the person with José despite the hard hat that concealed wheat-gold hair. Faded jeans hugged slender legs and shapely hips like a second skin, and though the plaid shirt was loose fitting and untucked at the waist, it could not hide the beautiful figure it covered. Even in the most casual and unpretentious of attire, Shannon Edwards looked sexy as hell.

Furthermore, Matt realized, the workmen standing behind him were as attuned to that fact as he was. He heard a smothered guffaw and an amused whisper, and they made his blood sizzle.

He didn't waste time quelling their open interest in her, though. That could come later. His mouth was dry with fear as he watched her inching along the scaffolding, pausing occasionally to speak to José. If she lost her balance and fell . . .

The thought, once in his mind, could not be banished. It terrified him beyond reason. True, she appeared to be as surefooted as a mountain goat, but all the same he held his breath. He didn't dare call out lest it precipitate the very thing he feared most, but mentally he willed her to step back between the support beams and onto the relative safety of the flooring inside.

At last, after what seemed like hours to Matt but in truth was only about five minutes, she returned to the inner framework of the structure. His breath returned in a huge gulp, and as José followed her, Matt swung around to face the work crew.

"Mrs. Edwards is a partner in this firm. If I ever see or hear any of you lacking proper respect for her again, you'll deal with me personally." His face was as ominous as a hurricane churning up the Gulf of Mexico.

He heard a collectively mumbled, "Yes, sir," as he turned and strode toward the building.

Inside the dim interior, Matt mounted the concrete stairway at one end. His boots made a scraping sound as he climbed. The sound of voices could be heard as Shannon and José carried on a conversation.

She saw Matt first and inclined her head politely as he came toward them. "Morning, Matt. José's been kind enough to show me around."

"So I noticed," Matt said evenly. He was struggling to keep a tight rein on his temper in front of José. Unwillingly his gaze followed her hands as she removed her hard hat, handed it to José and then fluffed her hair by combing it with her fingers. It was an ordinary act in itself, but it seemed blatantly sensual to Matt. It made him wish those were his fingers threading through the silky tresses.

Hastily he looked away and spoke to José, "Maybe you should go down to the men. They're standing around as if they have nothing to do."

"Is that so?" José's face took on a forbidding expression. If there was one thing he didn't tolerate, it was goofing off on the job. "I'll take care of that in a hurry," he stated decisively. He touched the brim of his hard hat in a brief salute toward Shannon, saying, "It's been nice meeting you, Mrs. Edwards."

Shannon smiled. "Same here, José. Thanks for everything."

A nerve in Matt's jaw twitched. He waited in cold silence until he heard José outside, shouting at the men. Then he moved abruptly, like a panther poised to spring.

His fingers clasped Shannon's arm and he pulled her toward him with more force than he'd intended. It brought her close, dangerously close, and instantaneous fire leaped through his body as her soft breasts made contact with the hard, flat surface of his chest. Their faces were only inches apart. The scent of her, soap and toothpaste, was morning fresh, and somehow more provocative to his senses than if she'd been wearing perfume. It made him hate himself—and her—and he spoke so harshly it surprised even him.

"Just what the hell were you doing, clamoring around out there?" he grated through his teeth. "Trying to get yourself killed? You had no right to be taking such chances and endangering José as well!"

Her eyes grew large in utter astonishment and her shell-pink lips formed a perfect circle, mirroring her surprise. They looked soft as velvet, and Matt fought against the overwhelming urge to taste them. They quivered ever so slightly, tantalizing him all the more. If he just inclined his head the smallest bit more...

The temptation was removed when Shannon ended the torturous intimacy. She wrested her arm free and stepped back. Swift relief swept over Matt that he hadn't, after all, made a fool of himself.

Her eyes narrowed with indignation. "You've got some nerve to say I was endangering anyone's life! Don't tell me *you've* never gone out on the scaffolding yourself to have a look!"

"That's different," Matt said quickly.

Shannon tilted her head and put one hand on her hip. "Don't be silly," she snapped. "Just because you're a man?"

"No. Because I know what I'm doing."

"And I don't?"

"Do you?"

"Apparently so. I'm here, aren't I? Alive and breathing." She shrugged. "I can't see why you're so stirred up about it, anyway. If I had managed to get myself killed, your problems would be over, wouldn't they?"

She shouldn't have said that. She realized it too late. Fury darkened Matt Tyson's face, even before he stepped toward her.

His hands came down on her shoulders. Through the cotton fabric of her shirt, she could feel his fingers almost on her flesh, pressing against her shoulder bones.

"How dare you?" His voice trembled hoarsely. "How dare you accuse me of actually wishing you dead?"

Shannon licked her lips. "I'm sorry," she said contritely. It *had* been a horrid thing to say and she regretted it. "I didn't mean it. I'm really sorry."

Like heavy stones, Matt's hands fell from her shoulders. He heaved a deep breath and said at last, "Me, too. I'm sorry you ever came here. All you've done since you've been here is disturb me and my employees. I ought to throw you off the premises!"

"Just try it!" Shannon snapped back. Contrition was forgotten in a flash. "You seem to have trouble remembering that they're *my* employees, as well, and that I have just as much right to be on these premises as you!"

"You're a disruptive influence," Matt said doggedly. "It'll be better for everyone if you stay away."

"Better for you, you mean," she countered swiftly. "What are you afraid of? What are you trying to hide?"

"Nothing!" He shook his head. "I swear it. You're just in the way, that's all!"

"It's too bad you feel that way," Shannon said, "because the only way you're going to be rid of me is if you buy me out!"

Matt rubbed his hand across his head with a frustrated gesture. "Don't think I haven't thought about it."

"Fine." Her voice was brisk. "You're welcome to make me an offer!"

Matt sighed and admitted slowly, "I'd give my eyeteeth if I could. Unfortunately I just can't swing it."

Shannon's eyes narrowed. "In that case, I suggest you try to be a little more cordial. It might make life easier for the both of us."

Spinnaker's Run, the development that Matt's company was working on, would be a first-class resort when it was completed. It was by far the most ambitious and prestigious project Anchor Development Company had ever undertaken, and Shannon mentally congratulated Matt. He had a right to be proud of it. The condominium currently under construction was only one part of the picture. There was also a single-dwelling residential section. The two areas were distinct and separated by a marina and a large parklike piece of land that would one day boast a clubhouse, a pool, tennis courts and a riding stable. Another tract of land abutting the condominium site was slated to become a golf course.

Matt had turned Shannon over to a young salesman named Ron, and for the past two hours they had toured the entire place. Ron showed her what had already been done and pointed out areas of future development.

Several homes already completed were occupied; several more were completed but unsold, and Ron took Shannon inside a couple of them.

She was impressed by the quality and creativity. Each house was distinctly different from its neighbor, yet all were well built, and much attention had been given to details.

Bedrooms and baths were opulent, kitchens well arranged, spacious and equipped with the finest appliances on the market. These were homes meant for easy, summertime living, and wide expanses of windows overlooking the bay reflected that purpose. At the same time the condos were meant for gracious entertaining, with elegant living rooms and formal dining rooms. Each home was set on an acre of land and behind them, boat channels led to the marina.

The salesmen working on Spinnaker's Run reported to a separate office from the one in town for Anchor Development, its parent company. A small on-site office was located near the main entrance gate of the resort, and as Shannon and Ron walked toward it at the end of the tour, he explained that the sales team consisted of three men—the sales manager, another salesman and himself.

When they entered the office, Ron introduced her to the sales manager, who had not been present earlier when Matt had left her with Ron.

Slightly overweight and red-faced, he had thinning hair and puffy eyes. His name was Malcom Judson. "Ah, Mrs. Edwards." He drawled her name as they shook hands. "I'm sorry I wasn't here earlier to take you around the development myself. If I'd been advised of your visit beforehand, I would have made a point to be here."

Smiling, Shannon said, "That's quite all right. Ron was an excellent guide."

"Of course, of course. I'm sure he was," Judson said heartily. "However, he hasn't been with us very long, so there might be questions he was unable to answer. If there are, I'll be more than happy to fill you in."

"I appreciate that, because I still have a lot of questions."

"Good, good. Won't you sit down?" While Shannon took a chair in front of the desk, he told the salesman, "Pour Mrs. Edwards a cup of coffee." Taking his own seat, he said magnanimously, "Now, what can I clear up for you?"

"Recent sales. I'd like to see the records covering the last quarter. Also, samples of the advertising and promotions being done."

Judson's smile vanished. He leaned back in his chair and aligned the fingers of both hands together, steeple fashion. "Uh, well, I don't know precisely where the records are at the moment. However, I must explain that real estate has been slow for some time now, what with interest rates so high and the whole economy down and—"

Shannon interrupted, her voice soft, but firm. "Surely you can tell me how many sales have been made in the past couple of months?"

Judson looked taken aback. The steeple came apart and his hands went to the arms of his chair, rubbing backward and forward in a nervous gesture. "Oh, we're holding our own as far as sales go, I assure you," he said quickly. "You mustn't worry your pretty little head about that. Mr. Tyson understands the intricate problems involved in merchandising a place like this and—" He broke off as Ron brought the coffee and set it before Shannon on the edge of the desk. "That'll be all," he told Ron in a clipped voice. "Go ahead and take an early lunch break while Mrs. Edwards and I get acquainted."

Ron looked surprised. "I'm sort of expecting a call from the couple I showed around yesterday. They said they'd probably phone around eleven."

"If they do, I'll take care of it." Judson had clearly dismissed him.

"Thanks for all your help, Ron," Shannon said with a quick smile.

He smiled back. "It was my pleasure."

After he left, Shannon spoke before Judson had time to resume his speech. "You still didn't answer my question. How many unit sales did you make the last quarter . . . two, three, a dozen?'' Again her voice was low and gentle, but there was a glint of something like steel in her gaze.

The large man shifted uncomfortably in his seat and tried another tack. ''One quarter's figures don't give an accurate picture, Mrs. Edwards. You have to take a lot of variables into account—the state of the economy, as I mentioned before, the season, the weather, local elections and how those will affect the tax base, etcetera, etcetera, etcetera. I could go on and on, but you get the picture, I'm sure. Resort homes like this can't be sold like so many hamburgers, you know. It takes time and patience.''

''Both of which I'm very quickly running out of today,'' Shannon said with meaning. ''Let's get something clear, Malcolm. I know when I'm getting a runaround. Now I happen to have a vested interest in Anchor Development Company and therefore I'm worrying my pretty head about everything concerning it, particularly sales. I don't want speeches or excuses, just facts. Naturally I can see the duplicate records at the main office, but I would much prefer it if you would oblige me and show them to me yourself.''

Judson was silent for a long moment. Then he shoved back his chair, stood up and said stiffly, ''Whatever you say.''

For the next hour Shannon looked at the records and asked hard questions Judson didn't like. He didn't like her, either, and the feeling was mutual. She also didn't like the numbers on the records nor the way Spinnaker's Run was being promoted. By the time she finally left the sales office she was filled with misgivings.

Shannon went home for lunch since it was so near the development. She made herself a quick sandwich, poured a glass of iced tea and went out to the sun deck to eat.

But it took some time for her to wind down from the battle of nerves she'd endured all morning, and for a long time the food remained untouched as she lay back in her lounge chair and gazed at the bay waters. Only by slow degrees did she relax.

She'd known when she'd come that it would be difficult, that she wasn't likely to be welcomed with open arms. But the continual hostilities between her and Matt were beginning to take their toll, and as for the rest of it, standing up to Matt's secretary and Malcolm Judson, the sales manager... Shannon sighed. She wasn't cut out to be the stern, executive type. It took all the courage she had to stand up to them, to assert an authority they were reluctant to concede to her. Yet she had no choice but to brazen it out. If Matt Tyson would only back her up, none of the employees would dream of challenging her or throwing stumbling blocks in her way.

But, then, if Matt Tyson had been open and willing to deal with her all along, there would never have been the need for her to try to take on something she'd never been trained to do. She would have been content to leave it in his hands.

Shannon ate her sandwich at last, then went inside to take a quick shower and change into something more business-like than jeans before going to the office.

As she rubbed soap over one shoulder she remembered the sensation of Matt's hands as they'd rested against her blouse. The scene in the condominium came back to her in vivid detail—that first encounter when Matt had pulled her against him, then a short time later, his fingers pressing into her shoulders when he'd been so furious.

Her face warmed as she recalled with almost painful intensity that brief moment when she'd been pressed against him, when their faces, their lips had been so close. In spite of her shock over his unexpected action, she had actually *liked* his hard, strong body touching hers. Even now she could feel the crispness of his shirt, feel his body heat flowing into hers, experience the electrical jolt that had quivered through her as she'd looked at his lips so close to hers and wondered if he was going to kiss her.

It was terrible of her to have such thoughts where he was concerned, and as she stood beneath the spray of hot water, Shannon vowed to herself that there would be no more of such nonsense!

Later, when she arrived at the office, she was gratified to find Anne eager to be friendly and helpful. She was further gratified to discover that a second desk had been wedged into Matt's office.

"It'll be a couple of days before we can get another telephone installed, though," Anne told her, "but we've done the best we could on short notice."

"This is fine," Shannon said as she sat down behind the desk.

Matt was not in, and Shannon congratulated herself that for the time being, at least, she had a respite from his disturbing and contentious personality.

She asked Anne for the sales records for the past twelve months and began poring over them with earnest attention.

Two hours later Matt entered his office to find Shannon Edwards as he had the previous day, head bent as she concentrated on the papers before her. The only difference was that this time she sat at her own desk instead of his. It was bitter gall for him to see her making herself entirely at home, but there wasn't a darned thing he could do to prevent it. Still highly conscious of Mike's warning that he'd already caused himself enough trouble with her as it was, he kept his thoughts to himself.

"Hard at it, I see," he said, unable to keep the sarcasm from his voice.

"Umm," she murmured, apparently not having caught the note of irony. Or else she chose to ignore it. Suddenly she glanced up and said politely, "Thanks for the desk." Then she bent her head once more and seemed to forget his very existence.

Matt had never seen anyone so earnest about studying since his school days, when Freda Mae Jenkins always had her nose in a book. Only Freda Mae never had such rich, honey-colored hair or such a ripe figure that it invaded a man's dreams.

Yet incredibly, Shannon genuinely seemed not to realize her effect on men. This morning he knew that she couldn't have been aware of the reaction of the work crew. Not once had she done anything that could be construed as flirtation. Her husband was a lucky devil. So why, he wondered curiously, had the man let her come to Texas without him? Were they separated? Or was it, he thought with hope suddenly rising, that she simply hadn't planned to stay here long?

He was distracted by the buzzer on his telephone. He picked up the receiver. "Yeah?"

"Mona Mosley on line one," Anne said.

Mona, divorced like himself, owned a local hobby shop. Matt had dated her only a few times. She was okay, he supposed, trying to be fair-minded, but she really wasn't his type, and when she'd gone away a few weeks ago to visit relatives, he'd promptly put her out of his mind.

Now she was back, and on the phone, waiting for him. Matt was reluctant to accept her call, but as his eyes flickered over Shannon's bowed head once more, he changed his mind. He punched the lighted button on his phone, leaned back in his chair and forced warmth into his voice. "Hi, Mona. How was Austin?"

Mona told him, long-windedly, and it was some time before she finally got to the reason for her call. "Caroline Avery invited me to their barbecue on Saturday. She said you'd been invited, too. I just wondered whether you'd like to go together."

Matt could think of little he'd like less. He'd already decided to cool it with Mona. But as his gaze fell on Shannon, a perverseness came over him. He resented his unreasonable, unwilling attraction to her.

It annoyed him so much that almost before he knew what he was doing, out of sheer pique, he'd agreed to take Mona to the barbecue.

"It'll be wonderful seeing you again," she purred in a more intimate voice. "I missed you while I was away."

What was he supposed to say to that? Matt wondered irritably. That he'd missed her, too? It would be a lie. Even if it were true, he could scarcely say so with Shannon sitting nearby, listening to every word.

He felt his face grow warm. "Umm, I'd better let you go now," he said, feeling self-conscious and uncomfortable. "I've got work to do. I'll see you Saturday...say around three?"

"Do we have to wait till then?" Mona's tone became low and suggestive. "I'd love to see you tonight."

"Sorry," Matt lied, "but I can't make it tonight."

"That's too bad," Mona pouted. "I'll try to be patient until Saturday."

When Matt hung up, Shannon looked across at him. Liquid gold amusement bubbled in her creamy-brown eyes, and her lips were twitching with the urge to laugh. It made him so furious he wanted to throttle her! He also had the most dreadful gut feeling that she'd been able to hear both ends of the conversation and had read his thoughts, as well...that she knew his own cussed stubbornness had just backed him into yet another corner.

"Something funny?" he asked coldly.

Her lips quirked and the laughter won. At the dark look in his eyes she controlled it hastily, however, and shook her head. "I'm only glad to know my arrival isn't interfering with your love life, that's all," she said in a voice that shook with enjoyment.

"Don't worry about that," Matt snapped. "That'll never happen, I assure you. You may have fifty-one percent of my business, but you'll never have one percent of my personal life."

Her amusement vanished. "You're so bad tempered, I wouldn't want it," she countered. "I'm only a bit surprised to hear you making a date."

Matt sneered at her. "Why? Am I so unattractive you think I can't get a date?"

"Oh, now, come *on*," she shot back. "If that's a hint for me to stroke your ego, forget it. I'm sure you're very well aware of your effect on women. No, I was only surprised because I thought you were married."

Matt stared at her blankly. "I'm divorced. Whatever gave you the idea I had a wife?"

Shannon shrugged. "Well, that little boy was with you in the supermarket. Is he your son?"

Matt shook his head. "I don't have any children. Jason's my nephew."

"Oh."

The news that he was unattached interested Shannon far more than it should have. After all, Matt had been nothing but consistently horrible to her.

All the same, his making a date with someone named Mona somehow intensified her loneliness and heightened her awareness of her own dismal, solitary existence.

Shannon resented him for that—for being so damnably attractive, for making her conscious once more of the sort of physical magic that can exist between a man and a woman. It only made each day a little bleaker, each night much, much emptier.

Chapter Four

T hat's right," Matt said into the telephone. From the corner of his eye he saw Shannon entering the office, but he didn't acknowledge her as he concentrated on what the person on the other end of the line was saying. "What? Yes, that's right. Nights and weekends." He listened closely and scribbled on a note pad. "What'll that cost?" Listening again, he scratched figures beside the notes he'd written, then leaned back in his chair and stared at the ceiling. "All right, send somebody tomorrow morning if you can swing it that soon. Get back to me on that, will you?"

He cradled the phone and looked around, but Shannon had vanished. He rubbed his eyes wearily, and when he opened them once more, she came through the doorway, carrying two ceramic mugs of coffee.

Matt's eyes were bleary from lack of sleep, yet she was still a magnet of loveliness drawing his gaze. She wore a white cotton sundress with a short-sleeved, red bolero jacket over it. A wide red belt encircled her waist and below it the skirt flared becomingly over her hips and legs. On her feet were attractive sandal-type high heels. In one brief glance, he took it all in, the cool, crisp summer look, her shiny hair and, finally, her face. Her eyes sparkled like sunshine on gold and her berry-red lips were parted into a pleasant smile.

"Good morning." She crossed the room and set one of the mugs in front of him. "I bought some doughnuts to go with our coffee. I hope you're hungry."

As she went around her own desk and began opening a paper bag, Matt watched her, trying to deny her beauty, the lure of her smile, and most of all, he tried not to admit his feelings for her. No matter how hard he battled against it, he couldn't shake the longing to touch her, to kiss those rose-petal soft lips, to run his fingers through that golden halo of hair.

The fantasy was a pleasant one—and an agony. Shannon Edwards was not for him, Matt curtly reminded himself. Even if she weren't married, she still wouldn't be for him. Though she was his business partner, she was also his business enemy. He must never let down his guard and forget that. He must never forget the hard lesson Vicky had taught him.

Still, he recognized a peace offering when he saw it, and he was as tired of hostilities as Shannon apparently was.

Carrying two doughnuts on a paper napkin, Shannon brought them to his desk. Her arm grazed his as she bent to place the offering before him, and the softness of her skin touching his sent a tingle of yearning along his nerves.

Matt caught his breath and held it. Today she wore perfume, and the faint scent of jasmine assaulted his senses, undermining his determination to remain indifferent to her. Impulsively, following his desire before he had time to reason, Matt caught her hand in his.

The slender fingers caught within the circle of his fluttered and then were still. Shannon's eyes darkened with surprise—and wariness—as she gazed down into his.

"Thanks," Matt said huskily.

"You . . . you're welcome," she answered uncertainly.

Instead of releasing her, Matt's fingers tightened around hers. He liked the silky smooth feel of her hand, the slender shape of it, the long delicate fingers, the warmth it gave to his own.

He cleared his throat. "Look," he said in a serious tone. "I'm sorry I've been acting like a jerk. I'd like to start over again." Her eyes widened, as though she didn't trust what he said, and Matt mentally kicked himself. After the way he'd behaved so far, who could blame her? He went on quickly, "I mean it. You're a partner. You have a right to know what's going on, to make decisions, too. I won't try to block you anymore."

Shannon's hand quivered ever so slightly within his. The tip of her tongue darted between her lips, moistening them, and the unconsciously sensual action entranced Matt. "Why did you?" she asked softly. "Block me, I mean?"

Matt sighed and shook his head. "It's a long, sordid story you really don't want to hear. I was taking something out on you that had nothing to do with you. All I can do now is apologize."

Shannon was extraordinarily conscious that her hand remained captured by Matt's. All her senses were alert to it, to the strength, yet gentleness of his long fingers, the mesmerizing warmth that flooded through her. Strangely, his grip felt comfortable, right somehow, almost as if her hand belonged there, sheltered within his, although she had no idea why she should feel that way.

As she stood beside him, her eyes drank in every detail of his appearance. A pale-blue pullover knit shirt, open and providing an enticing view at the throat, enhanced Matt's muscular shoulders. One strong, bronzed arm rested on the edge of the desk, while the other was propped on the armrest of the chair as he continued holding her hand. Shannon began to wonder whether he'd forgotten he was holding it.

Although she fought against the almost involuntary reaction, her gaze kept returning to his face. She memorized every detail of it, the softening of his lips, the tired lines that grooved his forehead. His hair was slightly mussed, but his face was freshly shaven.

Yet it was his eyes that drew her attention the most. They were slightly bloodshot, evidence of the fact that he'd had little sleep. As his gaze met hers steadily, she saw the sincerity in them. The apology was genuine.

"I accept your apology," she answered at last.

Matt's fingers tightened once more about hers. "Good," he said, sighing. "Good." Then slowly, as though he were reluctant to do so, he released her hand. "This morning's probably as good a time as any for us to talk things over. I'll fill you in on everything."

"Fine. I appreciate that." Shannon nodded briskly and returned to her own desk. It felt safer there, and she found that once she was away from Matt, she could breathe more freely and think more clearly.

Matt lifted the mug of coffee and took a sip. Then he rubbed his hands over his eyes once more.

Shannon said gently, "You look tired. Didn't you sleep well last night?"

Matt smiled wryly. "The fact is, I didn't sleep at all. I was patrolling at Spinnaker's Run."

Shannon stared at him. "Why? Is something wrong?"

Matt's face was grim. "There's plenty wrong. Someone is trying to sabotage the work, and he's doing a damn good job of it, too. Until last night it was thefts of supplies. Now the men haul everything they can back to the warehouse to lock up overnight. Last night one of the homeowners heard noises and called the sheriff. Someone got into one of the empty houses and did a lot of damage—broke some windows, ripped out wiring, sprayed paint on the walls. I went as soon as I got word, and spent the rest of the night there.''

"This is terrible!" Shannon gasped. "Did they catch the person responsible?"

"Are you kidding?" Matt shrugged. "They don't have any idea who's been doing these things, and neither do I." He sighed heavily. "The losses are starting to mount up."

"What are you going to do?"

Matt leveled a smile at her. "*We*. Us now. Remember?"

Shannon smiled back. She liked the sound of that. "All right," she said. "What can we do about it?"

"When you came in this morning I was talking to a security agency in Corpus. Much as I hate to be out the extra expense of hiring guards at nights and on weekends, I don't see much choice. I sure can't stand guard every night, and I can't exactly see you doing it, either." He managed another rueful smile. "Of course, if you can come up with some other solution..."

Shannon shook her head. "No, you're right. It'll be expensive, but we can't keep sustaining losses from theft and vandalism. We'd go in the hole in no time."

"That's how I figure it." Matt's face was glum as he broke off a piece of doughnut, chewed it absently, then washed it down with coffee. He looked at Shannon again and grimaced. "There's an investor who owns the land to the east of the development, who's been after me to sell him the two hundred acres adjacent to it—the area where we'd planned the golf course. If we keep having these kinds of problems, we may have to consider the offer just to stay afloat. The loans we have already are steep enough without having to go back for more to cover something like this."

"It's an option," Shannon conceded, "but let's not do anything hastily. Maybe with the guards the problem will end."

"I hope so." Matt drained his coffee. "Well, on to other matters."

For the next hour they poured over various records. Matt explained everything concisely, answered every question clearly and fully. Despite the fact that he was open and agreeable today, Shannon was somewhat suspicious at the sudden change in him. She wasn't ready to bestow complete trust in him.

Yet she could pinpoint no area in which she'd found him dishonest. As a matter of fact, in the records she'd taken home last night, she had discovered something that indicated just the opposite. It was that alone that thawed her more than anything.

Six months ago Matt had cut his salary and stopped taking his dividends as a shareholder, yet he hadn't cut off Shannon's or her father's. This was forcing her to reassess her notion that Matt was attempting to conceal some funny business. Rather, he'd been working hard to pare expenses to the bone, and he'd cut himself most of all. She was no business expert, but even she could see that such an action appeared contrary to what a crook might be expected to do.

Shannon kept waiting for Matt to bring up the subject, but he never did, and finally she felt compelled to mention it herself.

"Tell me, why did you slash your salary and stop your dividends but not mine or my father's?"

Matt's head shot up and he demanded, "How'd you know about that?"

"I found it in the books I took home with me last night."

"It's no big deal." Matt shrugged and looked back at the papers on his desk. "Now this—"

"I want an explanation." Shannon's voice was determined.

Matt sighed. "Sales have been too slow for months. I had to cut back somewhere, and the logical place was with myself."

"Agreed. But why not my father and me, as well?"

"I was hoping things would get better soon and I wouldn't have to do that."

Shannon drummed her fingers on her desk. "Do you think that's fair?"

"Fair?" Matt stared at her. "What do you mean? I didn't cut your income. You ought to be pleased."

"Well, I'm not," she bristled. "Partners share both the good times and the bad. If your dividends are suspended until sales improve, mine should be, as well."

"I don't see it that way," Matt argued. "As it is, you don't draw a salary, so why should we cut off your only income from the company?"

"Because we can't afford it just now, that's why. As of today my dividends are on hold along with yours for as long as we both deem it necessary."

"That's ridiculous!" Matt exclaimed. "That way you're drawing nothing out of the business. Unless you'd rather we put you on salary, too?" His eyes narrowed. "If you're staying permanently, that is?"

Shannon ignored the question. "I'm not asking for anything right now. Let's just concentrate on what's important—getting the company's finances back into a stable position. Now," she went on, ignoring his glare, "about those slow sales. Matt, do you have full confidence in Malcom Judson?"

Matt frowned. "I did when I hired him. He had a good track record selling condos on Mustang Island, but I have to admit he hasn't done so well for us. What's your impression of him?"

She tilted her head. "The truth?"

He nodded. "The truth."

"He's a slick, snake-oil salesman," she replied promptly.

Matt chuckled. "Surely not that bad!"

"Practically. To be honest, he struck me wrong on a personal basis and I may be letting my prejudice get in the way of my judgment, so if I am, say so. But I also don't like his sales methods. All those gimmicks to get people to visit the resort . . . you know, free radios or telephones, drawings for TVs or microwaves. When I get such come-on mail, I throw it away. Those who do respond get a high-pressure sales pitch. To me, that's another turnoff. It must be to potential customers, too, because now that interest rates are more favorable, sales are still off.''

"It's not ideal," Matt agreed. "I hate gimmicks and hard sell, too, but it seems to move a lot of resort properties."

"Umm. Still, it doesn't seem to be doing the job here," Shannon pointed out. "You didn't use that type of scheme with the first condo you and my father built, did you?"

"No. It wasn't a complete resort such as this and it didn't require extra measures to sell it. Neither did the shopping center we built, of course." Matt leaned back in his chair and tapped a pencil against his knuckle. "You're right, though. Sales have been lagging and we need to change our tactics. I've been thinking the same thing for months, but I haven't come up with any solutions yet. Do you have any suggestions?"

Shannon eyed him thoughtfully, not knowing whether he really wanted her opinion or not. "Well," she hedged, "I realize I haven't had any professional experience at this sort of thing and I don't want to come across as if I'm trying to tell you what to do, but I do have an idea."

Matt nodded. "Point taken. Let's hear it."

"It seems to me that what's really wrong is the marketing angle. The thing is, Spinnaker's Run is first-class. Yesterday I was struck by how much care and thought has gone into every aspect of it."

Matt grinned. "If that's a compliment, I'll take it."

"It is," she assured him. "And because it's top quality, it should be promoted more tastefully. I see it's principal appeal to the well-off—people who can afford the best and who buy only the most exclusive, the most elite, the most prestigious addresses. It should be offered for sale in a more selective manner than is being done now and targeted to the right people, not necessarily to the public in general.''

"How would you do that?"

"I'm not exactly sure," she admitted. "The first thing I'd do is replace the sales manager with someone qualified to market it the right way. I know a man in Dallas who's been highly successful for a developer there. His wife is a friend of mine from college. I could ask him to come for an interview if you're interested."

"I'll think about it," Matt replied noncommittally. The truth was, he was too tired and sleepy to be able to think straight anymore, much less make a decision as important as the one Shannon was placing before him.

"Of course." Shannon quickly dropped the subject. For a little while they'd been discussing things as a team and it had encouraged her. But perhaps she'd overstepped the bounds, after all. Matt still wasn't ready to accept her as a partner.

Matt awoke refreshed from his two-hour nap. He flipped over in bed and peered at the clock—6:05. Yawning, he got up, padded to the bathroom and stepped into the shower.

After the lengthy session with Shannon, he'd kept a lunch appointment, then gone to the construction site to confer with José about repairing the vandalized house. Instead of returning to the office when they'd finished he'd gone home to grab some of the shut-eye he'd missed last night.

Now he felt alert and energetic as he finished his shower and began to dress. There was no point in returning to the office this late in the day, but he decided to drive out to Spinnaker's Run one last time. Tonight two of his own men would be guarding the place; tomorrow morning the new security guard would arrive.

Matt wished he knew who was behind the thefts and vandalism. As far as he knew he didn't have any enemies. Yet clearly someone was bent on causing as much trouble as possible. It could be some rebellious kids, of course, doing it for a lark, but somehow he didn't think so.

Bad as the situation was, Matt felt less morose about it now than he had early this morning. Ever since he'd discussed it with Shannon, he'd had a sense of a problem shared, a problem halved.

Which was a damn silly way to be thinking, he chided himself as he drove toward Copano Bay. Just because she'd seemed concerned about the problems of the company this morning, it didn't follow that she had any concern or sympathy for him, for the burdens he'd carried alone. It just underscored her primary interest—the success of Anchor Development Company.

But somehow Matt knew he was beating a dead horse with that attitude. Of course Shannon was interested in the company's well-being, possibly as much as he was. It was why she was here. But she *had* been concerned about him, as well. He'd been amazed, and grudgingly impressed with her sense of fairness, that when she'd discovered his self-mandated pay cut and dividend suspension, she'd insisted her share be withheld, too. Much as he might like to convince himself that she was as ruthless and selfish as Vicky had been, this one act alone played havoc with his convictions.

Too, for all she'd readily admitted that she knew little about business, Shannon had understood the most vexing problem of all—lagging sales. Though he hadn't admitted it to her when the subject came up, the truth was, Matt had been searching for another sales manager and a fresh approach to sales for the past two months. The problem was that the people he'd interviewed hadn't impressed him as having any more on the ball than Judson, and as for the fresh approach, the only ideas he'd come up with or that the couple of ad agencies he'd consulted had dreamed up had all seemed stale, instead.

Yet Shannon had recognized the problem with Judson at once and, more to the point, had suggested a solution that just might have possibilities. In spite of himself he was impressed by her idea, as well as the fact that she'd given it serious thought. He'd figured she'd only come to wring what she could out of the company, not to actively try to help it and certainly not to offer to put her own dividends on hold. It was causing him to have to seriously reassess his opinion of her, and it made him uncomfortable and a bit ashamed of himself.

Matt didn't stay long at the development. His men explained their plan for patrolling the area tonight, and, after approving it, he left them to it with instructions to call him at once if anything unusual did occur.

The resort wasn't far from Charlie Main's house—Shannon Edwards's now—and as Matt reached the road, he wavered for a moment, trying to decide whether to turn toward it or head in the opposite direction back to town.

There was no urgent need to consult with Shannon on a Friday evening, but Matt found himself driving toward her house, anyway.

Unlike most of the houses along the bay, clustered together in subdivisions, a few farther along the road were tucked away amid live oak trees, concealed from the road and from their neighbors. Charlie's house was one of these, with a couple of acres surrounding it, giving it complete privacy.

Evening shadows were falling as Matt turned into the private driveway. He saw Shannon's car parked in the space beneath the house, and a light burned in the living room window, beckoning, inviting.

She came to the door wearing pink shorts and a white knit shirt, and Matt caught his breath at the charming picture she made. The soft fabric of the shirt caressed her breasts, and below the shorts her thighs were enticingly curved. The golden-peach glow of her skin was sensuously exciting. Matt's mouth dried as he struggled to hide the effect she was having on him.

"Good evening," he said rather formally. "I hope I haven't come at a bad time."

"Not at all," Shannon replied. "Won't you come in?" She stepped back to allow him to enter.

Inside the living room, Matt gazed around silently for a moment, then said huskily, "It's the same as ever. Seems like Charlie ought to be sitting there in his favorite chair."

Something caught in Shannon's throat and she murmured, "Yes."

Matt turned. Compassion blazed in his eyes and he gently touched her arm. "Shannon, I'm truly sorry. I know I haven't shown much evidence of it since you've been here, but I cared about him, too. I miss being able to talk with him. He was always there for me whenever I needed him. He left a big gap in my life, so I can imagine what it must be like for you."

Tears moistened her lashes. She was touched, really touched, and it was a moment before she could speak.

"Thanks," she said at last.

Matt's hand fell away, and a tiny, awkward silence brought a strange tension between them. Finally he said, "I came to discuss your idea a little more about revamping our sales technique. Is this a good time, or am I interrupting something?"

"I was just about to start dinner, that's all." She smiled, then offered impulsively, "Would you like to stay and join me?"

Matt returned the smile. "Thanks, I'd like that."

He followed her into the kitchen and leaned against the counter, watching idly as she worked. Their conversation was casual and surprisingly easy, considering how they'd been at loggerheads almost constantly since they'd met.

Shannon put the chicken she'd been preparing into the oven, mixed a salad and made a broccoli dish. Then they went back into the living room to relax over drinks until the meal was ready.

Matt started toward the sofa, but he stopped in front of a shelf and gazed at a photograph of a smiling young man holding a baby. He knew instantly who they must be.

"Is this your family?" he asked as he paused to study it.
"Yes."

Matt heard something telling in that one word. It had come out flat, clipped, and there was pain behind it. He turned slowly and looked questioningly at her.

"I lost them three years ago in a car accident," she explained in that same matter-of-fact voice that attempted to conceal emotion. By the very lack of it, it gave away more than a flood of tears would have done.

Matt went to her swiftly and looked deeply into her eyes. "I had no idea. Charlie never told me, but, then, you know how he was—he never talked much about personal problems. How terrible for you!"

Shannon's expression was tight and controlled. She shrugged and said nothing.

Matt turned toward the photo again. "They were both very handsome," he said softly. "Tell me about them."

Her face thawed a little and her voice was more normal when she spoke. "My husband's name was Brad. Our little boy's name was Timothy. That picture was taken about two months before the accident, when he was just a little over a year old."

Matt's gaze was warm as he looked at her again. "Your son had your smile."

Shannon suddenly smiled. "And his father's eyes and even temperament."

Carrying their drinks, they moved toward the sofa and sat down at opposite ends. "What did your husband do for a living?" Matt asked.

"He had a computer programming company. It was becoming quite successful, but it took a lot out of him, too. Most of the time he worked ten and twelve-hour days."

Matt nodded. "Well, that's usually what it takes when you own a business." He lifted his glass and took a swallow.

"Yes."

Again there was the odd, flat quality to her voice. Matt sensed that in some way her husband's work had bothered Shannon, but he had a hunch it was best not to probe. Instead he delicately changed the subject.

The strain that had crept into Shannon's eyes when they'd talked about her family eased over dinner as they discussed business. They agreed that she would invite her Dallas friend to come for an interview, and that settled, the conversation became more general.

While they talked pleasantly about a multitude of impersonal subjects, Matt was slightly amazed at how much he was enjoying himself and how relaxed he felt in Shannon's company. He also felt more at ease with himself. He was genuinely sorry she'd lost her husband and child so tragically, but now at least he no longer felt like a heel for being attracted to her, as he had when he'd believed she was married. Now he didn't have to feel guilty for thinking her beautiful or wondering what it would be like to hold her.

He helped Shannon stack the dishes after dinner. "You're a marvelous cook," he said. "I can't remember a meal I've enjoyed better."

"Oh, come now," Shannon said, laughing at him. "You don't need to exaggerate. It was very simple."

"Simple, but good." Matt grinned. "My sister's a darned good cook, but I think you must have a magic touch she lacks."

"Flatterer." She wrinkled her nose at him.

Matt's grin widened and he teased boldly, "Will it get me anywhere?"

"Nowhere at all," she shot back.

Chuckling, he said, "Well, you can't blame a guy for trying."

"Sure, I can."

They continued the banter while Shannon washed and Matt dried.

When they were done, Shannon poured fresh-brewed coffee, and they carried it outdoors to the sun deck. "You're pretty handy with a dish towel," she teased. "Somehow you don't look the domesticated type."

"Oh, I'm housebroken," he replied with a grin. "When you live alone, you more or less have to be, unless you want to be a complete slob."

It was a dark night, but the lights from the windows cast a soft glow, so that the wooden table and chairs were faintly outlined. They went to stand, side by side, at the deck railing, and set their cups on top of it.

Shannon asked quietly, "How long has it been? Since your divorce?"

"A little over five years." Matt smiled wryly in the dim light. "The worst and the best five years of my life."

She looked at him curiously. "What an odd thing to say."

Matt shrugged. "Worst because of the aftereffects of the divorce, best because I'm no longer married to her."

"Was it so bad, then?"

He heard the gentle note of compassion in her voice, and unaccountably he was touched. He was silent for a long moment, and then he answered simply, "It was that bad."

"I'm sorry."

Matt inhaled a deep breath, then smiled at her. "Don't be. I'm just glad it's over."

"I'm glad you're glad." She smiled back, then suddenly glanced beyond him toward the dark fathomless sky. "Look! A falling star!"

He turned and together they watched the white streak of stardust plunge through the sky.

"Beautiful," Shannon breathed.

"Very. Are people supposed to make a wish on falling stars, too, or only those that stay put?"

"I'm not sure," she said with a little laugh. "Why don't we try it, anyway?"

As the shooting star disintegrated, she closed her eyes as though making a wish, and a tiny smile curved her lips.

Matt had fought temptation ever since the day he'd helped her up from the supermarket floor. Now he gave into it. While Shannon's eyes remained closed he bent his head and touched his lips to hers.

Her lips were soft and warm, just as he'd known they would be. Shannon went very still, and then her mouth parted slightly, as though in surprise.

Matt's arms went around her waist. Gently he drew her to him until their bodies were just touching. Again there was the velvet softness, the inviting warmth of her, and Matt was captivated by her alluring sweetness.

His kiss deepened with sudden, unexpected urgency, and Matt's hands moved slowly up her spine until he buried one in the thick waves of her hair. His tongue slid between her lips and he tasted her intimately.

Shannon gasped softly at the familiarity and she shuddered within his embrace. Then, almost as though she were a novice, unsure of herself, her hands went to his arms and fluttered there for a timeless moment before boldly moving up to his shoulders and finally encircling his neck.

The evening breeze cooled their feverish skin. Beguiled by the wonder of her, the taste and texture of her, the molten-hot power of her lips as she responded to his kiss, Matt became lost to everything except the rapture of holding her. Shannon was at once innocent and seductive—an angel and a siren.

Slowly he raised his head so that he could look at her. Growing desire caused his heart to thunder inside his chest, and holding her so closely, he could even feel the answering cho of her erratic heart. He smiled and whispered huskily, 'Shannon, I—''

He got no further. Shannon gasped as though in shock nd abruptly pushed him away. He was taken off guard by he unexpected action, and his arms fell to his sides as she tepped back, putting an unbridgeable distance between hem.

In the semidarkness her eyes were dark and luminous, her ace somber, her lips trembling. Her breathing was shallow nd labored as she lifted an unsteady hand to her mouth.

"I wish . . . I wish we . . . hadn't done that."

She didn't sound angry, frightened, affronted or coy— ust terribly sad, as though some tragedy only she could nderstand had just occurred.

Matt scarcely knew what to think. He was still half- emused at the depth of emotion that had come over him. Ie'd kissed a lot of women in his time and he'd never been ffected quite like this, as though somehow all the puzzle ieces of the entire universe had suddenly fallen into place. Now, inexplicably, he felt betrayed. He'd thought, just for n instant, anyway, that she'd felt the same. Obviously he'd een mistaken.

"Why?" he finally managed to ask. "Was it so unpleas- nt?"

"No! Of course not!"

"Then why?"

She shook her head. "I just wish it hadn't happened, hat's all!" She looked more upset than he'd first realized, ut before Matt could decide what to do or say next, she 1urmured huskily, "Good night," and vanished inside the ouse.

For a long minute Matt stood frozen beside the rail, too hocked at her unexpected reaction even to move. At last he 1rned toward the stairs and went down, wondering what 1e hell he'd done wrong.

And then the anger came, an enormous tidal wave surging over him. First she'd behaved warmly and sweetly, as though she'd liked his kiss. So why had she ended it this way? Answer: to make a fool of him.

What made it all the worse, he realized belatedly as he sped toward town, was that like it or not, he'd have to see her again.

They were in business together. Partners. He was trapped with no way out.

Chapter Five

Saturday morning Shannon attacked the housecleaning with a vengeance, as though civilization itself hinged upon it and might collapse if every speck of dust were not eliminated, every smudge eradicated, every cushion or throw pillow or drape not vacuumed so thoroughly that it qualified as hospital sterile. That there was no one to see or appreciate the immaculate results did not even occur to her.

She was fleeing from herself, from the chaotic state of her mind. Last night she'd tossed and turned for hours as her disturbed thoughts tumbled about in her head. This morning her emotions were still confused and erratic, warring with one another.

Matt's unexpected kiss had been an emotionally shattering event. The moments she'd been in the shelter of his arms, feeling his lips on hers, had been highly charged with a growing sexual tension that had left her limp when the kiss was over. She still cringed with shame at the thought of how, for a time, she'd forgotten herself and become immersed in the heady pleasure of his embrace.

Today she told herself that it was because he was her business partner that an involvement with him would be wrong, since it would only complicate an already precarious relationship. What she didn't want to face was the truth—the guilt she felt because she was so drawn to Matt.

She could never forget, never stop berating herself over the foolish, childish fight she'd provoked with Brad the night before he'd died. She would remain forever unforgiven for that, for the ugly, meaningless threat of divorce that had wedged between them those last hours. And Timmy, her precious baby—even now she had to choke back tears of sorrowful regret because she hadn't picked him up earlier from her mother-in-law's home that fateful day. If she had, her husband and her son would both still be alive.

The burden of regret Shannon carried was always with her, heavy, fatiguing, without relief. She'd grown accustomed to it, learned to live with it, like a constant dull ache that wouldn't go away. She could never make it up to her beloved family, but neither could she free herself from the memory and the everlasting guilt.

By afternoon, it was a relief to escape from her gloomy thoughts. When she'd spoken to Caroline Avery a couple of days ago, she'd been invited to a barbecue at her home, and now, heartily sick of her own company, Shannon was glad she'd accepted. Caro had insisted she arrive early so they could have a private visit before the other guests arrived.

The Averys had a charming brick home on the outskirts of town. Lovely old live oaks graced the front lawn and lush, gigantic elephant ears filled a planter near the door.

Caro greeted Shannon with a hug and they both laughed as their eyes took inventory after nine years apart. "You look terrific!" Caroline exclaimed. "Slimmer, I think, with an air of sophistication."

"You look pretty wonderful yourself!" Shannon returned. Caroline was cute rather than pretty, with short auburn hair, twinkling brown eyes and a sprinkling of freckles across her nose. It was her winsome personality rather than her looks that had always drawn people to her, and Shannon was delighted to find she hadn't changed at all. She was as buoyant and friendly as ever.

"Come meet the gang," Caro said, urging her inside. She led Shannon through a lovely formal living room, then through a paneled family room and outside again to a wide terrace that meandered around a large swimming pool.

Two children were playing with a dog on the lawn and a man stood before a smoking barbecue pit, turning meat.

"Here she is," Caroline sang out. "Come here, everybody, and say hi to Shannon."

Immediately the two women were surrounded. Shannon was introduced to Mike Avery, whose voice she recognized from their frequent telephone conversations. He had an easy smile and a friendly manner that she liked immediately. As for the children, Cathy and Mikey, Shannon found them adorable. Both had thick mops of bright-red hair and even brighter, guileless smiles.

"Mommy says you're an old, old friend," Cathy said. "Mommy, I don't think she looks old. She's not crinkled or anything."

"Crinkled?" Shannon laughed. "Caro, have you been telling your children I'm old and crinkled?"

Caroline chuckled. "Well, it has been nine years. I wasn't sure what to expect, you know, so I had to prepare them for anything."

"Ignore her, Shannon," Mike said. "Now come here and give me your opinion on how this meat's coming along."

"Well, I'll try to hobble over, but it won't be easy, decrepit as I am." Shannon sniffed the air. "Umm, I'm no expert, Mike, but if that heavenly scent means anything, you're doing a superb job."

"That's what I think, too, but Caro said maybe I didn't marinate it long enough." He sliced a sliver of brisket and offered it to Shannon.

She tasted it and murmured blissfully, "Don't listen to your wife, Mike. Obviously it's her brain that's been marinated too long. This is wonderful."

Caro grinned at them. "While you two rake me over the mesquite coals, I'll get us something to drink."

"None for me, hon," Mike called as she went toward the house. "I'll wait until I get back from Mom's." To Shannon, he explained, "She's going to keep the kids for us tonight." He lowered the barbecue pit cover, then looked steadily into Shannon's eyes and asked somberly, "How's it going between you and Matt?"

She smiled ruefully. "I guess you could say we've called a truce—for the moment, anyway. Yesterday we actually sat down and discussed business in a civilized manner."

"Good. You're making progress."

"If it lasts," Shannon said doubtfully. Especially after the fiasco of last night. But she kept that to herself.

"Matt's really okay," Mike said. "He just has a few hang-ups about women where his business is concerned."

"So I've noticed. He even said he'd been blaming me for something someone else had done. What's it all about, Mike?"

"I'm not sure—" Mike was distracted by Caroline's reappearance. She carried two tall glasses of iced tea. Mike spoke again, saying simply, "I wouldn't worry about it, Shannon. You've made a start, so I think the two of you'll work things out all right. Matt knows he can't really keep you out of your own business."

"Business!" Caroline wrinkled her pert nose. "I did not invite Shannon here today so you could waste time discussing dreary old legal matters. We've got years to catch up on!"

"I'll let you get started, then." Mike grinned indulgently at his wife, then shouted at the children, "Come give Mommy a kiss before we go to Grandma's."

A few minutes later Caroline and Shannon were alone, seated in comfortable cushioned patio chairs near the pool, and, as they were prone to do on occasional late-night telephone conversations, they plunged straight into a heart-to-heart talk. Though it had been years since they'd seen each other, they'd remained close by telephone and mail.

"So how are you holding up under this latest blow...really?" Caro asked bluntly, referring to Charlie Main's unexpected death.

"Fine sometimes, not so well other times," Shannon replied, equally frank. "Sometimes I feel I've lost all sense of direction. There's no anchor anymore, and I honestly don't know what I want to do with my life."

Caroline squinted against the sun. "Maybe you shouldn't have quit your job."

Shannon shrugged. "It was just a job, and I can always get another. Actually, there were so many details to attend to the first couple of months after he died there wasn't time for anything else. I had to get his house ready to sell and settle all his business affairs. It was no easy task, believe me."

"I know," Caroline murmured sympathetically.

"And then there was the situation here when Matt wouldn't cooperate with me, so I had to come get it straightened out."

"And is it?"

Shannon shrugged again. "Who knows? Maybe. Maybe not."

"You know," Caroline said thoughtfully, "in a way I think all the problems you've had with Matt have been good for you."

Shannon stared at her. "Are you kidding? It's just been one more headache on top of all the others."

"True, but it also got you good and mad, and you were able to vent some of your emotions at an enemy you could fight, instead of holding all your feelings inside. It made you angry enough to break out of your rut and come to confront him."

Shannon grinned ruefully and conceded, "Well, it did that, all right. He roused all my fighting instincts!"

Caroline laughed before they moved onto other topics. A little later she asked curiously, "Is there a man in your life yet?"

Shannon shook her head, although unbidden came the thought of Matt, of the disturbing kiss they'd shared last night. Yet he could scarcely be described as a romantic interest in her life. His kiss had taken her by surprise; his reaction afterward left her in no doubt that it would be the last. And she wanted it that way.

"No. No one," she said firmly.

Caroline made an impatient sound and scolded, "Shannon, I know you went through a dreadful time when you lost Brad and Timmy, but that was over three years ago. It's high time for you to start taking an interest in men again."

"Maybe someday." But Shannon knew she still had to work her way through a fog of guilt.

"Someday!" Caroline snapped. "You'll be an old woman someday and life will have passed you by! The way you're afraid to have anything to do with men—it's not natural, Shannon! Can't be very healthy, either," she added with little effort at subtlety.

Shannon grinned at Caro's impassioned tone. "What would you have me do, marry the first man who comes along? For the sake of my health?"

"I didn't say you had to marry one," Caro pointed out reasonably, "but at least it wouldn't hurt to *date* the first one who asked . . . or even the second or third."

"I don't know." Shannon shook her head, unconvinced. "I'm just not ready yet."

"And the longer you wait, the harder it's going to be," Caroline said sternly. "Honey, no one can take Brad's place, but that doesn't mean someone else can't be right for you, too. But you'll never know if you don't go out and give yourself a break."

Shannon smiled. "Rationally I know you're right, but..."

"But," Caro finished for her, chiding gently, "you're an irrational gal, even though you're lovely."

"Right." Shannon changed the subject and asked what had become of another local girl she had known as a youth.

Caro took the bait. "She's living in Austin now, teaching school."

The mention of teaching brought a wistful longing to Shannon. She'd enjoyed teaching until Timmy had been born. Then she'd elected to stay home with her baby, with the idea in mind that a few years down the road, once he was older, she'd return to the classroom. But after his death, she'd known she couldn't go back to being with children all the time—other people's delightful, healthy, lively children—and so she'd found a humdrum office job, instead.

Lately she'd begun to wonder whether she was emotionally ready to go back to teaching again. Certainly the office work she'd done in Denver had been unsatisfying by comparison, and really, so was her involvement in a company of which she was a part owner. Now, with her father gone, too, there was nothing—no person, no place, no work, no sense of purpose—to give meaning to her very existence. Her family had given her that once; so had teaching. But could teaching fill the emptiness of her life now, or would it be a mistake to try to go back? Shannon knew that somehow she had reached a crossroad, that it was time to steer herself in a new direction.

The question was—which direction?

Many of the guests were already assembled by the time Matt and Mona arrived at the Avery's barbecue. Caroline met them at the door, along with several other new arrivals, so for a little while there was a confusing babble as everyone greeted everyone else.

"Make yourselves at home," Caroline bade them all. "There's a bar in the family room and I think a few people are in there playing billiards. There's another bar outside, and if you want to swim in the pool, please do." The doorbell rang again and she went to welcome more arrivals while those who had just entered conferred about what they wanted to do.

Matt and Mona went outside to the terrace. Mona wore shorts and a brief top and said she wanted to sunbathe by the pool. Matt, in jeans and a casual cotton shirt, wasn't interested in basking in the sun, but he figured he could keep Mike company while he tended the meat in the barbecue pit.

A new hubbub arose as they met other acquaintances as they slowly made their way toward the bar. They inched past one group and drew level with another, when suddenly Matt was face to face with Shannon. He halted abruptly, so surprised to see her that for a moment all thought was suspended.

Despite the relentless glare of the sunshine and the heavy heat of midafternoon, somehow Shannon managed to look cool and crisp. She was wearing the same white sundress she'd worn to the office one day, except that today the covering red jacket was absent. Tiny straps hugged her creamy shoulders above the simple, unadorned bodice, and around her throat lay a single strand of pearls. A tie belt at her waist added a bright red splash of color against the white folds of her skirt. She looked so fresh and lovely that it was difficult for Matt to stop gazing, to remember that there were others around them; difficult, too, to forget the feel of her in his arms last night or the taste of her incredibly soft lips.

Just now her lips parted into a smile, but the smile was hesitant, uncertain, and he knew that she, too, was remembering last night . . . and its unhappy outcome.

"Hello, Matt," she said slowly. The polite words seemed forced. "I had no idea I'd see you here today."

"Neither did I. I didn't realize you knew the Averys."

Shannon's smile deepened, becoming genuine and unaffected. "I only knew Mike from speaking to him over the phone, but Caro and I've been friends since we were about ten years old."

"How about that!" Matt smiled, too, and forgot for the moment, as he enjoyed the pleasure of just looking at her, just *being* with her, that he was supposed to be angry with her. "That's great."

Shannon offered a shy smile to his companion and this jarred Matt into remembering his manners. He introduced the two women. "Shannon's here from Denver," he elaborated for Mona's sake.

Mona acknowledged the introduction with what to Matt was a surprising lack of warmth, though her words were civil enough. "How long will you be visiting the Averys?" she asked.

Shannon's eyes widened. "Until the party ends, I suppose."

"I meant how long are you staying with them?" Mona said impatiently. "Before you return to Colorado."

Shannon laughed softly. "I'm not staying with them. I'm staying in my father's vacation house."

"Oh." Mona looked taken aback. "You're here for the summer, then?"

Shannon smiled. "It's a little indefinite."

"Shannon and I are business partners," Matt explained.

"Partners?" Mona's surprise was obvious.

Matt nodded. "Charlie Main was her father. She inherited his part of the company and she's here learning the ropes."

"I . . . see." Mona looked thoughtfully at Shannon. "I would think you'd leave the business matters for Matt to handle."

"Would you?" Shannon asked sweetly.

Mona shrugged. "Well, he's been doing it by himself all along, hasn't he? Your father left him alone. I'd think you'd do the same."

"Is that so?" Shannon asked calmly.

Too calmly. Matt knew Shannon well enough now to tell that the flash of light in her eyes spelled danger. The thorny subject was about to bring fresh trouble.

He interceded hastily. "Shannon's already come up with some good suggestions."

"Really?" Mona asked skeptically. "But, then, it's always easy to advise from the outside looking in, isn't it? Or is she an authority on resort developments?"

"Not at all," Shannon answered smoothly. "I'm just a very interested party."

Mona nodded. "I suppose it *is* fun to dabble in business if you don't need to make a living. And you don't, do you? I've heard Charlie Main was worth a lot. I guess you can pretty much afford to do whatever you want, including playing at a business you know nothing about."

Matt was suddenly incensed. Who the hell did Mona think she was meddling in *his* business... *Shannon's* business! He'd never seen Mona like this before, catty and deliberately rude, and he just didn't understand it. What he did know, however, was that after today he would never have anything more to do with her.

That didn't solve the immediate crisis, however. His eyes sought Shannon's. Mona's unprovoked verbal attack had caused Shannon to stiffen, and she was no longer smiling. Her lovely golden-specked eyes had darkened to murky brown, though whether from pain or anger, he was unsure. When she finally met his gaze, his spoke a silent apology.

For a moment they went on looking at each other, he quietly beseeching, she with a curious expression that he couldn't fathom.

Then abruptly she tossed her head, blond hair bouncing, and she laughed aloud, and he knew even before she spoke that the apology had been refused.

"Well!" she exclaimed in an amused voice as she looked at Mona once more. "You've managed to take my breath away! I was under the impression that business matters were between Matt and me. He didn't warn me that he'd appointed an outsider as his lobbyist." Mona didn't reply, and Shannon's gaze returned to Matt. Her eyes were cold, chilling him, and her voice was icy. "It's been *so* nice seeing you both. Excuse me, please."

"Shannon!"

But it was too late to stop her. She ignored his entreaty as she hurried away.

Matt was hard put after that even to be civil to Mona, much less friendly. He was outraged that her interfering remarks had driven yet another wedge between Shannon and him. He dutifully got Mona a drink at the bar, carried it to where she'd taken a chair near the pool and, since she was talking to another woman, made good his escape.

Back at the self-serve bar, he got himself a beer and broodingly glanced around in a vain attempt to locate Shannon, but she was nowhere to be seen.

"How're you doing, Tyson?"

Matt turned to see Jack Waring beside him.

"Can't complain," Matt replied briefly. Waring wasn't one of his favorite people.

"Stiff upper lip, eh?" Jack laughed, revealing a mouthful of even, white teeth. They went well with his golden-tanned skin and sun-bleached hair. "The way I hear it, you've been having a few setbacks at Spinnaker's Run."

Matt tensed and wondered angrily who'd been talking to Waring. He slowly lifted his can and took a long drink of his beer. In a flat voice he said, "Nothing I can't handle."

"That's good," Waring said in a sympathetic tone. "But if it gets to be too much for you, my offer's still open. Matter of fact, I'd be willing to up the bid a little if you'll sell now. I really would like that land.''

Matt struggled to hide his dislike of the man. After all, Waring had never done anything to him personally, and he was only making a legitimate business offer—the same offer he'd been making for at least six months. There was nothing wrong with that, even if Matt didn't want to sell. It was just that Waring had always struck him wrong. He was the son of a wealthy Houston oilman, and though he had, with his father's financial backing, locally built an apartment complex and an office building, Matt's main impression of him was of a spoiled playboy who drank too much.

''Thanks,'' Matt answered, ''but the answer's still no. I need that land myself.''

Jack turned toward the bar and replenished his empty glass. ''Well, can't blame a man for trying,'' he said mildly. ''We've all got to look out for number one, you know. Say,'' he drawled in a completely different tone of voice, ''what have we here? New blood, and *what* a looker!''

Matt glanced in the direction Waring was looking. Shannon, carrying a large tray of hors d'oeuvres, was coming out of the house, followed by Caroline Avery, who carried another tray.

''See you later,'' Jack said with a leering grin. ''I've got to check this one out before she gets taken!'' He walked toward the two women.

Matt's muscles tensed as he watched the unfolding tableau.... Waring flashed his you're-the-only-girl-in-the-world smile at Shannon, and she smiled back. Then he gallantly removed the laden tray from her hands and carried it to the table for her as she cheerfully accompanied him. The final maneuver came as Waring touched her arm and leaned forward to speak to Shannon in an intimate manner. But she didn't seem to mind as they took a couple of chairs and sat down together. Matt burned, yet there was nothing he could do to alter the situation. Shannon was a free agent and had a right to do as she pleased—even if it meant falling into a wolf's clutches.

Not that he cared personally, one way or the other. Shannon's rejection of him after their kiss last night had cured him of any romantic notions. It was only that he wouldn't wish Jack Waring on any unwary woman. Someone really ought to warn Shannon, he thought grimly as he polished off his beer, but Matt knew he was the wrong one to do it. He was the last person on earth she was likely to listen to now, after the unpleasant episode with Mona.

Fresh anger spurted as he thought about that. Mona's comments couldn't have been more damaging. It had sounded exactly as though he'd complained to her about Shannon's involvement in the business, which he hadn't done. But he had a hunch Shannon was never going to be convinced of that!

"You have to come," Jack said with emphatic charm. "We'll have a great time. I'll pick you up at ten."

"It's been years since I've done any water-skiing. I'm not sure I even want to try again," Shannon answered dubiously. "Besides, there are some things I need to do tomorrow. We'd better leave it open. Why don't you call me in the morning and we'll talk about it?"

For a fraction of an instant, Shannon saw displeasure flit across Jack Waring's handsome face, but as quickly as it had come, it was gone. Instead of arguing, which she'd thought he was going to do, he relaxed and said with an easy smile, "Fine. But I have to warn you, I don't give up easily."

Shannon smiled back. "And I don't give in easily," she retorted.

Jack tossed his head back and laughed. "I'll remember that," he told her.

They were seated together, having dinner, at a long picnic table along with a number of other guests. For the past two hours Jack had been continually at her side, and it seemed, she thought ruefully, that he intended to stay there throughout the evening, as well.

She didn't really mind. Jack was easy to talk with, good-looking and likable. Yet there was something about him that bothered her, though she couldn't quite put her finger on it. Maybe, she decided at last, it was because he was coming on too strong, too fast. He'd made it clear enough that he was interested in her and he had a tendency to find excuses to touch her too often for her liking. He had the air of a practiced flirt, as well as of a man who too often got his way, and warning alarms had sounded off in her mind.

All the same, she was grateful for his attentions now, juvenile as she knew that to be... because of Matt. Several times she had felt his eyes upon her, and the few times her gaze had accidentally met his, she'd found his disapproving. It was salving to the pride to have an attractive man showering her with attention while the man who'd kissed her last night, who'd confided his dislike of her presence in the company to his girlfriend, looked on.

Not that he was in any way jealous. Naturally she knew that. Why should Matt be jealous when he had a beautiful woman hanging on his arm and giving him loving glances? But it was still comforting to Shannon to know men found her attractive, though he no longer did.

But if he no longer did, a tiny voice whispered, she had only herself to blame. Last night... last night... But she couldn't bear to think about that. It was embarrassing enough that she'd fluttered away from him like a nervous sparrow, but in the light of day, seeing Matt with another woman, it was painfully humiliating, as well. He must think she was an idiot and probably regretted his impulsive kiss.

Yet why had he kissed her in the first place if he was involved with Mona? And why did he keep looking her way? Even now Shannon felt Matt's gaze upon her. Her skin prickled, and finally, almost unwillingly, she looked across the way toward the picnic table where Matt sat.

His eyes were but dark shadows across the distance, yet they were penetrating. His gaze held hers for a long time, saying something to her, but what? That he was still furious with her over last night? That he hated her? That he didn't hate her? That he wanted to kiss her again?

Shannon's face warmed at the unbidden thought. Or was it an unconscious wish? Mortified with her own wayward mind, she wrenched her gaze away and turned back toward Jack.

When dinner was over and everyone was milling around, Shannon stood quietly beside Jack, mentally debating whether to leave, when Matt, accompanied by another couple, surprised her by coming toward her. A smile crinkled the skin around his eyes, erasing the grim expression he'd worn all evening whenever he'd looked at her.

"Shannon, I'd like to introduce you to my sister and brother-in-law, June and Harry Madison. They're the parents of Jason, the tornado that you had the unfortunate encounter with in the supermarket."

June Madison's face reddened. "Oh! You're the one! Please accept our apologies. We're so sorry about what happened!"

Shannon smiled at the woman. "Forget it. You can see there's no harm done."

"That's kind of you," Harry Madison said. "All the same, we feel responsible. Is there anything we can do to make up for it?"

"Nonsense, I'm fine," Shannon assured him. "Be sure and say hello to Jason for me, though, will you? He's a real doll."

June cut her eyes toward her brother, then grinning, looked back at Shannon. "Thanks. He liked you, too, especially since you were so nice to him after what he'd done. He called you the 'pretty lady.'"

Shannon laughed. "I'm flattered."

"Hey, guys, I need some strong arms over here," Mike Avery shouted. "Let's move these tables out of the way to make room for dancing."

All the men responded, leaving the two women alone. June turned eagerly to Shannon and asked in a confidential tone, "So how's it going at the office? Is the bear letting you into his den?"

"Ah, I see he told you who I am," Shannon said. At June's nod, she admitted, "I've entered the den, but there's still some growling going on, though he's not showing his fangs as much as he did at first."

June smiled broadly. "Take some advice from the bear's sister—growl back and stand your ground."

Shannon chuckled, liking June Madison in spite of the fact that she was Matt's sister. That, she thought wryly, couldn't be helped and shouldn't be held against her. "That's exactly what I've done, though not without a few qualms."

"Matt can growl awfully loud," June conceded, "but he's basically harmless. It's been a blow to his pride having to make room for you, but he'll play fair as long as you do."

"I've discovered that myself," Shannon said. "But I still don't understand why he's been so adamantly against me. If it's just because I'm a woman, then he must be living in the Dark Ages!"

June's eyes flashed. "Believe me, it has nothing to do with the classic image of the macho man holding down the woman. Actually, it's the reverse." She broke off and added in a rush, "The men are coming back. Why don't we get together sometime soon and get better acquainted?"

"I'd love it," Shannon replied.

"So would I." To the approaching men, June said, "After all that heavy lifting, I hope you've still got energy for dancing."

Because of Jack's entreaties, Shannon stayed for another hour, dancing several times with him and a few times with other men.

It became increasingly clear that Matt would not add to their number. Shannon saw him dancing with Mona, with June, with Caro, with a few other women whose names she could not recall, but not once did he approach her.

When she finally left to drive home, she told herself she was glad, that he had saved her the trouble of refusing, that the last thing she could possibly want was to be held in his arms again.

But as she lay in the darkness once she'd gone to bed, she acknowledged that she'd been lying to herself.

Chapter Six

On Sunday morning Shannon decided it was a good day to sort through her father's belongings. It was a task she dreaded, a familiar task she'd already done far too many times. There'd been the sorting after Brad and Timmy died, then of her father's possessions in Denver. Now there were all the things he'd kept here at the summer house. There were a few clothes, his fishing gear, his large collection of books and magazines. It was a job that had to be done, and putting it off wouldn't make it any easier.

She divided his clothes into piles, one with things that were worn or outdated, to be thrown away, and a second with still useful items that she would give to charity.

Shannon worked quickly and efficiently, utterly engrossed in what she was doing, so that when she heard a knock at the door, she was startled.

The visitor was Jack Waring. He was dressed casually in a pair of white shorts, white tennis shoes and a blue shirt that hung open over his bare, tanned chest.

"Morning," he said, favoring her with a wide smile. "Are you ready to go?"

"Go?" Shannon stared at him blankly. She'd completely forgotten his invitation until this very moment. "Oh, the skiing! I'm afraid I forgot all about it. I thought you were going to call before we decided."

Jack shrugged. "So I came, instead. What difference does it make?"

"A lot," Shannon replied. "I'm really busy this morning. I don't have time to go."

"Then make time!" Jack coaxed with another winsome smile. "It's a beautiful day. Let's get out and enjoy it. Anyway, you have to come! A couple of my friends are waiting for us, and we're holding them up."

"I'm sorry." Shannon stuck to her guns. "I really am too busy."

Jack went on trying to persuade her for a few more minutes, but at last he seemed to realize she meant what she said. His former easy smile altered abruptly into dark displeasure before he went away, and Shannon, amazed over the change in him, was left to wonder whether he'd been *that* attracted to her or was simply not used to being turned down. She had a strong feeling it was the latter.

She could have made the time to go, of course, but she hadn't wanted to spend the day in Jack Waring's company. The hours with him at yesterday's barbecue had been more than enough. Jack just wasn't her type.

But, then, was anybody? she wondered morosely as she resumed the chore of going through her father's things.

Caro had scolded her yesterday because there was no man in her life, and she *was* lonely. Strangely enough, the sense of loneliness had increased since coming here.

Face it, she snapped at herself, the loneliness had intensified since meeting Matt. It was knowing him, seeing him, being near him, more than any other cause, that had brought about all this uncharacteristic preoccupation with

motives and guilts and needs . . . needs that for years she'd
denied having. And Caro had been right. It was an unnat
ural, unhealthy state of being.

Despondently Shannon dropped what she was doing and
wandered back into her own bedroom, where she picked up
a photograph of Brad. She was filled with disquieting long
ings these days, yet now, silently, apologetically, she ack
nowledged that they had nothing to do with him anymore.
The memory of him had grown dim and distant. Even his
photograph seemed remote, for it was the image of an ever
young man who would never change. He was frozen in time
while she went on, growing a little older each year and
hopefully, more mature and wiser. Brad was no longer there
for her, nor she for him. She walked alone now, garnering
new experiences they could never share, while he remained
the same forever. She was alive, achingly alive, and no
matter how much she had loved him, it was over.

Yet she was still a woman with needs. That was becom
ing uncomfortably clear, and she despised her weakness. It
wasn't fair for her to appease those needs, even to want to,
after the way she'd denied Brad.

But no matter how hard she tried, she couldn't seem to
banish Matt from her thoughts, or erase the memory of his
searing kiss. It had awakened an urgent yearning within her
that refused to fade. The shock of such feelings surging
forth after all these years had alarmed her so that she'd run
away from him like a silly girl who didn't know how to
handle her emotions. And maybe that was the truth of it—
she didn't know how to deal with that side of her nature
anymore.

Matt must hate her now. What man wouldn't? But any
way, it scarcely mattered. He had the beautiful Mona, and
she mustn't forget that. Meeting Matt had reawakened her
awareness of herself as a woman, but he was not the man for
her. Not only was he involved with someone else, but he
didn't even want Shannon around. Their dealings with each

other must be strictly business, and she would just have to guard against any personal feelings toward him as long as she remained in Texas. Once she went away again, the problem would be solved by distance.

The question, though, as always, was where to go, what to do? There was nothing left for her in Denver; there was nothing for her anywhere. Such unfettered freedom was frightening.

The car sped past sorghum and cotton fields, greedily eating up the miles. Inside, radio music filled the uneasy silence that existed between the two occupants.

It had been that way all week—the wary truce, the burst of speech when business needed to be discussed, the long stretches of silence at other times. The tension was unnerving.

Matt wondered what Shannon was thinking as she quietly gazed out the window, her hands folded and still in her lap. His senses were acutely tuned to her—to the lovely curve of her neck, to the fluffy, shiny length of her hair, to the faint scent of her perfume. If only she weren't so lovely, he thought, aggrieved. If only her very presence didn't awaken all his senses. Whenever she was near, his entire body was aware of her. Already in the short time he'd known her his mind had memorized the varying expressions he'd seen on her face—anger, wonder, compassion. Already at night when he closed his eyes he could hear her velvety voice, see her face, feel the touch of her warm, soft body.

Shannon checked her watch, and Matt asked, just to break the silence, "What time is it?"

"Seven-twenty," she answered. "We have plenty of time."

Matt nodded, and a fresh silence fell.

After a few minutes Shannon broke it, saying anxiously, "I could be wrong. Kevin might not be right for the job at all. Promise you'll be honest with me about your opinion of

him. You shouldn't feel pressured to hire him just because I
suggested we interview him.''

Matt smiled, and for Shannon it was as though the day
had just turned sunny. She felt a little flutter in her stomach as his warm gaze met hers.

"I promise," he said. "I don't want to make a mistake,
either. The stakes are too high."

Shannon returned his smile. "All right."

It had been a long, awkward week with the element of
strain between them at the office and now she sensed a
thawing in Matt that melted some of her own icy reserve.

Another silence, yet somehow a friendlier one, settled
over them as they hit the straight stretch of road toward
Portland. For a little while, Matt was preoccupied with
traffic, but when it became less demanding, he said hesitantly, "Shannon?"

"Yes?"

Matt shot her a quick, penetrating glance before looking
at the highway once more. "About what Mona said..." He
paused.

Shannon tensed. "You don't have to—"

Matt cut off her words and his voice was unexpectedly
harsh. "Yes, I have to. What she said was out of line and
unforgivable. I apologize for it. It should never have happened."

Shannon laced her fingers together and studied them intensely. "She was merely echoing your sentiments. You'd
told her how you felt about my coming here."

"She wasn't echoing anything!" Matt exploded. "I never
said a word to her about you! She just jumped right in on
her own! She was nothing but an interfering busybody
meddling in *our* business! It was inexcusable!"

Shannon turned to stare at him. "Is that true?" she asked
in surprise. "You hadn't been discussing me with her?"

"Not a word, I swear! Don't you remember my telling her
we were business partners when I introduced you?"

"Then what made her do it?" Shannon was honestly puzzled.

Matt threw her a wry look. "Can't you guess?"

She shook her head.

He concentrated on the freeway as they whizzed through Portland. Ahead was the Nueces Bay Causeway and beyond it, somewhat hazy in the distance, the skyline of Corpus Christi.

"Maybe," Matt said finally, "she was jealous."

Shannon stiffened. "That's absurd!"

"Is it?"

"Isn't it?" She refused to look at him.

After a while Matt said softly, "Yes. I guess it is at that. I'd already made up my mind that after Saturday I wasn't going to see her again. Her rudeness to you just set the seal on it. But if she blamed you for my loss of interest in her, she was way off, wasn't she? How could she know how distasteful you found me?"

This time Shannon did look at him. There was a tight set to Matt's jaw, and she realized for the first time how much her rejection after his kiss must have hurt him. And hurting Matt had never been her intention. She'd been too busy fighting the demons of confusion and guilt within herself to give much consideration to what she was doing to him.

She gazed unhappily at the bay. The morning sun glinted on the waters so brightly it was almost blinding. She swallowed painfully and said in a subdued voice, "That's not true. I know I reacted badly when you kissed me, and I'm truly sorry about it. I can't explain why I behaved that way without sounding like an idiot, but..." She sighed. For the life of her she couldn't look at him again as she forced the words that had to be said. "It wasn't what you think. I didn't... I don't find you distasteful."

"No?" There was a world of questioning bound up in the single word.

"No," she replied with gentle but unmistakable emphasis.

"Then that's how you behave with every man who kisses you?" The accusation was gruff.

Shannon curled her fingers into balls and stared straight ahead. "The...the truth is..." her voice was thick, "Matt, you're the first man I've kissed since . . ."

She couldn't finish after all. Her voice broke and she lowered her head and closed her eyes.

The shock of what she was saying jolted Matt. The car had reached the causeway; the traffic was heavy and he couldn't risk taking his eyes off the road to look at her. He silently cursed the situation.

"Since your husband?" he asked incredulously.

"Yes." Shannon's voice was faint, almost undecipherable.

Matt's heart—and spirits—lightened abruptly as understanding came. Shannon felt guilty, as though she were betraying the memory of the man she'd loved. Most likely she'd have felt this way the first time she was with any man, not just him. Yet he, dull-witted clod that he'd been, had taken it personally.

As he drove off the causeway and sped toward the harbor bridge, Matt was able to glance at her for a brief instant. Shannon sat erect, hands tight in her lap, head bowed, eyes shut as though to block him out. He realized that the admission had cost her a great deal, and he felt a swift rush of compassion for her as well as a melting tenderness that had nothing at all to do with compassion.

"I should have realized," he murmured, "but I never thought of it."

"Why should you have?" Shannon asked sharply. "Anyway, it doesn't matter. Except that I felt I owed you an explanation."

"I'm glad you did," Matt said quietly. He sensed her withdrawal, though whether from shyness, embarrassment or a desire to maintain a distance between them, he wasn't sure. At any rate, this wasn't the time or the place to go into the matter further.

They both fell silent for the remainder of the drive to the airport, where they were to meet their guest.

Once the tour of the development was over, the three adjourned to Shannon's house for lunch. She and Matt had agreed beforehand that it would be better than a restaurant because they wouldn't be disturbed and could talk as long as they wanted.

In the few hours he'd spent in Kevin Boyd's company, Matt had received a favorable impression. Boyd was affable, with the gift of gab so necessary to a good salesman. Yet on the subject of business, he was serious and thoughtful, and his comments and questions reflected a keen mind.

At the house, Shannon busied herself in the kitchen while Matt, at her request, mixed their drinks.

"Can I help?" Matt asked Shannon as he handed Kevin his drink.

She shook her head. "No, thanks. You two just relax."

Kevin was peering at the bay through the kitchen window. "I'd like to take a walk down to the water."

"Feel free," Shannon said cheerfully. "It'll be a few minutes before I have lunch on the table."

"Want to come?" Kevin asked Matt. "Maybe you can fill me in on the fishing prospects around here."

"Sure." Matt followed him out the door.

The discussion about fishing made a nice break from business for both men as they strolled to the water's edge. It also gave them an opportunity to assess each other on a different level.

They were still there fifteen minutes later when Matt saw Shannon waving from the sun deck. "Lunch must be ready."

As they leisurely retraced their steps across the lawn, Matt asked, "You knew Shannon in college?"

"Yes. She and my wife were roommates." He grinned. "Two greater cutups you've never met!" He sombered and went on thoughtfully, "Shannon's different now. More serious. Less ready to laugh. But, then, I guess I'd probably be the same if I lost my family the way she did."

"Yes. I doubt anyone who hasn't been through it can even begin to imagine how hard it's been for her." Curiously Matt asked, "Did you know her husband, too?"

Kevin nodded. "Not as well as Shannon, but I knew him. Diane and I used to double-date with them sometimes."

"What was he like?" Matt asked, unable to stop himself.

Kevin didn't seem to find the question odd, and he answered at once. "He was a real nice guy. He seemed crazy about Shannon, too, although I remember thinking at the time that they were mismatched."

"How so?"

Kevin shrugged. "Like I said, Shannon was different then. She was a fun-loving girl with a great sense of humor. She didn't seem to take life or herself too seriously. Brad did, though. He was ambitious. He worked hard for his grades, as well as at a part-time job. He set high goals for himself and he was dedicated to reaching them, while Shannon was more of the 'take-each-day-as-it-comes' type."

Matt couldn't even imagine the girl Kevin described. It was as though he were talking about a stranger instead of Shannon.

But over lunch, he thought he caught just the faintest glimpse of the person Kevin had described. Business discussions had been shelved temporarily, and Shannon and Kevin were reminiscing about old times. As she amusingly recounted some of her and Diane's exploits, her eyes lighted up like sunshine flooding through a windowpane and her smile wasn't just a smile anymore—it was a mirror of genuine, deep-down happiness. The lively animation of her features, her bubbly giggles, her slender hands fluttering in the air like a hummingbird's wings as they helped to illustrate a point, all combined to bemuse Matt. He'd thought her beautiful before, but now he found her truly dazzling. He wished he could always see her as she was at this moment.

He also wished she were his.

That thought stunned him. Oh, he knew the physical, sexual desire for her was there. It had been present in varying degrees ever since he'd picked her up from the supermarket floor. But this feeling was different—more intense, more profound. He wished Shannon belonged to him completely, not just for a night, not just for an interlude, but for good.

He was so upset at even entertaining such an unwelcome notion that it was all he could do to remain seated at the table, to laugh in the right places, to say a word now and then or nod to show he was listening. What he really wanted was to get away somewhere by himself and think this thing through. He couldn't, wouldn't, let himself fall in love. That was a fatal disease he had no intention of catching.

He was relieved when lunch was finally over and they went to the office to continue their conference with Kevin. Once the topic returned to business, he was able—temporarily, at least—to look at Shannon without thinking of his disturbing desire for her.

The three of them sat around Shannon's desk, on which a blueprint was spread. Kevin tapped it, saying, "I agree with what Shannon told me over the phone, Matt. You have a first-class place here and you don't need gimmicks to sell this type of property, at least not the kind you've been using."

"Let's hear your ideas," Matt said quietly.

"The first thing I'd do is print some elegant brochures and write personal letters on fine stationery, both to be sent to a select list of people. You'll probably need to buy a mailing list, but in the long run it will save you money, because you'll be weeding out the people who wouldn't qualify to buy this property, anyway. Next I'd build the clubhouse as soon as possible. Then you could host invitation-only events—champagne brunches, late-afternoon cocktail parties and the like...promotional affairs, sure, but soft sell. I'd also advertise in select newspapers and magazines, again with the emphasis on exclusivity.''

Shannon listened quietly, participating little as Matt and Kevin went over blueprints, sales records and tear sheets of prior advertising. She wished she knew what was in Matt's mind, but his face didn't reveal his thoughts. She had no way of knowing how he really felt about Kevin as a candidate to run their sales operations. She also had no way of knowing how he really felt about her.

She knew he'd been pleased when she'd been honest about why she had shied away from him that night, but that didn't mean he would want to kiss her again, and distressingly, she found herself wishing he would. There was something in her now that was unsettled, dissatisfied, and it was all bound up in Matt.

But Matt seemed more withdrawn and distant this afternoon than he'd been all week. This morning after her confession they'd seemed closer, and the closeness had lasted right up until lunchtime. Since then, however, he'd seemed colder, all business, and she didn't know what had brought about the change.

She suddenly realized she'd lost the thread of conversation, and with an effort she forced herself to pay attention. After all, this discussion was as important to her as to Matt.

''If I took on this job,'' Kevin said, ''I'd want complete control over the sales force. You have two salesmen in addition to the manager?'' At Matt's nod, he continued, ''That should be enough, and I'm willing to give the men already here a fair trial, but I'd expect them to meet quotas, or have the right to replace them. Of course I'd also expect to be able to offer them incentives over and above their commissions. Are there any now?"

"No," Matt admitted. "Judson never suggested it, and I'm afraid I never thought of it."

"Hmm. Well, I consider it vital. A team will only go the extra mile if you're willing to, too."

"What about you?" Matt asked quietly. "What sort of compensation do you expect?"

Kevin stated his wishes calmly, without arrogance, yet with obvious confidence in his own worth. Shannon winced inwardly. His salary and commission demands were steep, and they would be in addition to all the other expenses he was advocating—printing costs, new advertising, the promotional parties, the incentives for the sales staff—not to mention building the clubhouse much sooner than originally scheduled. It was going to take a lot of money up front, and she was filled with disquiet.

"You've given us a lot to think about, Kevin," she said. "I hope you don't mind if we don't give you an answer today. I think Matt and I should consider this carefully before we make any final decision."

Matt nodded. "Your presentation has been very interesting, but Shannon's right. We'll need a little time to talk this over."

"Of course." Kevin smiled easily. "I expected that."

"We'll call you next week with our decision," Matt promised. "By Wednesday at the latest."

"Fair enough," Kevin replied.

The meeting broke up, but it still remained for Shannon and Matt to drive Kevin back to Corpus Christi, where they would have dinner together. Anne had booked Kevin a hotel room there for the night and he'd be taking an early-morning flight back to Dallas.

While Kevin checked into the hotel and went up to his room to deposit his overnight bag, Shannon and Matt sat down in the lobby to wait. It was the first moment since meeting Kevin at the airport that morning that they had been alone together.

"Well," Matt queried, "what do you think?"

"The question is, what do *you* think?" she said, tossing it back to him.

Matt grinned and shook his head. "No fair. I asked first."

"Yes, but he's an old friend of mine. I mightn't be as impartial a judge as you. Let's stop fencing, Matt. Tell me your opinion before he comes back."

Matt shifted on the sofa and his knees accidentally touched hers. Shannon caught her breath at the contact.

"I think he's a very bright man who knows how to sell property," he said finally. "I'd like to have him on our team."

Shannon sighed. "So would I. But . . ."

"But?"

She felt Matt's gaze searching her face. "I just wonder about the financing of all this. It sounds expensive."

"You know," he said softly, "I'm beginning to believe you're really a girl after my own heart."

"How so?"

"You're demonstrating as much, if not more, concern about the health and welfare of the company finances as me."

"Well, of course!" she retorted with a grin. "I've got to keep you honest, don't I?"

Matt chuckled. "I guess you do. Never can tell when I might start siphoning off all those nonexistent profits."

"Speaking of which—if we do want to start seeing some of those in reality, we are going to have to change our ways. Kevin's ideas for marketing the resort sounded good, but can we afford him?"

"I don't see how we can afford not to hire him. Everything he has in mind will take a lot of cold, hard cash, but I think we're going to have to try it. I figure if we use some of the funds that had been earmarked for the golf course and landscaping, we'll do fine. And if we're right about what Kevin can do for us, when the time comes to finish the rest of it, we'll be able to swing it with the income from the increase in sales. The only thing is that our shares, yours and mine, of the profits from the sales may have to be reduced a little in order to cover the overall increased cost of doing business."

"Even so, that's better than no profits at all," Shannon mused.

"Exactly. So what do you say? Want to think it over some more, or should we offer him the job tonight?"

Shannon was silent for a moment, considering, and then she spoke in a rush. "I say let's go for it!"

"Good!"

The smile Matt gave her brought a light to his eyes that seemed to have nothing at all to do with a business decision. It made Shannon wonder and hope—though exactly what she hoped for she didn't dare analyze.

Over dinner they offered the position to Kevin; he accepted and they settled the deal by celebrating with champagne.

Afterward there were warm goodbyes as Shannon and Matt left Kevin. In two weeks he would be back for good, ready to tackle his new job.

The drive back to Rockport was a silent one, yet it was a comfortable, friendly silence. It had been a long day, and Shannon suspected Matt was as drained as she felt. All the same, she was satisfied about the course they had set. It would mean cinching belts a notch tighter for a time, but she believed Kevin would live up to their expectations and that in the long run, this move would be the best one they could have made for Anchor Development.

It was past eleven when Matt stopped the car in front of the summer house. "You asleep?" he asked softly.

"Almost," she admitted. "I'm afraid I wasn't much company to you on the drive back, while you had to stay alert."

"That's okay."

Shannon could almost feel him smiling, although she could only see his shadowy outline. "Well . . . good night."

"Good night, Shannon."

She was about to open the passenger door and get out, when a sudden impulse seized her. Without pausing to think, she leaned across the seat and brushed her lips lightly against his.

When she turned toward the door once more, Matt caught her arm. "Why did you do that?" he asked in a low voice.

Shannon's heart was thudding. Why, indeed? What on earth had come over her? Now she had to brazen the thing out.

She shrugged and said in a teasing manner, "It just seemed a fitting end to an important, joint business decision. And to show you I meant what I said."

"About what?"

"That you're not at all distasteful to me."

Before Matt could respond, she had opened the door and slipped out of the car. He sat in the darkened interior, watching as she hurried across the driveway and up the stairs. Amusement mingled with frustration inside him.

Beneath the beam of the porch light, she turned and waved before going inside the house.

Was he falling in love with her? Matt asked himself again. And if he was, was it such a terrible thing?

Chapter Seven

Shannon had to force herself to get ready to go to the office the next morning, because she dreaded seeing Matt. *Why did you have to make a fool of yourself last night?* she angrily asked her mirrored reflection as she brushed her hair.

The moment she'd entered the house, she'd regretted the insane urge that had made her kiss him, and she still wondered what had made her do it. Was it an ego thing? she wondered irritably. Had she been trying to prove she could win back his interest? Or was it because she honestly cared for him?

She didn't like to think her feminine vanity would carry her to such lengths, but neither did she want to think about the alternative. The truth was, she was afraid of the answer.

Anyway, what mattered now was that she had embarrassed herself and probably Matt, as well, by acting so rashly. She didn't know how she was going to find the courage to face him. She could hardly meet her eyes in the mirror.

She returned to her bedroom and slipped into a skirt and blouse, and as she tried to work the buttons, she was astonished to find that her fingers were trembling.

Shannon sat down on the edge of the bed and buried her face in her hands. The truth, the real truth, whether she wanted to deal with it or not, was that she did care about Matt. A lot.

More than a lot, in fact. Too much. Physically she'd been drawn to him from the first, and that in itself was alarming. Just the sight of Matt made her want to be in his arms, to feel his kisses, to have him make love to her. But the more she got to know him, the more she liked other things about him, too. She liked the respectful way he dealt with the people who worked for him. He wasn't just a boss, but part of a team, and this was obvious in the way he was always ready to listen to other people's ideas. She liked his easy camaraderie with his friends, too. In spite of the distance she had kept from him at the barbecue, she had noticed how well he got along with the other guests. Though they'd had their own problems initially because he hadn't wanted her there, basically she admired the way he handled the business. She'd had enough time to see that he was serious about it and that every decision he made had been carefully thought out. Unhappily Shannon came to the conclusion that in all honesty, there was very little about Matt she didn't like. And that scared her.

She wasn't ready to care about a man again, any man. She wasn't sure she ever wanted to feel that deep, down-to-the-soul emotional entanglement, because if he were taken away, it would be like an amputation without anesthetic. Shannon didn't think she had the strength to withstand even the possibility of such a bereavement ever again. And even if she could see herself taking a chance on loving and losing again, did she have the right? She'd cheated Brad of happiness during his last hours, so who was she to seek her own?

Shannon was proud that she had a handle on her emotions by the time she left for the office. It would be awkward seeing Matt, but she'd get through it. The light touch was all that was needed. After all, it had been only a simple kiss, not, thank heavens, a declaration of love! She'd been making too much over nothing, which just went to prove that she'd been out of circulation so long she didn't know how to play the game anymore. Maybe, she thought wryly, she ought to consider buying a cat, orthopedic shoes and taking up knitting. Life would be a lot less stressful that way.

The bravado was uncalled for after all, because Matt wasn't there when she got to the office. Shannon set to work attempting to draft suitable copy for the new brochures they would be printing. Kevin had given her some suggestions and she needed to get started before the ideas got cold.

She was utterly engrossed in her task when Anne knocked briefly at the door and entered. "There's a phone call for you on line one."

Shannon tensed in spite of her earlier courage. "Is it Matt?"

Anne shook her head. "No. Do you want me to ask who it is?"

"No, that's all right," Shannon replied. "I'll take it."

She reached for the phone, but before she could pick it up Anne asked, "Is it all right if I go to lunch now?"

"Is it that late already?" Shannon exclaimed, looking at her watch. "Sure, go ahead." Anne left the room as Shannon picked up the receiver and spoke into it.

"Hi, there." It was Jack Waring. "How about having dinner with me tonight?"

"Thanks, but I can't. I already have plans." She didn't, but Shannon could hardly say that she preferred an evening alone to his company. She didn't want to hurt Jack's feelings, but she simply wasn't interested.

"Maybe some other time." Jack took her refusal with good grace, a nice contrast to his swift, dark mood the other time she'd turned him down. Then he surprised her by changing the subject entirely. "I hear you're now the senior partner at Anchor Development."

"I'm hardly a senior anything," Shannon told him with a chuckle. She swiveled her chair around so that she could gaze out the window. "I'm the new kid at school."

"Maybe so, but as a majority stockholder you hold the balance of power. You can overrule Tyson in decisions when it's necessary."

Shannon didn't like the direction of the conversation. "What point are you trying to make?"

"Your company owns a strip of land between Spinnaker's Run and a piece of property I'm about to use to construct a condominium. I'm interested in buying that land from you and I'm willing to pay an above-market price for it if you'll sell it to me now."

"Ah, yes. Matt told me someone wanted to buy that land, but I didn't realize it was you."

"What do you say?" Jack's voice was persuasive. "I guarantee it'll be a lucrative deal for you. One you won't regret."

"You've already discussed this with Matt. What was his answer?"

Jack made an impatient, hissing sound. "Matt can be very stubborn and unreasonable. He doesn't always see what's in his own best interest."

"And selling this land to you is?"

"Of course it is!" Jack exclaimed. "I've already told you that I'm willing to pay top dollar for it. And—" he lowered his voice to a confidential tone "—from the gossip I hear, you may need that money before long."

Shannon stiffened. "What do you mean?"

"Just that I've heard there's been a lot of vandalism going on at the development and it's creating unexpected expenses. Sales have also been slow, haven't they? With those kinds of troubles, you ought to think twice before turning down a generous offer like mine.''

Shannon was suddenly, blazingly angry. How dared the man presume to tell them how to conduct their business? His snide remarks went far beyond the bounds of decent manners. In addition, he was blatantly trying to play divide and conquer between her and Matt by attempting to get her to make a major decision alone. She was so incensed that irrationally she thought that if this minute she had the choice between bankruptcy and selling that land to Jack Waring, she'd choose bankruptcy.

Fortunately she was able to restrain her temper, although she was trembling from the effort. It was a good thing Jack couldn't see her. Shannon forced a semblance of amusement into her voice and said, "You really shouldn't listen to gossip, Jack. It's not very reliable. Anchor Development doesn't have any troubles that can't be solved."

"I'm glad to hear it," Jack said heartily. "Still, it's smart business to do something that can turn you a good profit. Will you consider selling me that land?''

"I'm sorry, but we have plans for it ourselves. Besides, I wouldn't think of selling anything without my partner's okay.''

"I figured as much," Jack said with heavy sarcasm. "You're afraid to make any decisions on your own.''

"I'd be a fool to make any major business decisions without consulting Matt. After all, he's been doing a fine job of running this company for years, while I'm new at the game. But I'm not at all afraid to make decisions and I'm about to make one now. I find this conversation unpleasant, Jack, so I've decided to end it.''

Shannon whirled her chair around and smashed the receiver down into its cradle.

"Bravo!"

The sound of a single pair of hands clapping echoed across the room.

Shannon looked up, startled, to see Matt standing in the doorway. He wore jeans and a red-and-white shirt, and he looked as fresh as though he'd just stepped out of the shower. Just now his eyes glittered with laughter and his lips were stretched into a broad grin.

"I guess we're not selling our land to Waring," he observed.

Shannon made a sound of exasperation. "So you heard that, did you?"

"Every word." The grin deepened. "I especially liked the part about what a fine job I've been doing. They say eavesdroppers never hear any good about themselves, but—"

"I didn't say it to flatter your ego," Shannon snapped irritably. "I wanted to deflate his! *Who* does he think he is, anyway, trying to tell me what to do? Why, he was practically threatening dire consequences if we don't sell him that land! He's got one hell of a nerve if he thinks I'd be underhanded enough to go behind your back and sell just because he happens to want it! The guy has more gall than—"

"Hey!" Matt chuckled and came around the desk. "Don't yell at me! I'm on your side, remember?" Without any warning, he pulled her to her feet, wrapped his arms around her and kissed her.

All the pent-up anger inside Shannon dissipated like steam escaping from a boiling kettle, and Jack Waring was forgotten in a flash. The steady warmth of Matt's lips on hers transported her into another dimension where nothing mattered except the magical sensations that flooded through her. Her lips parted beneath Matt's, and gentle heat abruptly flared into leaping flames.

After a time Matt lifted his head, and teasing amusement lurked in his dark gaze. He raised her arms and placed them around his neck, and then his hands were at her waist again, drawing her closer.

When he spoke she could feel his soft breath fanning her cheeks. "Now," he said with an air of satisfaction, "we can do this properly." He bent his head toward her once more.

"Or improperly," Shannon gibed. "We *are* just business partners, after all!"

Matt laughed softly. "But *close* business partners, right?"

"Are we?" she countered.

Matt nodded. "Very close. Now it's your turn to kiss me, and it had better make up for that totally inadequate, breezy little peck that passed for one last night. All that did was whet my appetite!"

"Did it?" Shannon asked with unconcealed delight. She caressed his cheek with one finger, finding great contentment in the action. "I thought it might have embarrassed you."

Matt's eyes widened. "Embarrassed me? Are you kidding? How?"

"I thought maybe you weren't interested," she said frankly. "I thought it would make things awkward because we'd still have to see each other here at the office."

"For a smart woman, you sure do think an awful lot of silly things," Matt told her. His smile was wistful. "It was all I could do to keep from following you inside that house last night."

Shannon caught her breath. He was telling the truth. It was there in his eyes. "Oh, Matt," she whispered, "ever since I met you, I've been so confused I can hardly think straight."

"Tell me about it!" he said with a hint of irony. "Confusion's my middle name these days." In a rough voice he added, "I haven't wanted to be drawn to you, and heaven knows my life would be a whole lot more peaceful if I weren't, but . . ."

His face was very near hers, and Shannon was charmed by this close-up view of him. His brown eyes were as dark as midnight, yet his gaze was as soft and liquid as syrup. His strong, sensual lips were incredibly gentle, and their nearness mesmerized her.

"But?" she prompted.

He sighed. "But you are here and you fascinate me more than any woman I've ever met. Now, Shannon, are you going to kiss me, or what?"

She kissed him, and the potency of her kiss almost took his breath away. Matt's hands slid up her back, down to the seductive curve of her hips and finally, when he could resist no more, around to her enticing breasts.

Shannon gasped softly as his fingers stroked her breasts, but she didn't draw away. Matt felt the heat of desire flood through his body as she fitted herself more perfectly to him.

There was no telling where it might have ended. They were both lost to everything except their acute awareness of each other. Gone was a sense of time or place. Until the telephone rang.

Reluctantly they drew apart, breathing unsteadily, their eyes smoldering. "Damn," Matt whispered. "I suppose we'd better answer it."

Shannon nodded, too shaken to speak.

Matt's arms fell away from her and he turned toward the telephone on the desk.

A minute later, when he'd finished the call, Matt looked around to find her standing at the window with her back to him. "Shannon?"

"Yes?" Her voice was muffled.

Matt went to her, touched her shoulder and gently turned her around to face him. "What's wrong?"

She avoided his eyes. "Nothing. I think the phone call was timely, that's all. Things were getting out of hand."

Matt raised her chin so that her gaze had to meet his. His eyes twinkled. "Indeed they were, considering we're in the office. But you're not really sorry, are you?"

"No," she replied huskily. "Maybe I should be, but . . ." She stopped and shook her head.

"Listen—" Matt's voice was patient "—I'm not going to try to rush you about anything before you're ready. Okay?"

He won a smile from her then. "Okay," she murmured.

"Now . . . this is a hell of a time for me to be taking off, since all I want is to be with you, but I've got to leave for San Antonio in an hour. Harry's brother is getting married tomorrow afternoon and Harry, June and I are all in the wedding party. I'll be back late tomorrow night. Can I see you Sunday?"

Shannon nodded and smiled once more. "I'd like that," she told him.

"Good. We'll spend the day on my boat, and don't you dare back out on me."

"I won't," she promised.

All day Saturday, Shannon wavered about whether she should go. Things *were* moving too fast and it frightened her. She just wasn't ready to get involved with a man. Maybe a nice tepid relationship with someone would be nice—someone to have dinner with on occasion, or to go to the movies with—someone who wasn't a threat to her emotional well-being. There was no sense pretending Matt fell into that category. Just the sight of him or the sound of his voice sent tingles through her, while his touch... It was best not to dwell on that!

She still hadn't made up her mind what to do by the time he called her Sunday morning, but in the end she decided to go. It was, after all, what her heart prompted her to do. Recklessly she decided she could argue with reason later.

When he arrived to pick her up, Shannon was glad she'd decided to be with Matt. It was so good to see him. Just

knowing he was away had made the time drag. But now here
he was, solid and real, morning fresh, emanating energy and
vitality. He was dressed casually in cutoff jeans, a sky-blue
shirt, and wearing a dark-blue cap at a rakish angle. His
arms were a magnificent bronze in the sunlight, and his bare
legs, long and powerful, were a shade lighter. He was an
undeniably impressive symbol of masculinity at its best and
the sight of him knocked her senses awry.

His eyes flitted over her, also clad in shorts and a casual
shirt, and suddenly he smiled. "Umm," he murmured,
"you look good." Before she could reply, he bent forward
and kissed her lightly. "Taste good, too," he added as he
drew away.

Shannon was suddenly, crazily, happy. Her emotional
response to a man had been locked away in a dark dungeon
for so long that now that light was beginning to penetrate
that prison, she felt greedy for more.

"Thanks," she said with a little laugh. "You taste good,
too. Toothpaste and coffee."

Matt grinned. "Ah, the kiss itself meant nothing."

"Nothing at all," she assured him, grinning back. "How
was the wedding?"

Matt told her about it as they drove to his condominium.
Behind it, in the channel, was his boat, a sleek, beautiful
cabin cruiser.

"This is magnificent!" Shannon exclaimed as she climbed
aboard. "I'm impressed."

"Don't be," Matt said wryly. "She's a white elephant.
But," he added fondly, "she's my white elephant."

"Why do you call her that?" Shannon asked, amused.

"After we'd built this condo—" Matt waved a hand, indicating the building behind him "—and the shopping center, I was feeling flush. The business had far exceeded what
I'd imagined. So to celebrate, I bought the *Lady June*. Not
long after that, Bud wanted out and—" he shrugged "—you
know the rest. I couldn't afford to buy his shares because all

my excess cash was tied up in another investment in Houston. So your dad bought the shares, instead." He smiled ruefully.

Shannon chuckled. "So now you're stuck with two white elephants—*Lady June* and a female partner."

Matt's mouth twisted in amusement. "Oh, I don't know. I'm finding that having a female partner has its compensations."

The light in his eyes was disturbing, very disturbing, so Shannon said hastily, "So does a boat like this, I imagine. Do you take her out often?"

A few minutes later they were underway. The *Lady June* took to the open waters as naturally as a fish, and soon she was slicing through the bay, leaving civilization behind.

They talked little because their words were swallowed up by the sound of the waves crashing against the bow. It had been many years since Shannon had enjoyed such an outing, and she felt invigorated by the combination of warm sunshine, salty air and the stinging spray of salt water. In the distance she saw a few gulls hovering in the wake of a shrimp boat and even farther away was the receding shoreline.

It was one of the most relaxing mornings Shannon could ever remember. Neither she nor Matt was in the mood to fish, so instead they lounged in deck chairs and basked in the sun. Matt had removed his shirt and Shannon now wore a white bikini. Only occasionally did they stir to spread more suntan lotion or to speak, and then only idly, about nothing in particular. Neither made any demands upon the other. It was enough that they were together.

At noon they roused themselves enough to munch sandwiches and sip cold soft drinks. Then inertia overtook them again. Matt spread beach towels on the deck, and they stretched out on them and promptly fell asleep.

When Shannon awoke a while later, she looked straight into Matt's penetrating gaze. "What are you doing?" she asked, though it was perfectly obvious.

"Looking at you," he said. "Thinking how beautiful you are."

Shannon's heart stopped. So many years had passed since she had seen that special look in a man's eyes, a look that told her how desirably feminine she was, a look that said without words that he wanted to make love to her. She started to speak, but found that there was a lump in her throat.

Matt extended a hand and lightly brushed her cheek. Then he bent over her, his eyes drinking in the vision of such refreshing loveliness. Her hair, wind tossed and billowing, was a golden halo surrounding her head. Her golden-brown eyes seemed to reflect the sunlight, yet they were also earnest, shimmering with a waiting expectation. Her face, untouched by cosmetics, was vibrant with dewy youthfulness, and her lips, naturally rosy, were soft and tempting.

Matt had promised himself that today would be low-key, that he would keep it light and companionable. He realized that Shannon was nervous about the attraction between them and that the best thing he could do was let her set the pace. But the lure of her proved irresistible.

His kiss was gentle, cautious, because he was still conscious of the need for restraint. When she didn't resist, he embedded one of his hands in the silky strands of her hair while his other stroked her arm. It was smooth and supple and sun warmed to the touch.

After a moment he lifted his head and smiled down at her. Shannon smiled back, and then she captured his hand and brought it to her lips, kissing the valley of his cupped palm before moving on to the tips of his fingers.

Matt caught his breath. Her actions, so innocent in themselves, yet so erotic, drove away every ounce of the rigid self-control he'd struggled all day to maintain. He smothered her face with kisses—trailing across her skin from her lips to her cheeks to her closed eyelids to her brow and down again to her alluring mouth. Yet his thirst for her could not be quenched, and he sipped at her parted lips in a greedy effort to get his fill.

His own fervor seemed to ignite a matching one in her. Shannon's hands clasped about his neck, and then the fingers of one hand wove their way through his hair. A moment later, breathlessly, she pulled away from his feverish kisses so that her lips could nuzzle his throat. Her hands followed suit and then fanned out across his bare chest.

It was too much. She was driving him mad. Urgently Matt's hands slid downward, along her waist, over the enticing curve of her hips and on to her shapely thighs. The reality of her far exceeded his imagination, and he took deep pleasure as his fingers slowly learned the terrain of her exquisite, lush body.

At last his hands traveled upward again until they found the round, full thrust of her breasts. They were soft and pliant and fitted perfectly in the cup of his hands, yet he sensed their tautness, too.

When his fingers went to the knot behind her neck and untied the straps of her bikini top, Shannon closed her eyes briefly and shivered. It was time, she told herself. Time to be a woman again.

She felt the cloth break free, felt the sun wash over the tender, pale flesh, but only for an instant. Then Matt's powerful shoulders blocked out the sun as he gathered her into his arms and crushed her to him. The crisp texture of the dark hair on his chest rubbed against her delicate skin, and the intimate contact sent strong vibrations of heat coursing through her. Shannon was suddenly consumed by ardent cravings that screamed to be satisfied.

When he lowered her once more to the cushion of the beach towel, he gave her a long look that was heart stopping in its eloquence. Then his gaze moved lower to her breasts and he murmured, "Lovely. So incredibly lovely."

He bent to kiss them, one and then the other. Shannon closed her eyes tightly, shocked at the strength of the feelings Matt aroused in her. Violent, earthy desire rampaged through her, white hot and relentless. There was no place on her entire body that did not burn and throb. She was a creature of tortured yearning, passion that could no longer be denied.

"Make love to me, Matt," she pleaded. "Please."

She felt him go still, and when she opened her eyes she met his somber gaze. "I want to," he said simply. "Are you sure?"

She couldn't bear to meet his gaze anymore. She lowered hers to his massive chest. "Yes," she said in a small voice.

"We'll go below to the cabin." Matt moved and got to his feet, and offered his hand to her.

By the time they were below deck, Shannon was even less able to meet Matt's eyes. What was she doing? she wondered suddenly. Had she lost her mind? She paused, reluctant to go toward the lower bunk bed.

Matt didn't appear to notice her discomfiture. He came up behind her and his arms encircled her waist. "I've longed for this since the first moment we met," he murmured before burying his face in her hair. "You're so desirable, Shannon." He laughed huskily and confessed, "You are even in my dreams at night."

His fingers slid beneath the elastic of her bikini panties, and slowly he began to push them downward.

It was that action, even more than her second thoughts, that snapped Shannon out of her passion-dazed state. Her hand covered his, stalling it from any further movement, and she was deeply grateful she couldn't see Matt's face.

"Don't!" she gasped huskily. "I . . . I'm sorry, Matt, but I've changed my mind. I don't want this."

Matt withdrew from her at once, and in the small, silent cabin his quick intake of breath was startlingly loud. "Don't want—" His voice broke off, and it was harsh when he finally continued. "You're the one who suggested it!"

Shannon winced at Matt's tone. Gone was the tender, loverlike quality; replacing it were clinking chunks of ice. She lowered her head in shame.

"I know I did." Her voice was but the merest whisper. "I'm truly sorry, but I just can't go through with it. I thought I could, but I can't."

"For God's sake, Shannon! You make it sound like a dreaded duty, something you were trying to force yourself to do! Thanks a lot! Thanks a whole, damn lot!"

"It's not—"

"Save your breath!" Matt snapped. "I don't want to hear it!"

An instant later his footsteps thudded on the deck outside the cabin. Shannon sighed, reached for her clothes and began to dress.

Chapter Eight

Monday morning Shannon awoke with the beginning of a cold. It seemed only fitting that her body should feel as grim as her thoughts. To add to the bright new morning, she made her coffee too weak and she snagged her last pair of panty hose.

She would have given almost anything for an excuse not to return to the office—ever. Matt had managed the business before without her help. She was certain he'd be delighted to do so again, especially after the disaster of yesterday, but she knew that was cowardly thinking brought on by desperation. Even if she packed her bags this minute and left town, they'd still have to deal with each other to some extent until another buyer could be found for her share of the partnership. No matter what had happened between them on a personal level, Shannon had no intention of being a passive, ignorant partner. Some situations simply called for rising above personal differences, but she had to won-

der if it were possible for either of them to rise above yesterday's fiasco.

She just hadn't been able to carry it off. She had wanted
to make love with him with all her being—she was still a bit
stunned at just how desperately she had wanted it—but in
the end she'd remembered Brad. It would have been the ultimate betrayal of him, and she just couldn't do it.

Ironically, she knew it wouldn't have seemed like such a
betrayal if she weren't so deeply attracted to Matt, if she
weren't already half in love with him. It was not the physical act itself that would have betrayed her husband's memory as much as the emotions that were intertwined with it.
How, in good conscience, could she give to Matt, and take
for herself, what she had denied to Brad?

Yet, a small voice challenged, was denying herself or Matt
the answer to her problems? It could not change history or
bring forgiveness. It was years too late to square things with
Brad. Nothing she did or did not do now would ever alter
the events of the past.

But she would know. She would know if she plunged
forward callously, grasping at happiness for herself while
Brad and Timmy no longer had that option. She would
know if she accepted the riches of life for her own selfish
gain when she alone might have spared their lives.

At the office Anne greeted her with the news that Matt
would be at the construction site all morning. Shannon's
chief emotion was relief. The dreaded confrontation had
been postponed.

She settled down to work, roughing out some ideas for
magazine ads. She was neither a professional writer nor an
artist, but she had some strong ideas about what their promotional materials should convey. When her concepts were
clear, she would show them to Matt and Kevin and get their
input before turning them over to an advertising agency.

Anne took an early lunch, and by the time she returned
at noon, Shannon was ready for a break. She'd been sneez-

ing all morning and she suspected she was running a temperature. She decided to walk the couple of blocks to the drugstore to buy some aspirin, hoping the medication along with a bit of fresh air might do her some good.

At the drugstore, she'd just finished paying for the aspirin and a box of tissues, when she heard her name.

"Shannon Edwards? Is that you?"

She turned to find Matt's sister, June Madison, in line behind her. She smiled back and said, "Hi. How are you?"

"Fine. You?"

Shannon shrugged. "Coming down with a summer cold, I think."

"That's too bad." As Shannon moved to the side of the counter to replace her wallet in her handbag, June stepped forward, taking her place. The pharmacist placed a small paper bag in front of her and she began to write a check. She talked to Shannon at the same time. "I'm picking up a prescription for my mother-in-law. Say, have you got time now for that lunch we were going to have?"

Shannon hesitated. With the current strain existing between her and Matt, she wasn't sure it was a good idea to get too chummy with his sister. On the other hand, what harm could it do? She wasn't going to tell June what had happened yesterday—that was for sure—so no potentially embarrassing situation was likely to develop.

"Why not?" she replied easily. "I'd like that."

Since Shannon had left her car at the office, they took June's and drove to a Mexican food restaurant.

"Ah," June said, sighing with pleasure after they'd placed their orders. "This is the first time I've sat down to rest all day. Cleaning up after a young tornado every morning isn't easy." She grimaced. "Neither is running a hundred errands."

"Where *is* your tornado today?" Shannon asked.

"At the day-care center. He goes three mornings a week. It works out nicely because it gives him the opportunity to play with other children and gives me a break. He stays until nap time is over."

"He's really a cute little fellow. If you find yourself needing a baby-sitter sometime, just give me a call. I'd be happy to stay with him."

Shannon was shocked at her impulsive offer. She could scarcely believe that she, who had avoided children for the past three and a half years, should suddenly put herself in a position where she might spend time with one.

June looked as surprised as Shannon felt. She said slowly, "That's awfully kind of you, Shannon. Considering."

"You know?" Shannon asked bluntly. "About my family?"

June nodded somberly. "Yes. I'm terribly sorry."

"I suppose Matt told you."

"No. Actually, it was Caro. I hope you don't mind."

"Of course not. It's no secret." Shannon smiled suddenly. "Jason's about the same age as my Timmy would have been. I guess that's why I'm so drawn to him."

"In spite of his running you over."

They both laughed, and June went on, "If you really mean it, I'll keep you in mind—about the baby-sitting. But don't wait until I need you to visit. Stop in anytime."

Their guacamole salads arrived and June asked, "How are things at the office now? Has Matt stopped growling and accepted you?"

Shannon shrugged. "To a degree. I think Mike Avery convinced him I'd cause more trouble than it was worth if he didn't."

"And would you?"

"Yes," Shannon admitted honestly. "I would. I've come to respect Matt's integrity and business judgment, but that doesn't mean I'm going to roll over and play dead. I've got a right to know what's happening and to make my own contributions to the success of the business." She shook her head. "I didn't come to tear down the company, or to take

Matt's place, so I don't understand why he resented me so much.''

"It would be more surprising if he hadn't," June said. "Back in Pennsylvania Matt was a builder, and he worked hard to make his business succeed. But when he and his wife divorced, she got just about everything in the settlement—the assets of the business, the equipment, their house, most of the cash, etcetera. By the time it was all over Matt had been picked clean. You can't really blame him for being bitter or for fearing that another woman—you—intended to repeat the process."

Shannon inhaled deeply and her voice was soft. "I had no idea."

"I know. I'm not telling you this just to gossip about my brother, but because I hope it'll help you to understand how Matt felt when, out of the blue, you suddenly became a majority stockholder in yet another company he's worked so hard to establish. It was bad enough that through a stroke of fate he should lose his own majority status, but to lose it to a woman was just too much. It wasn't you personally he resented. How could he, when he didn't even know you? It was the threat you represented—and still do, for that matter."

It all made sense now—Matt's hostility and resentment over her share of the business. And she had only added fuel to the fire by her determination to take her rightful place. It must be galling indeed for him to be forced to accept her, especially as a majority stockholder; while when her father had been alive the shares had been divided and Matt had been in control. In his place she mightn't have taken so kindly to someone else's suddenly holding all the cards, either. Technically she now had the right to outvote him on any issue. How was Matt to know whether she would exercise that right and possibly even try to push him out of his own company?

When lunch was over, June drove Shannon back to the office. In front of the building Shannon got out of the car, and the two women made a promise to repeat their get-together soon.

Just as Shannon closed the passenger door and stepped back, June flashed a smile and waved to someone behind her, then pulled away from the curb and drove off. With a heavy dread settling over her shoulders, Shannon turned around.

There was Matt, parking the company pickup truck in its usual spot. An instant later he was striding toward her, and vibrations of hostility flowed ahead of him.

"What were you doing with my sister?"

"We had lunch together," Shannon answered, trying to form a smile. "June is—"

"And I suppose you entertained her by gloating over yesterday!"

"I did no such thing!" Shannon cried vehemently. "You must really believe I'm a terrible person if you think I'd talk about that to anyone!" Suddenly she, too, was angry. And impatient. "If you weren't so darned obstinate and would just listen to me for a minute and let me apologize, you'd understand that I—"

For the second time Matt's outburst cut off her words. He was too incensed to hear her out. His eyebrows were crushed together, giving his face an ominous ferocity. "Why should I listen to you?" he growled. "I believed you and you made a complete fool of me! I don't intend to make *that* mistake again!"

"Unreasonable!" Shannon was shouting back now. "Muleheaded! You don't want to let me talk to you? Fine! I've tried to apologize, but you wouldn't accept it, so now I take it back! You know what your trouble is, Matt? You're angry because your ego got a good, swift kick! Apparently you expect to score with every woman you take out, and when you don't, it's a jolt to your overinflated pride! Well,

Mr. Macho, that's one for me!'' With her forefinger she marked a straight line in the air, then turned and walked away from him.

Three days later Matt still smarted with rancor. He'd been rejected and humiliated, and he wasn't likely to forget it, much less forgive it.

The past two and a half days, ever since their heated quarrel in the parking lot, the temperature inside the crowded office he shared with Shannon had turned cold and the atmosphere was bleak. They spoke only when obliged, and the rest of the time they tried to pretend the other didn't exist.

It hadn't been easy for Matt to pretend Shannon wasn't there. She sneezed and sniffled at her desk, battling a cold. Besides his awareness of her physical misery, he was, quite simply, aware of her. Period. He couldn't get her out of his system. The allure of her tugged at his senses whenever she was near.

Most of the time Matt managed to stay out of the office, thereby avoiding her. Shannon usually visited the development herself around two o'clock each afternoon, so it was easy enough to evade her there, too. Yet some of the time, of necessity, they occupied the office at the same time.

On Thursday morning Matt reached the office around ten-thirty, and Anne handed him a sheaf of messages, including one asking him or Shannon to return Kevin Boyd's call.

Matt looked at Anne with mild surprise. ''Shannon didn't take his call?''

''She hasn't come in this morning.''

That seemed a little odd, but Matt shrugged it aside. Shannon could, after all, suit herself about her comings and goings. Still, her absence was strange. Ever since she'd arrived in town she hadn't missed a single workday.

...be tempted!

**See inside for special
4 FREE BOOKS offer**

Silhouette Special Edition®

Discover deliciously different
Romance with 4 Free Novels from
Silhouette Special Edition®

A FREE
Folding Umbrella
and Mystery Gift
await you, too!

↳ Clip and mail this postpaid card today! ↲

Mail this card today for

4 FREE BOOKS
(a $10.00 value)
this Folding Umbrella and
a Mystery Gift *ALL FREE!*

← Clip and mail this postpaid card today! ←

Silhouette Special Edition ®

Silhouette Books, 120 Brighton Rd., P.O. Box 5084, Clifton, NJ 07015-9956

☐ **YES!** Please send me my four Silhouette Special Edition novels along with my FREE Folding Umbrella and Mystery Gift, as explained in the attached insert. I understand that I am under no obligation to purchase any books.

NAME _____
(please print)

ADDRESS _____

CITY _____ STATE _____ ZIP _____

Terms and prices subject to change.
Your enrollment is subject to acceptance by Silhouette Books.

Silhouette Special Edition is a registered trademark.

CAS086

He went into his office, *their* office now, returned Kevin's call and the others, and by the time he'd finished dealing with them all, Shannon still hadn't shown up. Matt settled down to do some paperwork, and cursed himself roundly whenever he found himself glancing at his watch and wondering where she was. In spite of the cold war between them, she hadn't let it interfere with business, so surely she wasn't suddenly staying away because of him.

Finally Matt broke down and asked Anne to call her house. A few minutes later the secretary reported that there was no answer.

Now really annoyed with himself for worrying, Matt left to keep a lunch date with friends. What did it matter where Shannon was? he asked himself. Why should he care?

But it did matter, and when lunch was over he telephoned the office from the pay phone in the lobby of the restaurant. "Have you heard from Shannon?"

"Not a word," Anne replied. "There've been a couple of other calls for you, though. Let me see, there's—"

"Are they urgent?" Matt asked impatiently.

"No. They—"

"Then never mind. They can keep." Matt rang off and went outside to his truck.

He drove straight to the development, thinking Shannon might be there, but he got the same story from the men as from Anne; no one had seen or heard from her all day.

His anxiety overcame his reluctance and he turned the truck in the direction of her house. And when he pulled into the driveway, relief flooded over him. There in the carport beneath the house was her car.

Feeling like a fool for having been so concerned but determined to satisfy himself that she truly was all right, Matt went up the stairs and knocked on the door.

She took so long to answer that he was beginning to get alarmed again, but then the door swung open.

One penetrating glance told the story. Shannon was covered by a shapeless blue robe. Her eyes and nose were red in an otherwise pale face, and her hair was disheveled, although it looked as though she might have attempted to brush it hastily before coming to the door.

"You're sick!" Matt breathed sharply. "Why in hell didn't you call the office and say you wouldn't be in? I've been half crazy worrying about you!"

Shannon's shoulders shrugged beneath the voluminous robe and her moist eyes met his levelly. "It never occurred to me you'd care, so I didn't think to bother."

Matt felt instant shame as he recalled his abrupt, unfeeling behavior toward her all week. "I suppose I had that coming," he said, chastened. He paused, then asked, "Can I come in?"

"Why not?" Shannon seemed utterly indifferent. As he stepped inside, she padded barefoot to the sofa, where she sat down and curled her legs beneath her.

Matt stopped in front of her. "Anne tried to call," he said. "She got no answer."

"I unplugged the phone so I could sleep."

He nodded. "That makes sense, but I wish you'd let me know you were feeling so bad."

Her eyes rounded. "Why?"

Why? Damn it, Matt thought, she had a point. *Why?* At last he grinned feebly. "Because we're partners."

He saw her stiffen. "Since when does that count for anything?"

Matt expelled a long breath and grimaced. "Okay. You're right. You're absolutely right. So far it hasn't counted for much of anything, particularly civil behavior on my part! I'm sorry, Shannon."

She lowered her gaze to somewhere about the middle of his chest, and soft color crept into her cheeks. "I deserved it this week," she said flatly.

Matt found himself smiling. "Well, maybe some of it," he conceded, "but not all of it. How about a truce? What do you say?"

Slowly she lifted her gaze to his face, as though searching for the truth. After a time she nodded. "All right. Truce." The last word ended on a sneeze. Shannon pulled a tissue from her pocket and blew her nose.

Matt was more touched by that prosaic action than he had any business being, and in that instant, he knew he was a goner. He was in love with this woman, like it or not, and when she hurt, so did he. It was as simple—and as complicated—as that.

He went to her and gently clasped her arm. "Come on," he urged in a quiet voice. "Let's get you to bed where you belong. Is there a chicken in the house?"

Shannon allowed herself to be led into her bedroom. "A chicken?" she sniffled.

Matt grinned at her bemused expression. "For soup. I make a wonderful chicken soup that's guaranteed to cure the common cold."

"Is that so?" For the first time Shannon smiled.

"Sure. The patent's pending, and when I market the product, I expect to make a fortune. So, do you have a chicken or do I need to go shopping?"

"I'm afraid it'll take shopping, but honestly, you don't need to go to all that trouble. I don't feel much like eating, anyway."

"It'll do you good, so don't argue." In the bedroom Matt pulled back the bedcovers. "Now in you go," he ordered.

Her fingers went to the tie belt at her waist and as she slipped out of the robe, Matt took it from her. She wore a silky pink gown beneath it, and he caught his breath as he saw her. The sunlight from the window made the thin cloth transparent, and in that one moment before she slid into bed, he had an enticing view of her shapely body.

He turned away quickly from the tempting vision and draped the large robe over the back of a chair. "This is too big to be yours. Was it your husband's?" he asked gruffly.

"No, it was one my father had left here. I forgot to bring one with me."

"I see." Matt felt it safe to turn around again, and when he did, to his relief she was covered from the chin down by the blankets and she looked drowsy. "Get some sleep," he murmured.

"Yes." Shannon closed her eyes. When he was about to leave the room, she said, "Thanks, Matt."

He halted in the doorway and turned. "For what?"

She opened her eyes briefly. "For...for just being here."

She slept for nearly three hours. When she awoke, late-afternoon shadows were darkening the room. Shannon turned over in the bed to glance at the clock and saw that it was a little past six.

Through the open doorway came the muted sounds of the television, and she remembered that Matt had come, that he had promised to make soup.

She got up and bundled herself into the robe again. A peek into the mirror appalled her. She looked awful. She could do nothing about the runny eyes and red nose, but she could and did brush her hair thoroughly.

Matt was sitting in her father's easy chair, watching the evening news on TV when she entered the living room. He stood up, smiled, and absurdly, it warmed her all over. "Hi. How're you feeling?" he asked.

"Better. I think the nap helped."

He nodded. "Sit down and I'll bring you some orange juice. Are you cold?"

"A little."

"I'll bring a blanket, too."

That evening Shannon was pampered in a way she hadn't been since Brad had spoiled her when she'd been pregnant. Matt served her dinner on a tray, brought pillows to tuck behind her head as she stretched out on the sofa afterward and made sure she took her aspirin and had plenty of juice. His kindness was almost overwhelming, and it choked her up. But when she tried to thank him Matt wouldn't let her.

"Partners don't have to thank each other," he said almost brusquely.

"Don't they?"

"Nope. They just need to be there when they're needed."

Shannon sighed. She didn't understand him in this new, gentle mood, but she decided to seize the moment and try to make her peace with him. She owed it to him.

"Matt, about that day on the boat—" she began.

"Look, we don't have to talk about that," he said quickly.

He was seated in the easy chair beside the sofa, near enough to reach out and touch, but when he looked away from her, Shannon suddenly felt as though a million miles separated them.

"Yes," she pleaded. Her voice was husky with unshed tears. "I do."

Matt shrugged indifferently, but Shannon could tell by the set of his shoulders that he was tense and defensive.

"What's to talk about? You simply changed your mind, like you said."

"There's a little more to it than that." Shannon stopped looking at his averted head and stared across the room at the blank screen of the television. "I went about it all wrong, I'll admit. But honestly, it wasn't you I was rejecting that day, but myself. I . . . I didn't set out to hurt you."

"Can't we just drop this?" came the muffled reply. "It's not a subject I care to rehash."

"I'm not enjoying this, either!" she exclaimed. "But I need to say these things, so please, just bear with me, will you?"

Shannon looked toward him again and saw that his face was still turned away from her. But at least he was silent, and that gave her fresh encouragement.

"I . . . I haven't been with anyone since my husband."

"I know that," Matt groaned. "You told me that after I first kissed you." He swung around suddenly to look at her, and his eyes were dark and intense. "Did you love him that much, Shannon, to the point that this many years later you can't bear to have another lover? Or is it just me in particular?"

His gaze seared her face, and Shannon found herself looking away this time. Her throat ached as she struggled with the words. "I loved him very much, and I still love his memory. I always will. But something happened just before he died that still—" She broke off and inhaled deeply before she forced herself to meet Matt's gaze. "I wanted you that day, Matt," she said boldly. "I wanted you very badly. I'm very attracted to you and I'm not going to deny that. But I can't lie to you, either. I couldn't allow myself the pleasure of making love with you then, and maybe I never can. But it had nothing to do with not wanting you."

Matt's voice was quiet. "Do you want to talk about it?"

She shook her head, and when she smiled at him, it was through a haze of tears. "I can't," she said huskily. "It's something I have to deal with by myself. It's my own private demon."

"Maybe you need someone to help set you free."

"I'm not sure I can ever be free of it," she said sadly.

"So in the meantime you'll go through life denying your own feelings and needs?"

"I don't know," she said softly. "I just don't know."

Matt was silent for a time. Finally he asked, "And what about me?"

Shannon looked at him in surprise. "I thought I'd explained."

"You've explained exactly nothing except that you don't know what you really want. You say you want me, yet you turn away from me. I want you, too...sexually, sure, but that's only a part of it. I want to get to know you—all your moods, your likes and dislikes. I want to spend time with you, to find out why you interest me. I want you to know me, too." He shrugged. "Maybe there could be a relationship in this thing for us, and then again, maybe not, but if you're going to stonewall us at every turn, what chance do we even have? Where do I fit in, Shannon? Or do I?"

"I wish I knew," she answered unhappily. She lifted a hand and pushed her hair away from her face. "Matt, after Brad, I never thought I'd be interested in another man. Well, I was wrong. I've come to care about you very much. But I'm not ready for a relationship, so it wouldn't be fair to you to kid myself otherwise. I don't want to create any false hopes for either of us."

"So what does that mean? Just forget how we feel about each other?" he asked harshly.

"Just that I don't want to make any promises I can't keep. Don't you see? I'm trying to protect you!"

"Are you?" he demanded. "Are you really concerned with my feelings or about your own? Isn't it rather that you're afraid to step back into the mainstream of life? Look at your left hand! You're still wearing your wedding rings. It's a defense, Shannon, and a dishonest one, as well. It's like wearing a big sign that says No Trespassing!"

Shannon looked down at her rings, somewhat dazed, and then she argued vehemently, "No! I never even thought about that!"

"Didn't you? It's an effective barrier, believe me! You weren't wearing them that day on the boat, or I could never have—" He broke off impatiently and got up to pace the room. Suddenly he stopped and hurled a challenge at her. "I dare you to start living again!"

Shannon moistened her lips. "Matt, please..."

He cut through her protests. "If you have any courage at all, you'll see me, go out with me, spend time with me, give us both the opportunity to discover how we really feel. But if you don't . . ." He came over to her, took her left hand in his and gazed down solemnly at her rings. "I'm leaving now, Shannon. If you're interested," he added heavily, "I'll know it when you stop wearing these."

Chapter Nine

As her cold improved, Shannon battled a new problem. Matt's ultimatum. She was in such a state of turmoil she didn't know what to do. In the end, she did nothing. For the next week she continued to wear her rings, and whenever she saw Matt at the office, he was polite and impersonal, as any business associate would be, no more, no less.

He had meant what he'd said.

Her resistance at first was as much sheer stubbornness as it was indecisiveness. She didn't like ultimatums. Who was Matt to tell her what to do? Brad's rings were a part of her, and she wasn't going to remove them at anybody's demand. They meant too much. They were proof of the love she and Brad had shared, and she would never part with them.

But gradually she came to the disquieting conclusion that Matt was right about her motives. She *had* continued to wear her wedding rings as a subconscious defense. They represented a past over which she still grieved, and she realized she'd also worn the rings as an amulet, a visible symbol of her unavailability. They were a charmed protection against having to deal with herself as a woman—a functioning, complete woman.

It was a deeply disturbing discovery, and she resented Matt for forcing her to delve into herself this way. He had snatched away every shred of mental comfort she'd possessed since Brad's death and now she was no longer satisfied with the status quo. Brad was her past; Matt was the present, and she could not continue to ignore the turbulent emotions he aroused within her.

Late Saturday afternoon she could bear the emptiness no more. For two hours she paced the floor before she finally summoned what courage she had and drove toward Fulton. There was no guarantee he'd be home, of course. Shannon had no idea how Matt spent his free time. If he wasn't home... Well, that would be that. She doubted if she'd have the nerve to seek him out a second time.

The day was hot, humid, and the brilliance of the sun was dazzling against the white stucco building. Shannon felt herself drooping as she walked toward it, and her heart thudded painfully.

At the door, she wavered and came very close to turning back. What if he rebuffed her? Worse, what if he laughed at her? Most frightening of all, what if he demanded more than she had the capacity to give?

But if she didn't try, she would never know and she would despise herself for the rest of her life. The courage that had brought her here today would never resurface if she didn't go through with this now.

Shannon knocked timidly and then waited in agony.

The door opened and Matt stood there in jeans. No shirt, no shoes, damp tousled hair. The sight of him half dressed was powerfully provocative. Shannon's gaze was drawn to the strong shoulders, the bare, golden chest, the slim tapered waist. She moistened her lips and struggled with the unnerving sensations that swept over her. It was another moment before she could finally bring herself to meet those dark quizzical eyes.

He wasn't going to help her. He just looked at her and waited.

She tried to speak, but her throat was too dry. Yet she had to do something. The silence was dragging on awkwardly. At last she did the only thing she could think of. She thrust out her hands so that he could see for himself that her fingers were bare.

The expression that altered his face was instantaneous. The smile came, first warming his eyes, then softening his lips, until it brightened his whole face. Before Shannon could catch her breath, he clasped her outstretched hands and pulled her inside, straight into his arms.

Shannon quivered spontaneously as Matt kissed her. His mouth was firm and demanding on hers, and his arms crushed her to him with more strength than perhaps he realized. Potent excitement set her blood afire and she snuggled even closer, pressing herself to his bare chest as her hands slid around to his smooth, warm spine.

The intensity of his kiss caused them both to tremble. Shannon felt as though she were melting as her body leaned against his for warmth and support, and she never wanted his embrace to end.

But finally the kiss mellowed, becoming gentle and soft before Matt lifted his head. One hand caressed her face and throat, and the light in his eyes was unsettling, burning, almost as though it branded her. He whispered huskily, "I'm glad you came. I'd begun to think you never would."

Gently Shannon broke the embrace and stepped backward. It was easier to talk without looking at him, so she turned toward the living room behind them. It was a pleasant room, done in sea green and oyster white, but Shannon was almost blind to it.

"You were right," she began huskily, "about the rings. About why I was wearing them. About a lot of things." Matt came up behind her and touched her arm, but she drew away. "No, please don't . . . until I've said this."

"All right." Matt's voice was quiet.

"I do want to try what you said the other night, seeing each other, getting to know each other. The truth is, I can't seem to think about anything else except you. But . . ."

"Go on."

"You'll have to be patient with me, Matt, not push me or expect too much of me. I'm honestly not sure I'm ready for this, for anything, and . . ."

"And you're afraid," Matt finished for her.

Shannon nodded.

Matt didn't touch her but he did walk around to stand in front of her. "Look at me, Shannon," he ordered softly.

She looked up, and saw that his face was thoughtful and serious. "I don't know what you're so afraid of, but if it's me, you can relax. I'm a patient man. We'll just take things one step at a time and see how it works out. No strings, no expectations. If it's lovemaking you're so worried about, I'll leave it to you to decide when. I want you, Shannon, but I want you to want me just as much, and I'm content to wait until you do."

Shannon nodded stiffly. "Thank you. You're very understanding. It's more than I have any right to expect of you."

Suddenly Matt grinned and teased, "Very true, but, then, I'm perfect, you know."

"Perfect, hmm?" She laughed and the tightening in her throat eased. "I had no idea."

"That's because I don't like to brag about it," he said in a deprecating manner. "It makes lesser beings feel inferior."

"Your modesty is admirable," Shannon shot back.

"Naturally. As you get to know me better, you'll find that everything about me is admirable. You'll be quite unable to resist my many charms."

"Is that a threat?"

"Oh, I hope so!" Matt declared with a disarming grin. Then he swept his arm toward the living room and said, "Make yourself at home while I finish dressing. I just got out of the shower."

"Am I stopping you from anything?" Shannon asked, thinking about that for the first time. "Were you about to go somewhere?"

Matt shrugged. "I planned to go out later to eat, that's all." His eyes narrowed thoughtfully. "How about it? Have dinner with me tonight?"

Shannon nodded. "I'd like that."

While Matt was in his bedroom, she went over to the sliding glass door and stepped out onto the balcony. It boasted a small table, a couple of comfortable outdoor chairs and a few pot plants.

Just below was the boat channel, which meandered between the buildings, and to the left was the bay. The salty air lightly grazed her face, pleasantly cooling it, and Shannon leaned against the rail and watched a sailboat in the distance.

When Matt joined her a few minutes later, dressed in slacks and a royal-blue shirt, she still stood in the same place, admiring the view, enjoying the breeze and feeling too content to wonder where the next minute or hour or day might take her.

Matt made coffee, which they drank while sitting on the balcony. They talked companionably about a number of things, and Shannon was faintly surprised at how relaxed she felt. All traces of her anxiety were gone, even about the ultimate outcome of the step she had taken. She was too grateful for the moment. Happiness was unique to her, a rare occurrence, and now she savored it.

An hour later, they went to a seafood restaurant for dinner. Shortly after they'd placed their order, Matt, who was facing the entrance, let out a low whistle. "I hope," he said with a wry grin, "that you don't want our being here together to be a secret."

Shannon raised her eyebrows questioningly. "Why?"

"See for yourself." Matt nodded in the general direction behind her. "We've got company."

She turned in her chair and immediately recognized the two couples coming toward them—the Averys and the Madisons.

Hastily she swung back to Matt and whispered, "Looks like the cat's out of the bag, all right." She wasn't pleased, and she could tell by his expression that he wasn't, either. They were in for a time of it, and this thing between them was still too new, too fragile, to be intruded upon by outsiders. Shannon nibbled her lip in frustration.

Just then the others saw them and clustered around their table.

"Hey, since when has this been going on?"

"Tyson, you sly dog, you!"

"Why so secretive?"

"You *could* let your family know what's going on!" came June's aggrieved voice.

Shannon pretended astonishment. "I don't know what you're all so excited about! Matt and I met to discuss business."

She saw Matt's eyes twinkle with appreciation before he played along. "Things were too hectic at the office, so we thought a dinner would be better. Quieter. More private. Though as it turns out..." He sighed as if he were put out at having a serious business discussion interrupted.

Caro looked crestfallen. "Oh, darn! Shannon, you're hopeless. Really hopeless."

"No more than her partner," June said dryly. "Honestly, Matt, business on a Saturday evening? Can't either one of you find anything better to do?"

Matt met Shannon's eyes over the flickering candle in the center of their table. At the same time, they both burst out laughing.

"I think we've been had, folks," Mike Avery said with a chuckle.

"That's what you get for being nosy," Matt told them.

In the end, Matt and Shannon moved to a larger table along with the other two couples, and dinner was a festive, talkative affair. Shannon couldn't recall a time she'd enjoyed herself more. The food was wonderful, the company lighthearted and fun, and she was with Matt. Every now and then their eyes met, and when they did and he smiled at her, her heart skipped a beat. It was almost frightening—being so happy. She wasn't used to it.

After dinner the other two couples were going on to a nightclub and they insisted Matt and Shannon go along, too. Matt looked at Shannon quizzically. "Want to go for a while, or have you had enough of these clowns' company?"

Shannon wrinkled her nose as though considering. "Umm, maybe we could tolerate them another hour or two."

"We can try," Matt agreed. "Just let me warn you—if he asks, be prepared with an excuse not to dance with Harry. He has two left feet."

"Not true!" Harry growled. "He's just jealous because all the women line up to dance with me."

"Don't you wish, Mr. Astaire," his wife said, laughing. "Come on, gang, let's go."

The couples split up to go to their separate cars. Matt clasped Shannon's hand lightly in his as they walked toward his car.

He opened the passenger door for her and she slid inside. A moment later he got in on the other side, slammed the door and inserted the key into the ignition.

But instead of turning it on right away, he glanced toward her, though they couldn't see each other clearly in the darkness. "You were a good sport about all that razzing we got in there."

"So were you." All at once she chuckled.

"What's so funny?" Matt demanded.

"Did you really go on your first date when you were nine years old?" June had provided her with that bit of trivia.

She heard him laugh softly. "If you can call being forced by your mother to accompany a very shy eight-year-old girl to a birthday party because she was new in the neighborhood and didn't know the other kids, yeah." He held up his hand, revealing a tiny space between his curved thumb and forefinger. "I came that close to running away from home that day."

Shannon giggled.

"What about your first date? I bet it was with the most popular boy in school and," he added in a voice mimicking teenage girls, "You had the *dreamiest* time in the world."

"You lose," she said promptly. "It was a blind date set up by my supposedly best friend, and he was a creep with pimples and bad breath."

Matt laughed. "Tough luck."

"It was. I've been more careful about choosing best friends ever since, and thank heavens, my luck has improved." Impulsively she leaned across the seat and kissed him.

"Hey," he said, sounding enormously pleased. "What's that for?"

Shannon shrugged. "I just felt like it."

Matt slid his hands beneath her hair, just at the nape. "I like your feelings," he whispered before he leaned toward her and kissed her again.

Matt sat alone, drumming his fingers against the table in time to the music, watching Shannon dance with Mike. Her head was tilted back as she laughed at something Mike was saying, and Matt felt a fresh stirring in his heart. She was enjoying herself and he was enjoying himself simply by watching her. How and why she'd captured his love he had no idea. He only knew it for a fact.

He'd promised he was a patient man and he hoped he'd be able to keep that promise. More than anything he wanted to be able to show her how he felt, to be able to make love to her, but it wouldn't be any good unless she wanted it, too. He had a feeling that Shannon would have to be in love, really in love, before she could commit to that, and though she openly admitted she cared for him, he was not at all sure she cared as much as he did.

Even if she did fall in love with him, would she ever get over whatever it was that held her back from freely expressing her feeling? He frowned in frustrated speculation. He knew Shannon to be a passionate woman. She'd proved that the day on the boat before she'd done such an about-face. But somehow, she was still hung up about her husband, and it wasn't only because she'd loved him so much. It was more than that—but what?

He sighed and jerked himself out of his reverie. The music was still playing and Shannon was still dancing with Mike. Caroline was dancing with another mutual friend, and Harry and June were table-hopping. Matt decided to buy a fresh round of drinks, but restlessly he got up and went to the bar across the room to order them, instead of waiting for the waitress to notice him.

At the bar he fell into conversation with an acquaintance and for a little while he was stuck. The music ended, then started up again, and out of the corner of his eye, Matt saw Jack Waring approach Shannon. A moment later she accompanied him to the dance floor.

Matt didn't like it, but there was nothing he could do about it short of making an ugly scene, so instead he tried to pay attention to what his companion was saying.

After he'd ordered the drinks, to be sent to the table, Matt was finally able to break away. He headed back across the room, but was stopped a couple of times by still other acquaintances. He sighed inwardly. That was the trouble sometimes with small-town living. Everybody knew you and it would be rude not to say hello.

At last he was able to make it back to his table. The rest of his group was seated, except for Shannon. The dance with Waring was over, and now she stood behind her chair, talking with him.

Neither of them noticed him because a small group of people were also milling close by, and Matt couldn't help overhearing them.

"If not tomorrow, how about Monday night?" Jack was saying.

"I'm sorry, but I can't," Shannon answered.

Waring frowned. "Look, I'm getting pretty tired of all your put-offs. Why won't you go out with me? If you're concerned about who I am, let me assure you my family is one of the most prominent families in the state. Anybody can tell you that I . . ."

Matt didn't like the belligerent tone of the man's voice. He was about to step forward and intervene, but Shannon spoke before he had the chance.

"Of course that's not it!" She interrupted Jack. "I'm flattered that you've asked me out, but I'm involved with someone, and I'm not seeing anyone else."

"Involved? You mean with someone back in Colorado? So what? We'll just go out a few times and have some laughs. He'll never know the difference."

"That's not my style, Jack," Shannon said in a straight-forward manner.

Matt saw Waring shrug. "Then you're a fool," he said flatly. "I'll bet whoever he is, he isn't sitting around pining away for you while you're gone."

"Even if it were a man in Colorado, I wouldn't go out with someone else behind his back. But the man I'm seeing lives here. It's Matt Tyson."

Matt's heart had skipped a few beats with growing elation. Whatever was between them was only beginning, yet already Shannon felt enough loyalty toward him not to go out with another man. The difference between her and his cheating ex-wife was so dramatic that he could scarcely credit it. Shannon was unaware that he was hearing any of this; Vicky, in the same circumstances, would have jumped at the invitation, especially from a man with as much money and social position as Waring.

"Tyson!" Jack's face twisted into a sneer. "He can't possibly offer you what I . . ."

Matt decided it was time to make his presence known. He skirted around a couple blocking the way and stepped behind Shannon. He put his hand possessively at her waist, and it gave him an enormous sense of satisfaction to be able to do that. He nodded amiably at Waring before smiling down at Shannon. "Sorry I was gone so long. I got waylaid talking to a few people. Have you been enjoying yourself?"

Shannon smiled back, and Matt was pretty sure that what he saw in her eyes was relief. "Immensely," she returned. "Jack was nice enough to ask me to dance while you were away."

"My pleasure," Waring said stiffly. "Excuse me, will you? I see someone waving to me from the bar." He inclined his head in a gesture of goodbye and left them.

A few minutes later Matt and Shannon left the club and drove back to Matt's condominium, where Shannon's car was parked. Matt parked next to it and then turned to Shannon in the semidarkness.

"It's still early," he said. "Would you like to come in?"

He heard her quick breath before she answered softly, "If you don't mind, I think it's better if I pass. I'm a little tired."

They both knew better, both knew that she was wary of what might happen in an intimate setting. Matt decided not to push his luck, so despite his disappointment, he accepted her refusal gracefully. He ran a finger down the side of her face and smiled. "Another time, then. Can I see you tomorrow? Now that we're officially 'seeing' each other."

"You overheard my conversation with Jack!" she accused.

Matt chuckled. "Frankly, I enjoyed every word of it."

Shannon became defensive. "I wasn't making rash assumptions, honestly. We agreed there'd be no strings and I don't want you to feel that I . . . well . . . it just seemed like a good way to get rid of Jack without making him angry."

"Hmm," Matt said, considering. "And I was hoping there was at least a grain of truth to what you said."

Shannon went still. "Were you?"

"Um-hmm."

"But I thought we'd agreed . . ."

Matt sighed. "We agreed to what you want, Shannon. Not to what I want. The last thing on my mind right now is going out with any other woman." He added with a gentle, teasing note, "Lord knows you're enough trouble all by yourself. I sure don't need to borrow more."

Sunday evening the Madisons had Matt and Shannon to dinner. It was fun and Shannon found herself having a wonderful time. Each time she was with Matt's sister, she liked her more, and Harry, too, was good company. As for Matt, it went without saying that she was where she wanted to be—with him.

Covertly she watched him as he chatted companionably with his brother-in-law. She liked the strength of Matt's profile, the dark richness of his hair, the even resonance of his voice. She liked the way his eyes smiled when he talked to his young nephew, the bantering that went on between him and his sister. It was easy to see that Matt loved his family very much.

Sometimes, when she caught him looking at her in a special, intimate way that was very private between them, she thought, she hoped, that he loved her, too. But then she'd grow angry with herself for wishing that he loved her, because it wasn't being fair to him.

Truthfully, it wasn't fair to be taking up his time at all, to go on seeing him. What good would it do? Would she ever be able to give him what he wanted? What she wanted, as well? Did she deserve to seek happiness and fulfillment for herself, or must she go on denying that side of her nature forever?

As usual, there was no answer. All Shannon knew was that she was very tired of being alone, without a man, and that feeling had grown stronger and more urgent since she'd begun to care for Matt.

But if she surrendered to her inclination, what then? A brief love affair and then goodbye? What else could there ever be for her?

Yet she knew that things had to be resolved between them some way, and soon. She was asking too much to expect a virile, healthy man to wait forever for her to make up her mind. As for herself, the torture of being near him, caring so deeply for him, yet remaining frustrated and unsatisfied, was getting to be impossible for her to handle. The temptation of Matt was too powerful.

"Shannon, will you read me a story?" Jason interrupted her thoughts. The child had just returned to the room after his mother had given him his bedtime bath and now he looked sweet and huggable in his pajamas. In his hands he held a bright-colored book.

"Of course I will," she agreed readily. She made room for him beside her in the easy chair she was sitting in and patted the space. "Come sit here next to me."

"What?" Matt exclaimed indignantly. "Reading a bedtime story is my job whenever I'm here. You're not gonna turn on me now, are you, Jason?"

"Want Shannon," the boy said stubbornly.

Harry chuckled. "You've been replaced by a pretty face, old buddy. You may as well bow out gracefully."

Matt gave Shannon a menacing scowl. "I'll get even with you for this," he threatened. "I don't take kindly to stealing."

Shannon wrinkled her nose at him, then draped her arm around Jason's small body so that she could hold the book in front of him. "Never mind your Uncle Matt," she said. "He's just an old grouch."

"Old grouch!" Jason giggled with pleasure. "Old grouch!"

Matt pretended he was about to lunge for him, and Jason shrieked with delight and excitement before burrowing against Shannon. "Don't let him get me!" he squealed.

"I won't," Shannon assured him, laughing. She shot Matt a stern look. "Now behave yourself, Matt, or I'll stand you in the corner."

Matt tried to look meek. "Yes, ma'am," he said. "If I'm good, can I listen to the story, too?"

Their eyes met, and a softness came into his that made Shannon swallow hard. She was in love with this man. She was. The question no longer existed. And tonight, later, she suddenly promised herself, somehow she was going to reach beyond the past and start living in the present.

But it was not to be.

Thirty minutes later, while June was tucking Jason into bed, the telephone rang and Harry went to answer it. A moment later he returned and his face was somber.

"We've got a fire, Matt."

Matt was instantly on his feet even as they heard the fire alarm go off, clanging through the night. "Where is it this time?" he asked.

Harry hesitated for a fraction of a second before he replied.

"Spinnaker's Run."

Chapter Ten

Against the backdrop of the black night sky the orange flames glowed. The fire crackled and popped angrily as it devoured the house.

The air was sooty, smoke clogged; men shouted as they battled frantically to overcome the hungry flames.

From a safe distance June and Shannon watched in silence. Harry and Matt were both members of the volunteer fire department, and they were there on the front lines, fighting the blaze along with the others, but Shannon could not identify either one of them. They were too far away and anyway, every hardhat looked identical to the next one.

The night was hot. Dry, suffocatingly hot. There was a breeze, but it did nothing to ease the heat generated by the fire. Instead the wind caused concern that the flames might spread to nearby trees and grasses and thus endanger other houses.

Shannon shivered in spite of the stifling temperature of the parched air. She felt ill at the sight of the beautiful home being mercilessly consumed. The only thing she could find to be grateful for was that it was unoccupied, one of the unsold houses, and that none of the new families already living here had been threatened.

Yet.

She shivered again. Only two houses beyond the fire there was an occupied house. The family who lived in it were huddled together now, just a few yards away, staring in fascinated horror as the firemen worked to put out the blaze.

"I wonder what started it," June said.

"I'm almost afraid to speculate," Shannon replied.

June looked at her sharply. "Why is that?"

Shannon's voice was dull. "We've had thefts and vandalism out here, you know."

"Arson!" June breathed beneath her breath. "Surely not!"

"I hope not," Shannon returned. "But I can't understand how the fire could have advanced so far before it was reported. We have a security guard who's supposed to be patrolling the area."

"Did he call in the report?"

Shannon drew her gaze away from the mesmerizing flames and looked at the other woman. "Good question. You know, I haven't seen him at all since we've been here."

"Maybe he's helping the others fight the fire."

"Maybe." But somehow Shannon wasn't satisfied with that conclusion. "I think I'm going to walk over to have a talk with those people," she said suddenly, indicating the family standing nearby. "Maybe they can tell me something."

June nodded. "I'll sit in the car with Jason." She turned to take the few steps to the car, where her son slept in the back seat.

Shannon approached the family and introduced herself. The man extended his hand in a brief greeting.

"Nerve-racking, this," he said.

"Yes." Shannon's gaze followed his. "Do you have any idea how it started?"

"Not a clue. We'd gone out to dinner, and when we came back we could smell smoke. My wife went in the house to call the fire department while I started looking around."

"You mean you're the ones who discovered it?"

"I guess so," he answered. He looked at his wife. "When you called to report it, did they say anybody else had called?"

"No. The dispatcher sounded like it was the first they'd heard of it."

"Have you seen the security guard?" Shannon asked.

"Come to think of it, I haven't," the man told her. "There was nobody else around when I saw the fire." He shrugged. "There were huge flames visible through the windows when I first got here. The interior was already gutted, I suppose. Nothing I could do but watch."

A silence fell over them all as they stared soberly at the brilliantly lighted spectacle. After a moment the woman spoke, anxiety in her voice as thick as the smoke. "The wind's shifting. We'd better load some things in the car while there's still time."

While the couple and their children hurried toward their house to salvage what they could, Shannon went back to the car. "Do you have a flashlight?" she asked June.

June found one in the glove compartment and handed it to her. "Something wrong?"

"I don't know. I think I'd better look for the security guard. He may be at the fire with the other men, but I'm not so sure. Those people haven't seen him at all, and they're the ones who reported the fire."

"Do you want me to come with you?"

"No. There's no sense waking Jason up and dragging him around. I may be concerned over nothing. I won't be long."

She switched on the flashlight and strode toward the front of the development, where the sales office was located. The office was also the headquarters for the security guards on night and weekend duty. Shannon hadn't even bothered to glance at it on their way in earlier because all her attention had been focused on the fire.

When she reached the office she saw that the lights were on inside. Shannon doubted anyone was there, but she intended to check all the same. She knocked on the door, then opened it.

"Anybody..." Her words trailed off as she stepped inside, because she saw him right away.

When she'd entered, her gaze had been trained to the left, where there was a doorway leading into a small anteroom used for extra file cabinets and storage. It was also where the coffee maker and a small refrigerator were located.

The guard lay sprawled on the floor in that room, surrounded by a pool of liquid.

Shannon rushed over and knelt beside him. His face was ashen and there was blood matting his hair and streaking his forehead. The front of his shirt was drenched by a brown stain, and a coffee cup lay nearby.

"Can you hear me?" she asked anxiously. She sought for a pulse point. "Can you hear me?" she asked again, louder.

The man did not respond, but just then she found a pulse. Relief washed over her with the force of a surging tide. He was alive!

But clearly he needed help. Shannon left him to go into the other room, where she called for an ambulance. Then she hurried into the rest room, grabbed a handful of paper towels and wet them with cold water.

When she returned to the man, she gently applied the wet towels to his face with one hand as she sought a second time to locate his pulse. A minute later she was rewarded. His eyes opened and he stared up at her. "What...?"

"I'm Shannon Edwards, one of the owners of Spinnaker's Run. Your name's Bob, isn't it?"

"Bob Delbert. What happened?"

"You've been injured," she explained softly. "How are you feeling?"

"My head hurts."

He lifted a hand toward it, but Shannon caught it and drew it away. "No, don't. It's been bleeding and you might make it start up again. The ambulance should be here soon. Can you tell me what happened?"

Bob closed his eyes, as though trying to piece the puzzle together, but when he opened his eyes once more, he said slowly, "I don't... know. I was pouring a cup of coffee, when I thought I heard a noise. But before I could turn around, something hit me. I don't remember much after that. I came to a few times, but then I'd pass out again. We'd better call the sheriff. I—"

He tried to get up, but Shannon stopped him. "It's all right," she told him. "I'll make the call. You stay still and rest."

"Okay." When she didn't move he said urgently, "Call now. Whoever it was might still be on the premises somewhere."

Twenty minutes later the ambulance sped the guard to the hospital in Aransas Pass. By the time he left, Bob Delbert was more coherent and argued about going, but Shannon and the sheriff's deputies overruled him. Shannon knew she wouldn't feel at ease about him until the doctors pronounced him fit. Meanwhile, she promised to telephone his wife.

When she finished the call, one of the deputies speculated, "I'd say it's a fair guess this is connected with that fire out there."

"It's an awfully big coincidence otherwise," Shannon agreed unhappily.

"Any idea why? Or who?"

She sighed. "None at all, I'm afraid."

The second officer shook his head. "It's too bad the guard wasn't able to see who hit him. Give us a description, something to go on. There's not much we can do without it.''

"I know.''

"Who discovered the fire?''

"One of the residents. His wife called in the report.''

"We'll talk to 'em. With any luck, they might have seen something.''

Shannon smiled wanly. "I hope you're right, but I don't have much faith in luck right now.''

They all went outside, and Shannon was heartened to see a black sky again where ominous light had illuminated the night a few minutes earlier.

"Looks like they've brought it under control," one of the men said.

"Thank God!'' Shannon whispered beneath her breath.

She locked the office and rode in the deputies' car back to the scene of the fire. When they stopped, she pointed out the house belonging to the couple they wanted to talk to, and while they headed toward it, Shannon walked the short distance back to June's car.

Briefly she told Matt's sister what had happened, and then she went searching for Matt.

Several men were spraying water over the smoldering embers of the totally leveled house, while a few men were resting on a grassy area out of the drift of smoke. One of the fire trucks was gearing up to leave.

Shannon found Matt standing near the blackened ruins.

He'd removed his hard hat and yellow slicker and wiped his arm across his brow. Smoke and ash had sooted his skin and his clothing until he was barely recognizable. His despair was obvious by his partially bowed head, the weary slump of his shoulders, and her heart went out to him. All the work and effort he'd put into that house had vanished within minutes. She had an interest in it, too, but not to the same extent as Matt. By the sweat of his brow he had built that house, and by the sweat of his brow he'd helped put out the fire that destroyed it.

She hated what she had to tell him.

"Matt?" She touched his arm gently.

He turned toward her, startled. "I didn't know you were here," he said. His head swiveled so that his eyes were trained once more on the rubble. "Not a pretty sight, is it?"

"No," she said, choking back tears.

He brushed a hand across his eyes. "At least it didn't spread," he said wearily.

"Yes."

Without looking at her, without any change to his voice, he added, "It looks like arson."

She gasped. "That's what I came to tell you. What makes you so sure?"

"One of the men found a gasoline can." He shrugged and laughed humorlessly. "A gasoline can in an unoccupied house."

Shannon inhaled deeply. "It looks like that ties in with what happened in the sales office."

Matt looked down at her with a ferocious frown. "What are you talking about?"

Quickly Shannon told him what had happened to the guard. "He's been taken to the hospital. Unfortunately he couldn't give a description of his assailant."

Matt pounded his left fist into the palm of his right hand. "Where is all this going to end?" he demanded.

Shannon moistened her lips and probed delicately, "Matt, have you thought of anybody with a grudge against you for some reason? Someone you've made angry, who might be doing this out of revenge?"

"I've thought and thought, until my head's whirling. If somebody hates me this much, I just don't know who, or why." He sighed wearily. "All I know is that he, or they, are out to destroy me."

"And me," Shannon said quietly.

Matt shook his head. "Can't be anything to do with you," he declared. "The vandalism and thefts began before you ever arrived. Unless it's someone who had a grievance against Charlie and extended it to you and me?"

It was a startling idea. "I can't imagine Dad having any enemies."

Matt grimaced. "Neither can I, but, then, until all this started happening, I didn't think I did, either." He added gruffly, "Go home and get some sleep. Standing around guessing isn't getting us anywhere, and there's nothing else you can do."

"What about you?"

He shrugged. "We're short a guard, remember?"

The next day Matt didn't come into the office at all. He called and left a message with Anne that he was going home to get some sleep, and for the rest of the day Shannon and Anne had their hands full, dealing with their company insurance carrier, the authorities and the local newspaper reporters. In between they handled routine business matters.

In the afternoon Shannon drove to Aransas Pass to visit the hospitalized security guard, and spent fifteen minutes chatting with Bob and his young wife. He'd received a mild concussion, minor cuts and bruises. Since he wasn't badly injured, he would probably be released after another night of medical supervision. Shannon returned to the office feeling greatly relieved.

Anne filled her in on the calls she'd missed while she was away, including one from Jack Waring. "Matt called, too," she said. "He was concerned about whether we'd lined up another guard for tonight. I told him we had."

Shannon nodded. "How's he feeling? Did he get any sleep?"

Anne shrugged. "I didn't ask. He was at the development when he called. Said he wouldn't be in today because when he left there, he'd be going to the hospital to see the guard. I told him you had gone, but he seemed to feel he needed to put in an appearance, too.''

''I see,'' Shannon replied. Apparently Matt had left no word about whether he'd be in touch with her later.

At the end of the day she went home, changed from her skirt and blouse into shorts and a shirt, and started dinner. Since she thought sure Matt would be arriving sometime soon, she made a shrimp creole, rice and a salad.

She hummed as she worked. Cooking was such a blessedly ordinary thing to do after the past twenty-four hours, and the process soothed her nerves. She'd always enjoyed preparing meals, but for too long there'd been little incentive. She had to admit, it was nice to have someone to cook for again.

Matt still hadn't come or called by the time the meal was ready, so Shannon kept the food warm and settled down to watch a TV program while she waited.

A few minutes later the phone rang, and she went to answer it eagerly. But it wasn't Matt, and Shannon grimaced as she recognized the voice.

''Hi. How are you?'' Jack Waring asked.

''Fine. And you?''

''Couldn't be better,'' he answered. ''But I was sorry to hear about what happened out at your development last night.''

''Thanks,'' she said briefly.

''Any idea how it started?''

''I don't think they know yet.'' Shannon wasn't about to admit the suspicion of arson.

''Well, these things take time,'' he said smoothly. ''I just wanted to tell you that if there's anything I can do to help, I'd be more than happy to do it.''

''I can't think of a thing,'' Shannon said honestly.

''I was wondering if maybe this changes things a bit?''

''What things?''

"About your selling that land. I wouldn't bring it up, except I thought maybe this latest event might be making your financial situation uncomfortably tight, and I wanted you to know, my offer's still open."

"Thanks, but we're not quite in the poorhouse yet, Jack," Shannon said dryly.

He chuckled. "Didn't mean to imply that you were. But I did think this might make a difference. Since there's a question of arson, I mean."

Shannon froze. How did he know that? But a second later she answered her own question. This was a small town, and gossip was bound to spread faster than the fire had last night.

Carefully she asked, "Even if that were the case, what difference would it make?"

"I imagine it would make a lot of difference to the insurance company if they suspected you might have needed the money yourselves."

"That's a filthy thing to suggest!" she gasped.

"Hey, don't get mad. I'm just pointing out how an insurance investigator thinks. I'm sorry if I upset you! Look, let me make it up to you. Let me take you out to dinner tonight."

"I've already eaten," Shannon fibbed.

"Oh. Then how about going out and having a couple of drinks together?"

"I told you the other night that I'm seeing Matt Tyson."

Jack made an exasperated sound. "Don't you know he's just interested in you because you've got half his company? Everybody in town thought he was going to marry Mona until you showed up. He dumped her pretty fast when you came on the scene, and maybe you ought to ask yourself why."

"This isn't a subject I'm going to discuss with you, Jack," Shannon said with a chill in her voice.

"All right. Fine. But you think about it, because it's true." His voice softened persuasively. "Listen, beautiful, I'm crazy about you, and if you'll just give me half a chance I'll show you how much. Come out with me tonight. I promise I'll take you home whenever you say."

"Thanks, but I don't think so."

"Why not?" he insisted. "We could have a great time together if you'd loosen up! I just told you about Tyson. You're wasting your time on him."

Shannon sighed. Why was this man so persistent? There seemed to be nothing she could do except be blunt with him. "I'm sorry," she said, injecting as much kindness into her voice as she could muster, "but I'm just not interested."

Abruptly the conversation was terminated. Jack had hung up on her. It was too bad she'd had to make him angry, but Shannon had simply run out of ways to turn him down politely.

All the same, he had given her food for thought, and it destroyed her appetite for the food in the kitchen. Had Jack been telling the truth? Had Matt really been callous enough to break off with Mona simply because Shannon was valuable to him as a major stockholder in Anchor Development? Surely he wasn't so cold-blooded and calculating, but how could she be sure? There was no denying that his interest in her now was the exact opposite of his hostile attitude when they'd first become partners.

The ugly suspicion refused to be banished, especially as the evening hours crept past and Matt did not call or stop by. Shannon picked at her solitary meal, stored the remainder of the food, washed up and then went to take a long, hot bath.

The bath did little to relax her, though. She could not shake Jack's words from her mind, nor could she erase her feelings for Matt. She felt hurt and betrayed.

Unhappily she admitted the truth. She'd had so many hopes for this evening and she'd expected to be spending it with Matt. She had realized that by holding back from making love with him, she'd been cheating Matt just as surely as she had Brad. She'd come to the conclusion that because she loved Matt, heart and soul, it was wrong to deny him the full expression of her love. What she'd been doing, without realizing it, was making him pay for her mistakes, her sins of the past. But now she no longer knew what to think. If he'd been faking his true feelings about her, she was lucky that things had not gotten that far between them.

The late news was over, and still fully clothed as he sprawled across the bed, Matt switched off the television by remote control. Then he flipped over onto his side, and when he saw the telephone he glared at it, as though it were responsible for all his troubles. He'd felt torn all evening over whether to call Shannon, and the battle still raged.

He knew she was probably wondering what had happened to him. Though they hadn't had the chance to make any plans, he felt sure she'd expected him to show up at some point tonight. After all, they'd agreed they were developing a relationship, and when that happened, a man didn't neglect the lady in question.

But Matt was tired and depressed and he'd had a lot of thinking to do, so he'd gone home where he could brood, uninterrupted. Twice the phone had rung, but he hadn't answered it. If it was Shannon he wasn't ready to talk to her, and if it was more bad news, such as maybe a tidal wave had just washed the rest of Spinnaker's Run out to sea, he didn't want to hear about it.

His business was fast being strangled to death and he couldn't seem to find a way to save it. First had come the depressed sales; next the shock of Charlie Main's sudden death and the consequent discovery that he himself no longer owned controlling interest in his own company. Then the final blow had landed—the repeated attacks against the development project by someone who meant to grind him into the dust, someone who was, moreover, succeeding extremely well. Much more of it and there would no longer be a business for him to worry about at all!

Matt's thoughts scuttled around like a rat trapped in a cage as he tried to figure out who could be responsible for all that was happening. But he came up blank every time. Fleetingly he'd thought of Judson, since he'd let the former sales manager go, but he'd soon scotched that notion. Judson might have been an ineffective sales manager, but Matt didn't think he was a criminal. Besides, until the fire, Judson had been in his employ, so he'd have had no grievance before that, and after checking around today Matt had learned that the man was now in Houston, already working for someone else. It was carrying desperation for a solution to the extreme to think the man would have sneaked back to town last night just for the dubious pleasure of playing with matches. No, the responsibility lay elsewhere. But where?

And now there was a new worry to contend with: the insurance on the demolished house. While he'd been sleeping this morning, Shannon had called the insurance company to report the fire, and late this afternoon when he'd called them himself, he'd been told they'd be doing an extensive investigation before they settled. Though he hadn't been told in blunt words, Matt had gotten the picture. Arson was ugly, and they were going to try to pin the rap on him and get out of paying the claim.

Matt sighed. He guessed he was taking it too personally. Of course the insurance people had to be careful and check out every detail before they paid off a claim where there was a question of arson. After all, there were unscrupulous people in the world who torched their own property when they were in a financial bind. Matt couldn't really blame the company for being cautious. He would be, too, if he were in their shoes. It was just that it had seemed to be the straw that broke the camel's back.

If all that wasn't enough to make a man insane, there was Shannon and their so-called involvement. That was a joke on him. The truth was, Shannon didn't really care about him, at least not the way he wanted. Oh, she wanted hand holding and kissing and a little nuzzling, but that just wasn't enough for him. That was a game for kids, and they weren't kids. He'd told her he could be patient until she resolved whatever was holding her back from having an honest, mature relationship, but now he wasn't sure he could carry out that promise. Hell, maybe she was just stringing him along to make him look like a chump. That was certainly what he felt like right now.

But even though he told himself these things, he wanted her, wanted her so much that a terrible ache spread through his loins.

In the end he called her, even though it was late—already past eleven. The need to hear her voice overpowered everything else.

"Hello. This is Tyson," he said when she answered. His voice came out curt, revealing the anger and frustration that festered inside him.

He was a little stunned, though, to hear the sarcasm in her voice. "Well, well, fancy hearing from you."

"Why do you say it like that?"

"I thought maybe you were busy having a cozy evening with Mona. Or did you just leave her?"

Matt was taken aback at the accusation, and swiftly, like a furnace turned on full blast, he burned with anger. "Maybe I should have gone to her tonight. My reception's bound to have been a lot warmer."

He heard her gasp and he could scarcely believe what he'd said. He was about to apologize, but her words forestalled him.

"And I should have accepted Jack Waring's invitation to dinner. It would have been a lot better than the meal that got cold while I waited for you."

"Correct me if I'm wrong," Matt said, "but I don't remember us making any arrangements for dinner tonight."

There was a small silence, and Shannon said stiffly, "My mistake. I'd assumed that since we hadn't seen each other today, you'd—"

"Take a piece of advice. Don't make any assumptions where I'm concerned," Matt cut in ruthlessly. "I've got my own life to lead and—"

This time Shannon interrupted him. "Don't worry," she said distantly. "I'll never make any assumptions about you again. You just go right ahead and lead your life. You won't get any interference from me."

Matt sucked in a ragged breath. "Look," he said grimly, "I don't want to fight with you, but I've been thinking. This situation between us just isn't any good."

"You're right," she agreed readily, "so maybe it's better if we don't contin—" She broke off abruptly, and her voice when it came again was a whisper, a panic-filled, shaken whisper. "Oh, my God! Matt! So-somebody's trying to get in the house!"

Every muscle in Matt's body stiffened. "Grab anything you can find to use as a weapon," he barked. "I'll call the sheriff and be right over."

She hung up, and the terror in her last word echoed in his brain as he dialed again. "Hurry!" she'd pleaded.

Matt was sickeningly aware of the distance between his apartment and her house and that it would take vital minutes to cover it.

Minutes that might make all the difference.

Chapter Eleven

She wasn't breathing; her muscles and limbs seemed frozen. Her throat ached as she screamed silently. The darkness was suddenly her enemy, yet she dared not turn on a light lest it encourage and guide the attempts of whoever was outside the door. His efforts, soft and stealthy, magnified by her fear, seemed to reverberate through the house like the clash of cymbals.

As quickly as the paralysis came, it left her. Shannon sucked in a breath of air and focused her eyes in the darkness. When Matt had called, she'd already been in bed, not asleep, but her eyes had been closed. She hadn't bothered turning on a light while they'd talked. Now her night vision adjusted well and she crept out of bed and went unerringly toward the bedroom door.

There she paused, listening. The sounds were louder. From beyond the stretch of the dark, silent living room came the unmistakable rattle of the front doorknob and the scuffling of shoes on the wooden sun deck.

Weapon. Matt had told her to arm herself, but with what? Shannon's thoughts scurried frantically, racing in all directions, purposelessly, panic-stricken, accomplishing nothing. She had no gun. She'd never touched one in her entire life, yet it was the only word her mind seemed to associate with a weapon.

Then another word came. *Knife.* In the kitchen there was a large, dangerous-looking butcher knife. She should get it.

But Shannon didn't move. The kitchen seemed suddenly to be at least a mile away and the door leading into it was but inches away from the front door. If the prowler burst in before she got to the kitchen drawer where the knife was stored, she'd be helpless.

What then? Her heart swelled and hammered with fear, suffocating her. She had to do something! She had to! She couldn't just stand here and meekly wait for her fate.

Steady. Strangely it was Matt's voice she was hearing in her mind. *Steady.* It was as though he were standing right beside her, encouraging her, calming her.

Shannon inhaled another deep breath, and the cloud of confusion vanished. All at once she was thinking clearly, rationally, and she remembered the baseball bat, a relic of her childhood tomboy days. Only last week she'd discovered it hidden in the back of her father's closet, and unable to part with the souvenir of her youth, she'd left it there.

Now she was galvanized into action, and she hurried silently into her father's bedroom. Feeling her way along the wall, she located the door to the closet and opened it. A sob of thankfulness tore through her throat as her fingers made contact with the hard, sturdy wood and closed around the handle.

A moment later she was creeping down the hall and into the living room. Now the sounds outside were even more ominous. There was a scratching, scraping noise against the door, as though the prowler were using some object to attack the lock.

Shannon's mouth was dry with fear as she crept quietly to press herself against the wall beside the door. The baseball bat was gripped so tightly in her hands that it might have been an extension of her arms. Now there was nothing more to do except wait and be ready.

Where was Matt? she wondered frantically. Where were the authorities? She heard a tinging sound as the doorknob was again assaulted, and she knew instinctively that it would not be much longer before the intruder succeeded in his objective. Dear God, her mind cried, what was she going to do? What was *he* planning to do?

Matt punched the accelerator to the floor and the car tore along the highway at suicidal speed. The taste of fear burned his mouth and scratched his throat. The distance between his Fulton apartment and the summer house seemed to have stretched into unending miles. If something happened to Shannon before he got there...

The thought was unbearable and he willed it away. Keep calm, he told himself. *Hold on, Shannon. I'm coming!* He approached a car ahead of him like a speeding bullet. Fortunately the driver noticed him and pulled off onto the grassy shoulder of the winding road. Matt flew past.

At last Matt approached the turnoff into the Main driveway and he slowed his dangerous speed. When he did, his headlights picked up the glint of metal in the distance. A vehicle was parked on the edge of the road, near the entrance to the driveway.

Understanding flashed like lightning. The prowler had parked his car on the road so that the beam of his lights or the sound of his motor wouldn't alert Shannon. Most frightening of all was that it was still parked here, which meant the prowler was still here... at the house, perhaps in it by now... with Shannon.

Matt jerked his car to a stop behind the other one and quickly extinguished the lights. Then he was out and racing

through the darkness, careful to keep on the grass so that the
sound of his footsteps was muffled.

No lights were visible from the house and Matt worried
about what that meant. Was it because Shannon had kept
them off so as not to help the prowler to see, or was it because he was already in there?

He clamped a lid on that thought. Speculation was no
good now. He had to be alert for action. As he neared the
house, he paused to catch his breath, and when he went on,
it was with silent caution. He crouched like a riled panther,
ready to spring at the slightest provocation.

The noise came from above him, a scratching sound, and
then a rattle, as though someone were jiggling the doorknob. Matt's heart leaped! The person up there was still
trying—he hadn't yet managed to get inside!

It was all he needed to know. Confidence surged through
him, warming his blood, loosening his muscles, sending
adrenaline through him. Matt threw away all caution and
mounted the steps at a run. He had the other person trapped
now and there was no longer a need for silence. There were
only two ways for the trespasser to get away: down these
stairs, where he'd have to encounter Matt himself first, or a
leap from the balcony.

Matt was fast. Halfway up, he saw the form of the prowler, hovering beside the door. The form swung toward him,
murmured a curse and exclaimed, "What the—!"

Matt had both feet on the solid deck now, and his right
fist plowed into the midsection of the dark form. He heard
a grunt, and a weak blow grazed his head before the other
person staggered back.

Matt went after him and the fight was on. He landed another strong blow to his opponent, but the other man retal-
iated and Matt felt a stinging sensation on his left arm.

His adversary had a knife.

On the opposite side of the door, Shannon could hear the
ruckus of thuds and shifting feet. Someone had come, either

the law officers or Matt, and trembling with relief, she quickly flipped on the outside light, opened the door and rushed out to help. She still gripped the baseball bat and had every intention of using it if she had to.

But in a moment the rout was over. Matt's fist smashed into the other man's face and the intruder slumped to the floor of the deck. Shannon stared at him in shock as she recognized him.

Matt stood, half-bent, his chest heaving as he glared down at Jack Waring's prone body. He lifted his hand to wipe his perspiring brow and Shannon saw a rip in his shirt sleeve and blood running down his arm.

"You've been hurt!" she exclaimed in alarm. "Matt! Oh, Matt!"

She rushed toward him and threw her arms around his waist, pressing him close to her. Her own body was quivering and it only grew calm when Matt's uninjured arm encircled her.

"Are you all right?" Matt asked gruffly.

"Yes, I'm fine. It's you who—"

She never finished the sentence. Two sheriff's deputies pulled into the driveway and Matt released Shannon, his eyes soft as he looked at her. "Maybe you'd better go put something on," he whispered.

Shannon looked down at herself and realized she was clad only in a thin nightgown. She nodded and hurried inside.

When she returned with her father's thick robe enveloping her, one of the deputies, whom she recognized from the previous night at the sales office, was helping Jack Waring to his feet, and he wasn't being gentle about it. "What's your name?" he demanded.

"S's Waarin," Jack muttered. He was obviously inebriated.

"What'd he say?" the other officer asked.

"Waring," Matt said harshly. "Jack Waring."

"Waring?" The man shot Jack a quick look, then his partner. "Of the Houston Warings?"

"The same," Matt said curtly.

"What were you doing here bothering this lady?"

"Came ta'see Shannon. Wan' her. She won' go out wi'me. Wan' her."

Shannon looked away, disgusted.

The deputy she'd met last night stepped toward Shannon and asked in a low voice, "Do you want to press charges, ma'am? There could be trouble, being he's who he is."

She looked at Matt in confusion, not understanding the reference. "Who is he?"

Matt shrugged. "His father's a big shot in this state. He has a lot of money and power."

"I see. What do you think I should do?"

Matt's face, too, was filled with disgust as he looked at the limp man being held up by the other deputy. "I'd like to see the book thrown at the slob, but unfortunately it's your name that would get dragged through the mud."

"I'm sorry," Jack whined. He was fast sobering up to the reality of the situation, though his words were still slurred. "I guessh I 'ad too mussh t'drink. Diddn' mean t'make trouble. Jus' wanna see Shannon. Don' be mad at me, Shannon."

Unconsciously she moved closer to Matt, but her eyes were on Jack. "If I don't press charges, will you swear in front of these men that you'll never come near me again?"

"I . . . promish." Jack nodded emphatically.

The first deputy had a word with Shannon, while the other led a stumbling Jack down the stairs. "I know it goes against the grain to let him go free, but Mr. Tyson's right, ma'am. You did the best thing. If he does come back and bothers you again, that's the time to press charges."

Shannon nodded. "Thanks for everything."

The man grinned and teased, "We've really got to stop meeting like this every night. My wife's going to get suspicious."

Shannon laughed. "We can't have that, can we?" She explained to Matt that they'd met when the security guard had been injured, and he laughed with them. Then the deputy took his leave.

Shannon turned to Matt and said anxiously, "Let's get you inside and tend to that arm."

"It's not bad," he assured her. "It's only a scratch."

"I'll be the judge of that," she snapped. She led him into the kitchen, pushed him into a chair and then went away to rummage through the bathroom medicine chest.

When she came back, Matt was struggling to remove his shirt. She gasped softly at the sight of his bare chest, and then she jerked her gaze away and dumped her supplies on the table. "Here," she said as matter-of-factly as she could manage. "Let me help you with that."

Gently she eased the shirt sleeve down his arm, trying not to let the cloth rub against his wound. When it was done, she dropped the blood-stained shirt to the floor and reached past him to the table for the disinfectant. As she did, her arm brushed against his chest, and her skin tingled at the contact.

They were both silent as she took care of his arm, until finally Matt asked, "How is it?"

"Not too bad, considering he might have killed you!" Her voice trembled. "Thank goodness the cut's not very deep." She taped a bandage over the wound and stepped back. "Well, that's that." She carefully avoided looking at his half-naked body, and her gaze went instead to his face. The stormy expression on it shocked her. "What is it?" she asked anxiously.

"He could have hurt you," Matt said roughly. "I should have killed the son of—"

"Shhh!" Without thinking, Shannon wrapped her arms around his neck and bent to kiss him.

The unexpectedness of the embrace jolted them both. Matt's lips, granite hard with rage, softened beneath Shannon's gentle mouth. Her lips opened invitingly, like a rose petal welcoming the morning sun, and he followed her enticing lead. Her tongue ventured out, tracing the inner perimeter of his mouth, light and gentle, tasting him experimentally.

She withdrew slightly and their eyes met. Matt's gaze was silently questioning, and all at once Shannon went hot with embarrassment. Too late she remembered their telephone conversation just prior to Jack's unnerving arrival. "Sorry," she murmured huskily. "I—" She broke off, hastily removing her arms from his shoulders and tried to back away.

She couldn't. With his one good arm firmly around her waist, Matt held her imprisoned. "Where do you think you're going?" he asked gruffly.

"I shouldn't have done that," she said.

The beginning of a smile tugged at the corners of his lips, spellbinding her so that she forgot her efforts to get away.

"Why shouldn't you?" he asked, amused. "If I'm not complaining, who will?"

Shannon gave her head a minute shake. "On the phone," she reminded. "We decided . . ."

"To hell with what we decided," Matt growled. He drew her down until she was sitting on his knee. Now his injured arm slid around her, too, so that she was encircled by the warmth of him. His face was somber as his dark gaze held hers. "You know I want you, Shannon," he said frankly. "But what do you want? Do you even know?"

Oh, she knew all right. She wanted him desperately. But she wasn't quite ready to say so. She had to clear up something first. Shannon took a deep breath, trying to forget how wonderful it felt to be sitting on Matt's lap, wrapped in his arms, her face only inches from his.

"Were you planning to marry that other woman before I came?"

Matt leaned back and his eyes widened in astonishment. "What woman?" he demanded.

"Mona."

For Shannon, time was suspended while she waited for his answer. She braced herself to hear the worst. She didn't expect the response she got.

Matt burst into laughter. It was loud, hearty, welling up from deep within his chest so that it shook his entire body and hers with it. And it seemed to have no end. Matt was suddenly struggling with his breath as he whooshed and whooped.

"I'm delighted you find this so funny," she said frostily, not in the least amused.

"I can't help—" Matt gasped for air in between bouts of chuckling. "Sweetheart, where did you get such a bee as that in your bonnet?"

Shannon ducked her head and muttered, "Jack said so when he called earlier tonight to ask me out."

"Waring?" Matt want off into another seizure of laughter, while Shannon glared at him. "You mean you believed him?" He shook his head and suddenly he was over his amusement. "Damn it, Shannon, I did give you more credit than to think you'd believe anything that man had to say."

Shamefaced, Shannon couldn't meet his eyes anymore. She lowered her lashes and her gaze fell upon his chest. "Well, I didn't really believe him, but I couldn't help but wonder. He said everybody in town knew it—that you'd dumped her for me be... because of the business."

Matt's thumb forced her chin up so that she had to look at him. His eyes were piercing, his voice suddenly stern. "And what do you think? That I went after you because of your shares in the company?"

Shannon's voice broke. "I don't want to think that."

Matt sighed. "I don't know how I can prove it to you, except to remind you that in the beginning I wasn't exactly nice to you. If I'd been that cunning, wouldn't I have tried to win your favor right away?"

"Maybe. I don't know what to think about anything anymore."

"Neither do I. But I can assure you that if you ask anyone besides Waring, I think you'll learn that nobody has heard any talk of my marrying Mona. The subject never came up. She was just someone I dated a few times, Shannon, that's all. She doesn't interest me, and frankly, I wish I could say the same about you."

She knew he was telling the truth. It was there in his eyes, in his voice, in his expression. "I believe you, Matt. About both of us." Unhappily she met his gaze and added, "It would've been better if I'd never come here."

Matt returned her gaze in troubled silence. "Well, you did," he said at last. "Shannon, the truth is, I'm crazy about you, but I don't think you feel the same way about me. If you did, you wouldn't hold me off the way you do. I thought I could be patient while you worked out whatever it is that bothers you, but what happens if you don't work it out? I can't be dangled from a string indefinitely."

"I know that," Shannon said quietly. "I've come to that conclusion myself." She paused for a second, and her heart beat in a staccato rhythm against her breast. "Matt, I do care about you, more than you know. Will . . . will you stay with me tonight? Will you make love to me?"

She heard his swift intake of breath. "Are you sure this time?" he asked. "Are you sure you're ready?"

"I don't know if I'm ready," she admitted truthfully, "but I do know it's what I want more than anything on earth."

Shannon slid off his lap, held out her hand to him, and after a moment he accepted it. As they left the room, she flipped off the overhead light, and through the velvet darkness, she led him to her bedroom.

When they stood beside the bed, Matt stopped her. "You can still back out if you want," he said from behind her.

She knew he was thinking of that other time, the day on the *Lady June,* and she knew that whatever her own private demons were tonight, she had to see this through, for Matt's sake even more than for herself. She couldn't, wouldn't, hurt him again.

She turned toward him in the darkness and placed her hand flat on his warm chest. "Not this time," she whispered. "Unless you want to back out and pay me back."

Matt uttered a sound of anguish and she felt his arms close about her. "I want you," he told her. "Not revenge." His hands ran over her back and then he murmured, "I want to see you, Shannon. I want to see every beautiful inch of you when I make love to you. Turn on the lamp."

With an unsteady hand she obeyed, and when she turned back it was to find him gazing at her with unmistakable longing shimmering in his eyes.

Matt slid the bulky robe from her shoulders and it slithered to the floor. Then he bent to place tingling kisses at her throat. Shannon quivered as her fingers slid up his sleek, smooth shoulders and then buried themselves in his rich, dark hair.

His hands were gentle as they explored her curves. His fingers lightly traced the route from the tips of her breasts, along her rib cage, to span her tiny waist before fanning out across her hips. Shannon's heart pounded as he set her body afire.

Very soon Matt was discontent. He lifted the hem of her nightgown, and in one quick movement it was over her head, joining the robe on the floor. His gaze seared her as it flickered over her, and her pulses throbbed at the admiration she saw in his eyes.

Slowly he bent his head to her breast, and when his mouth found the nipple she gasped, filled with sudden, wanton pleasure. Her back arched, allowing him better access, and when his other hand slid down to caress her inner thigh, she thought she would die at the wild surge of desire that stormed through her.

Her hands raked his back in rhythm with the accelerating stampede of passion that raged through her. Swept away and forgotten were all her previous questions about whether she deserved to be a full and complete woman again. She was too utterly engrossed in the moment to give any thought to her doubts. Matt had released a part of her that had been forgotten until now—that she was a highly passionate woman who thrived when she was being true to her nature; that she had been born to satisfy the man she loved by satisfying herself at the same time; that without the intimate give and take of this most precious gift between herself and her man she wasn't even half alive.

Now Shannon came fully alive and she exulted in it. She had been reborn and she joyfully celebrated the occasion.

She cupped his face in her hands and lifted it. Matt's dark, slumberous gaze met her hot tawny one. She smiled, loving him with her eyes, and then she pressed her body to his, flattening her breasts against the hardness of his chest as her lips touched his face in a flurry of kisses.

"Hey, hey, what's this?" he said, laughing huskily when she stopped at last. His eyes were brilliant with warmth as he held her cushioned snugly within his arms.

"I want you," she said steadily. "So very, very much."

Matt groaned and buried his face in her hair. "What a woman you are," he murmured. "You keep my head spinning trying to figure you out."

Shannon laughed softly. "Maybe that's what I want to do—keep you guessing."

"You're doing a good job of it," he said as she nibbled his earlobe and amazed and delighted him when she let one hand stray beneath the waistband of his jeans at his hip. "I never dared to think you'd be like this—a tiger lady."

"Do you like it?"

Matt's lips quirked. "Oh, I more than like it."

A gamine smile flitted across her face. "Mister," she said, laughing, "you ain't seen nothin' yet!"

She had spoken the truth. Their lips met and Shannon's response was no less greedy, no less savage than his own. Her mouth opened with eagerness to the pressure of his, and as their tongues met, hotly erotic, Matt was shaken by the primitive sensations that assaulted him. Impossibly, here was an earthy woman with a fierce passion to challenge his own.

He released her long enough to shed the rest of his clothing, and he was amused to find that her gaze on his body was every bit as avid and appreciative as his had been on her. Uninhibited, unembarrassed, she wanted him, and when he was naked she stepped forward boldly and clasped her arms around his waist.

"You're a beautiful man, Matt," she whispered shakily. "Make love to me now."

With their arms wrapped around each other they fell into the soft nest of the bed. Matt's body half covered hers and he said, "I love seeing you like this, with your hair all over the pillows and your skin gleaming like soft gold." His mouth came close to hers and his breath was featherlight on her face. "I've wanted you so much for so long."

He kissed her gently, as though with a promise, and then he began to slowly make love to the rest of her. An aching welled within Shannon, an exquisite mingling of pleasure and pain as his lips roamed over the entire length of her body. Her breasts thrust forward with tortured sweetness as his tongue flickered over her rigid pink nipples, and when he buried his face between them, she uttered a moan and threaded her fingers through his hair.

When he began to kiss her sensitive inner thigh, spasms of violent yearning quivered through her. His fingers stroked her and teased her, bringing her to a feverish pitch that became unbearable.

But Matt was in no rush to take her, and his lips began to work their way upward again, over the flatness of her belly, over the ridges of her rib cage. He was deliberately torturing her beyond sanity.

"Please," she begged at last. "Oh, Matt, please..."

He laughed from deep in his throat. "Not yet," he murmured. "Not yet, my love."

But she had to have release from her agony. She wrenched free and, with an unexpected force that caught him off guard, maneuvered from beneath him even as she pushed him down.

A devilish glint lurked in her eyes. "You want to play mean? I'll give you mean!" she threatened breathlessly.

Matt chuckled, but the laugh died quickly as she began her sensual assault upon him. She nuzzled his throat, and the silky golden strands of her hair tickled his face while her slender, lovely hands moved down his chest, slowly, deliberately and provocatively. The touch of her fingertips was delicate and light, taunting his body as they danced across his ribs, curled themselves in the thickness of the wiry hair centered on his chest, then leaped like wildfire to his thighs before circling round to his hips and then jumping to crawl up his arms to his shoulders.

Meanwhile, her mouth was following the same path, inching down, her tongue darting out to tease now and then. Matt's entire body went stiff with urgent, shattering need. Never had he felt such intense and painful desire, never before had he been so ruthlessly, so dangerously brought to the edge of control. Every atom of his body screamed for an end to the growing pressure inside him. Shannon's feminine power over him was absolute.

But he held the same power over her, and he reveled in that realization when, ending her torment by pulling her beneath him, he saw it in the bright glitter of her eyes, felt it in the way she quivered expectantly. The truth was, they were at each other's mercy, both open and vulnerable.

They came together then, and Shannon welcomed him into her with a tiny cry of gladness. She buried her face in his shoulder and Matt was still for a timeless moment, deeply moved by the enveloping, womanly warmth of her.

Then they moved in unison as they climbed to the stars together. Higher and higher they rose until at last they reached their destination in a shower of fireworks.

Matt's arms tightened around Shannon and she clung to him as though she would never let him go.

Now they were floating on a glassy-smooth sea of love and contentment. No thoughts came to interfere with the blissful peace of completion. Their fierce embrace relaxed, but still they remained one, too spent, too filled with emotion, too content to move.

At last Shannon stirred, and Matt lifted his weight from her and rolled to his side, though his arms still held her.

"How do you feel, love?" he asked tenderly.

Amazingly her eyes misted. "As though I've just been reborn," she whispered brokenly.

Matt's throat choked up. He hadn't expected such a glorious answer. He gently wiped away a teardrop and asked, "Then why the tears?"

Shannon shook her head. "I never dreamed this could happen to me," she said in awe. "I've been frozen and dead inside for so long. Matt, I...I can't find the words to tell you how much this..." Her voice broke again. She longed to be able to tell Matt exactly what he'd done for her, the freedom, the release he'd brought to her, but she was too overwhelmed.

Matt leaned toward her and kissed her softly. "You don't have to say it," he told her. "I know, because I feel the same way. It was perfect, and how can anyone describe that?"

"I guess you're right," she said huskily. She knew he understood that she couldn't talk about it just then and that he would wait until she could. She ached with silent thankfulness for him.

He pulled the covers over them both, then switched off the lamp. As he snuggled down, he drew her head to rest on his shoulder. "By the way," he said conversationally, "there's something about me you ought to know."

"What?" Shannon giggled suddenly, regaining her equilibrium and sense of humor in the snug security of his embrace. "That you snore?"

Matt chuckled and slapped her bottom playfully. "No, smart aleck. That I love you."

Her equilibrium slid by the wayside.

"Oh."

"'Oh'? Is that all you've got to say about it? 'Oh'?"

"Hmm. I suppose I *could* say that I love you, too."

"Ahh!" He sighed with satisfaction.

"'Ahh'? Is that all you can say? 'Ahh'?" Shannon feigned indignation.

Through the velvety darkness, she could almost feel him smiling. "I say we're being very silly about a subject of such earthshaking significance."

"I agree." Her voice turned husky. "I never expected to feel like this again...to be in love again. It seems so strange. Am I dreaming, Matt?"

He chuckled softly. "This is real, all right. What just happened between us was real, too. I'm just as surprised as you are, darling. I was thoroughly convinced that I was immune to love. But then you came along and showed me I didn't know myself as well as I thought I did." His arms tightened around her and he rested his chin on top of her head.

"It scares me," Shannon confided. "I never planned to love you."

"And you think I did?" he asked, then sighed. "Love just wasn't included in our projected goals as business partners."

"That's for sure. It changes things, doesn't it?" she asked hesitantly.

"Yes. It changes things. For the better," Matt said firmly.

"I'll go along with that." Shannon caressed his warm, bare chest and her words were unsteady when she spoke again. "Until tonight, until this minute, I didn't realize quite how lonely I've been."

"I know exactly what you mean," Matt said fervently. "Holding you like this, having made love to you, just proved how empty my life has been until now. I didn't want to love you, Shannon." His voice softened and he kissed her forehead. "But I'm glad I do. I didn't think a man could ever be this happy." Unexpectedly Shannon laughed, and he demanded gruffly, "Now what's so funny about that?"

"Not a thing." Hastily she reassured him. "I was just thinking about how I came to Texas spoiling for a fight with you. I never imagined I'd end up falling in love with you."

Matt laughed, too. "The tables sort of got turned on both of us, didn't they? I thought you were beautiful and desirable from the first, but I was ready to fight you to the bitter end. Now I'm ready to fight anything or anyone who tries to take you away from me."

Shannon nestled more closely within the security of his arms. The warmth of him was infinitely soothing. "Nothing like that's going to happen if I have anything to say about it. But it's getting late and you've been through a lot this evening," she said with another hint of laughter in her voice. "We'd better get some sleep."

Matt bent his head and gave her a long, tender kiss. A moment later he whispered, "Good night, my love. Sleep well."

"You, too."

"Oh, I will. Because I'll be dreaming about waking up with you still in my arms."

Like a cat curled in an easy chair, Shannon shut her eyes and drifted off into the best night's sleep she'd had in years.

Chapter Twelve

Shannon awoke as the dawn's light splashed the deep indigo sky with streaks of brilliant orange, lemon yellow and flamingo pink. Her entire body was toasty warm. Like two spoons cupped together, she and Matt formed a comfortable curve. His chest was touching her back, his arm was arced across her hip and their legs were intertwined.

She was happy, totally, completely, utterly happy, and the realization that she was, surprised her. It was not a state of being she had aspired to entering ever again. It made her want to laugh out loud, to sing for the sheer joy of it, and if she could, she would have embraced the entire world, sharing with it her wondrous rapture.

A featherlight kiss fell on her exposed shoulder above the covers. "Good morning," came a resonant male voice.

Shannon flipped over so that she and Matt were facing each other. "Good morning yourself," she said, smiling. Matt's face was ruddy, still flushed with sleep, and she was enchanted by the tangled black forest of his hair. His chin was smoky blue with its overnight growth of beard and his lips were soft, sensual and entrancing. She appeased her desire to trace them with her fingertip.

Matt caught the finger, planted a kiss on it, then pulled her close. "I want my good-morning kiss," he stated.

"Sorry, sir. I'm fresh out. Someone stole them all last night."

Matt's eyes twinkled. "Then the thief will just have to give them back, won't he?"

"I suppose he will."

His lips captured hers and the kiss was poignantly sweet and warm, bringing a rush of tender emotions from Shannon's very soul. She felt transformed by it, as though she were on an arid desert lake bed suddenly filled with life-giving water.

Subtly the kiss changed, becoming demanding, charged with compelling ardor. Beneath the covers their hands sought each other and they became intoxicated on the dawn-fresh nectar of each other.

Their lovemaking this morning was different from the night. Though still urgent and powerful, it was less feverish and rapid. Now they savored each other languorously.

Sunlight had completely washed away the night before they arose at last and showered together.

"What would you like for breakfast?" Shannon asked a little later as she finished dressing in a pair of jeans and a white cotton shirt. "I can make pancakes or bacon and eggs."

"We'll go out to eat," Matt decided. "After we stop by my place so I can get a shave and some clean clothes."

Although Shannon didn't mind cooking, she acquiesced. She was too content to care much where they ate, what they ate or even whether they ate. When she said as much to Matt he laughed at her. "I love you, my sweet, but I'm not prepared to starve for you. Especially since you're directly responsible for my enormous appetite this morning, anyway."

Shannon's cheeks turned rosy and Matt laughed at her again before they left the house.

When they reached Matt's apartment, he called a restaurant and ordered breakfast to go.

"To go?" Shannon asked when he'd hung up. "Are you going to bring it here, then?"

Matt grinned and shook his head. "Nope. If we stayed here, I'd probably end up taking you back to bed, and without any food for strength, you might have a fainting man on your hands."

"That would be tragic," she admitted. "So where are we going?"

Matt's teasing manner disappeared and his eyes became piercing and intent as he looked at her. "Out in public where I won't be tempted by you, yet where it's private enough to talk."

Thirty minutes later they were seated at one of the covered picnic tables that dotted Rockport beach. At this hour of the morning they had the place to themselves. It was still too early for the picnickers, swimmers and skiers who would be out in full force later on. Behind them was the ski basin and the summer homes on Key Allegro; to their right was the harbor, where a few fishermen milled around their boats and the bait stands. Already a few sea gulls circled, searching for their own breakfast.

Shannon and Matt sat facing the bay, and the breeze was pleasant on their faces. Sunlight cast a golden overlay on the water and the sound of the surf gently lapping the shore was soothing.

The flavor of the food and coffee seemed to be enhanced by the tangy air—or possibly, Shannon decided, it was because her appetite was so voracious. She had discovered that she was as hungry as Matt.

She glanced toward him as he lifted his Styrofoam coffee cup to his lips and they exchanged glances. The love she saw glowing in his eyes made her breathless. It was a miracle, all this happiness, and Shannon wondered if it wasn't almost too much for one mere human being to grasp.

"What're you thinking?" Matt asked softly.

"About how happy I am at this moment," she replied honestly. Shannon hugged her arms about her shoulders in a possessive manner. "I wish things could stay like this forever."

"Why? Don't you want them to get any better?" he teased.

"They can't get better than this!" she retorted.

Matt's eyes smoldered as he held her gaze. "Want to bet?" he said suggestively.

"Oh, you! You know what I mean!"

Matt grinned and nodded. "Yes. I do know what you mean." He leaned closer to her and said in a soft voice, "I never knew golden-brown eyes could reflect the color of water."

"Do they?" She was mesmerized by the lips that inched nearer to hers.

"Umm-hmm. Tell you something else, too."

"What's that?"

"Your lips are adorable."

"I was just thinking the same thing about yours."

"Were you, now?" His head bent and he kissed her with the sunlight and the sea breeze and the gulls as witnesses.

"Our food is getting cold," she murmured some time later.

Matt sighed. "There you go, being right, being practical. You have no romance in your soul."

"Look who's talking! You're the one who said you couldn't live without food! I've never met a man yet who didn't think of his stomach before he thought about romance."

Matt grinned. "Well, got to keep our strength up, you know."

"And women don't, I suppose?"

"I never heard anybody say the way to a woman's heart is through her stomach."

Shannon laughed. "That's because they don't know how hungry I've discovered I am. We're supposed to go for diamonds and furs and the like, but this morning I'll take my breakfast over all the diamonds in the world." She broke off a piece of toast and popped it into his mouth. Then she turned back to her own food.

Matt was finding her more enchanting by the moment. Shannon was showing him new facets of her personality—she could be serious one moment and delightfully playful the next, as in the shower earlier, when she'd insisted upon sculpting a soap-bubble beard on his chin. In bed she'd turned out to be far more than he'd dared to dream of—a sorceress who bewitched him with her seductive charm. No sultan could have ever had a more expert temptress. She had driven him to frenzied desperation, and then she had carried him to hitherto unimaginable heights. She was beautiful, intelligent and altogether wonderful, and best of all, she returned his love, a love he'd never thought he'd bestow upon any woman again. Shannon had snared him, heart and soul.

When they finished eating, they removed their shoes and rolled up their pant legs. Hand in hand they went to the water's edge and began to stroll along it.

"Tell me now," Matt said quietly, "so you can put it behind you for good."

Shannon looked down at her feet. The damp sand clung to the bottom of her feet and then was washed away by the gently surging waves.

She knew what Matt referred to, and she swallowed painfully. Even now the memories cut through her heart like a sharp knife. She'd never told anyone about the burden of guilt she carried inside herself. She wasn't sure she could even now. And yet she wanted to be honest with Matt. She didn't expect absolution from him; how could she, when she couldn't give it to herself? But perhaps he'd understand more fully why she never would be free of the past.

She inhaled deeply and stared straight ahead, but the water and the sand blurred before her eyes as she recalled the past.

"Brad was . . . was a very good husband and father." She had to pause to clear her throat. "He loved Timmy and me very much, and overall I was happy with him. I loved him, too. He and Timmy were my life. I feel that it's important you understand that basically we had a very good marriage."

She looked at Matt and he nodded before she continued. "He was a good provider, generous, kind—everything a woman could want in a husband. We had a nice home in the suburbs, a little cushion of money in the bank, friends and a good relationship with both his parents and my father." Shannon sighed. "I guess you could say if Brad had one real fault it was that he was too ambitious, he worked too hard. My fault was that I resented his work taking up so much of his time."

"And so you fought about it," Matt said shrewdly.

Shannon nodded. "Yes, we fought about it. More and more as time went by. Brad spent long hours at work most days, although he did take off early sometimes so that we could go out to dinner or to a movie or visit with friends. But what angered me was that he wouldn't ever take any time off so that we could get away together for a few days. We hadn't gone anywhere for so much as a weekend since before I was pregnant. Brad reasoned that he was getting his business really established and couldn't afford to slack off. Since he was working to support his family and make a better life for us, he expected me to understand. But I didn't. I thought he needed a rest, that we both did. I was feeling bogged down in my role as wife and mother and I wanted a break. I felt as if life were starting to slip by us, that we hardly ever had real time for each other anymore." She sighed. "I guess what I really wanted was a second honeymoon and for Brad to show me that I was still important to him."

"That doesn't sound unreasonable," Matt said.

"No?" She shot him a look, then glanced away. "It was juvenile, selfish. I was thinking only of myself, not of Brad."

"I think you're being too hard on yourself."

"No, I'm not. I've had three and a half years to think about it. The...the last night we were together I created a terrible scene. My mother-in-law was keeping Timmy overnight and Brad and I went out to dinner together. Brad was excited because he'd just landed a new account he'd been trying to get for months, so we were celebrating that. Halfway through dinner I suggested we ought to take a few days off and go somewhere, but, as usual, Brad had a hundred reasons against it. So we had an argument right there in the restaurant. He called me frivolous and selfish and I called him a lot of hateful things, too. In the end I threatened to divorce him. I can still see how white his face went, how shocked he was. It was the first time the word had ever been mentioned between us."

Shannon shuddered and went on slowly. "Later, after we got home and went to bed, he tried to make up. He was really shaken by my rash threat and he promised that if getting away somewhere was that important to me, he'd make time and we'd do it. Then he...he tried to make love to me."

She couldn't speak for some time after that, and Matt squeezed her hand encouragingly. "And you wouldn't let him," he prompted softly.

Shannon lowered her head in shame. "No," she said in a hollow voice. "I was too angry by then to care what he was saying. He could have offered me a trip around the world and I'd have turned a cold shoulder. I didn't want him to touch me, and in fact, I got out of bed and went to sleep in Timmy's room. It was the only time in our entire marriage that I ever did that, the only time I ever refused him, the only time we didn't resolve our differences before we went to sleep. It was the cruelest thing I could do, and it made him think I was really serious about a divorce. The next morning he had already gone to work by the time I got up, but he'd left a note in the kitchen saying that if that was what I wanted, he'd find another place to live by the weekend."

"And then?"

"It wasn't what I wanted, of course. By morning I was ashamed of myself. I tried to call him at the office, but he was out installing a computer system somewhere, so I couldn't talk to him. I decided I'd make it up to him that night with a nice dinner and a romantic evening. I asked my mother-in-law to keep Timmy all day so I could shop and have my hair done, and she was happy to do it. I called the office again and left a message with Brad's secretary to have him pick up Timmy there on his way home from work. It wasn't very far out of his way, you see, and he usually did that whenever Timmy was at his parents' house. So I spent all day getting ready for the evening. I even," she added ruefully, "bought a new nightgown before I went home to cook dinner."

Her voice broke, and blinded by tears, she stumbled against Matt. He caught her to him and steadied her. "You've told me enough," he said huskily. "You don't need to put yourself through all this anymore."

She didn't even hear him, she was so caught up in the memories of that night. "It had begun sleeting and snowing late that afternoon, but I never gave it any thought. We're used to that in Denver. I didn't even worry when Brad didn't get home when I expected him. I just assumed he'd worked a little later or that he was spending a few minutes visiting with his parents when he went to get Timmy. But finally, just when I was about to call them to see if they knew what the delay was, the doorbell rang. It was a police officer with the news that another car had slid on a patch of ice and crashed into Brad's. He and Timmy were both killed instantly. I . . . I can never forgive myself for that."

"Forgive yourself?" Matt asked incredulously. "What did you have to do with it?"

Her eyes were brimming with tears as she lifted her head to look at him. "Don't you see?" she asked. "If I hadn't started that argument with him the night before, I wouldn't have been concentrating on how to make up with Brad, and I'd have picked up Timmy earlier in the day. And if I had, they would both still be alive. They wouldn't have been at that particular intersection at that particular time. It was my fault! All my fault!"

Matt shook her by the shoulders. "Shannon," he ordered roughly. "Snap out of it. You can't reason like that! It's insane. It's just something that happened. It could have been anywhere, at any time. You said yourself you often left Timmy at your mother-in-law's and that Brad would pick him up in the evenings. You can't blame yourself for what was an accident, just because you had a quarrel! It's tragic. It's horrible. It's heartbreaking. But it's not your fault!"

"Rationally I know what you say is true," she said, gulping for breath and wiping away the tears. "But how do you get over knowing you cheated your husband out of pleasure his last night alive? How do you get over knowing you said awful things to him, things you didn't mean, and that you never had the chance to tell him how sorry you were or how much you loved him? How do you get over knowing you won't ever see your ch-child learn to ride a bicycle or play in Little League or march in a graduation cap and gown? How do you—"

Matt crushed her to his chest, and his arms were steel bands around her trembling body. "Do you believe Brad would have forgiven you that night if he had come home?"

The question startled her, and she lifted her head from Matt's shoulder to look at him through damp lashes. "Why, yes, of course I do! He loved me."

"Then if you know that, you have to forgive yourself, darling," he said gently. "It's only fair to him. To his memory. You can't let your guilt over that night haunt you forever, or let a misguided sense of blame for the accident taint the rest of your life. You're letting it overshadow the good memories you have of him and of your son, and that's not right."

Shannon gazed at him in amazement. "I never thought of it that way."

Matt smiled tenderly. "Maybe it's about time you did. Do you think either of them would have wanted you to destroy your own ability to live fully because they're no longer with you? Is an unhappy, guilt-ridden life what you'd have wanted to condemn them to if it had been the other way around?"

"No, I'd want..." Shannon stopped and managed a woebegone smile. "I see what you're telling me," she said slowly. "Thank you, Matt."

He smiled. "Better now?"

She nodded. "Much." Her voice had a catch in it. "I'm glad I told you."

"So am I."

Shannon mopped at her eyes again. "I must be a mess."

"A beautiful mess," Matt said. He released her, glanced at his watch and sighed. "I guess we'd better be on our way. The insurance people are sending someone else out to look at the ruins this morning and I want to be there."

"Again?" Shannon looked at him in surprise. "Didn't they have someone out there yesterday afternoon? They told me that's what they intended to do."

As they walked back toward the car, Matt told her of his own conversation with them, and Shannon was indignant to learn that as owners they were suspected of igniting the blaze themselves.

"And did we also hit the security guard over the head!" she demanded hotly. "Besides, we can prove we weren't anywhere near the place when the fire started. June and Harry can vouch for that."

"June is also my sister," Matt reminded her. "An insurance investigator could argue that her alibi might be slanted in our favor."

That silenced Shannon. This was an alarming turn of events. If the insurance claim was denied and the company had to sustain the loss, it would put them in a precarious position financially, not to mention how damaging such an indictment would be to the company's business reputation. It was beyond thinking about! Everything Matt had struggled so long and so hard for would be wiped out overnight. Shannon was sickened at the thought.

Matt drove her back home, where Shannon could change into more businesslike attire and pick up her car. At midmorning she had a meeting with an advertising agency in Corpus Christi, and they both felt it was important that she keep it. Neither wanted to voice the underlying fear that at this stage this might be a matter of throwing good money after bad.

"How about dinner at my place tonight, love?" Matt suggested before she got out of the car.

Shannon smiled despite her heavy heart. "Still thinking about your stomach, eh?"

Matt grinned. "And yours. Besides, I'm trying to make up for that dinner you cooked last night that I didn't show up for. How about seven?"

"Fine. Matt?" she asked anxiously. "Should I give the go-ahead for those magazine ads if I like what they've done? They'll be awfully expensive."

Matt nodded. "Advertising's a fact of life, and Kevin is convinced we should aim at those magazines. Go ahead if you think the ads are good. The sooner we get results, the better."

But that afternoon, as Shannon left the advertising agency's office on the south side of the city and joined the stream of traffic on the freeway, she wondered if she shouldn't have held off, just until all this insurance business was over. The agency had taken her copy and a rough layout Kevin had sent down and turned them into a sleek, seductively beautiful magazine spread. Shannon had approved it and requested them to go ahead and place the ads with the selected magazines. Now Anchor Development was committed, whether they could afford it or not.

It was almost four when she got back to the office. Anne said Matt had been in, but had gone back to the development. "Good news about Bob Delbert," she said as Shannon went toward her office. "His wife called to say he went home from the hospital this afternoon. The doctor told him he can go back to work in a couple of more days."

"That's great." Shannon sighed with relief as she went into her office and closed the door. At least there was one piece of good news in the midst of so much that was bad.

Skirting Matt's desk, she went to the files and pulled out a stack of papers she almost knew by heart: the current financial statements.

At her own desk she looked them over and began playing "what if" at the calculator. She was trying desperately to figure out a way to make all the ends meet if the insurance judgment went against them. She was drawing no salary herself, and Matt had already cut his to the bone.

In a worst-come-to-worst case, she thought morosely, they might have to let Anne go. Shannon could take over the job of secretary herself, but she wasn't at all happy with the idea. Anne had been with the company for years and she was good at her job. Shannon would hate having to dismiss her. Besides, even if they didn't have to pay her salary anymore, it wouldn't make up all the difference.

One of the salesmen, too, perhaps. Maybe even Kevin himself, even though so many of their hopes rested with him. Despondently Shannon rubbed her hands over her eyes. Kevin wasn't even due to actually start working for them until Monday, and here she was thinking about his possible termination. She felt strongly that he would be good for the company, but on the other hand, Kevin didn't come free. He didn't even come medium expensive, if you compared his salary demands to what Judson's had been.

She sighed and stared unhappily at her figures. The bloom had most definitely been taken off a day that had begun so beautifully.

All the same her heart tripped with excitement at the thought of being with Matt again tonight. Her body warmed in a glow of anticipation.

He'd been right about the burden of guilt she'd been wearily dragging around with her for years. Why hadn't she ever been able to see that it was wrong for her to blame herself? Of course she would always regret the quarrel, the coldness that had existed between Brad and her that last night, but Matt was right that she couldn't justifiably blame herself for the accident that had taken Brad and Timmy's lives. If things had been right between her and Brad at the time, she would never have thought it was her fault. It wouldn't have made the loss any less, but her grieving wouldn't have been tainted by false self-condemnation.

Last night Matt had released her from her self-imposed imprisonment as a woman who didn't deserve to be loved; he'd shown her that she did; he'd opened up for her once more the wellspring of living. Today, with a few simple words, he'd freed her emotionally as well from a mental punishment she didn't deserve. She would never cease being grateful to him for that.

So now, what could she do to lift *his* spirits from the on-slaught of so many worrisome business problems?

Matt showered, dressed and went into the kitchen for the steaks. Mechanically he seasoned them, then went onto the balcony to start a mesquite fire in the grill.

He was tired, drained. He wished this thing between Shannon and him hadn't happened just now. The timing was off. He was too besieged by worries over the business to be able to concentrate fully on his feelings for her.

Yet it had happened and there was no going back. He was still in awe of the depth of the emotion she could arouse in him. He'd believed he was in love when he had married Vicky. Otherwise he wouldn't have been hurt so badly when she was unfaithful to him. But now he saw that what he'd felt for his wife had been a thin, ghostly version of what he felt for Shannon.

She loved him, too. After last night he didn't doubt that. But they hadn't known each other long, and Matt wondered if the feelings they had for each other could stand the test of time. Despite Shannon's loving response to him, he still had doubts, an insidious fear that whispered caution. He didn't want to make a second mistake.

Shannon was still bound up in her own past, too, and Matt couldn't help but wonder if she could truly extricate herself from it. Their cases were at opposite poles. He was afraid of getting burned again; her wounds still bled over her loss of the man and child she'd loved so much. Now she said she loved him, Matt, but enough to put her past behind for good? Could either of them really do that?

Yet the thought of a future without Shannon in it was suddenly impossible. Last night had shown him that she was the only woman he wanted. Any other woman would be a sorry substitute, a cheap synthetic as opposed to sterling quality.

Fortunately his brooding thoughts were interrupted by the sound of the doorbell.

Matt went to open the door and there stood Shannon, a beautiful business executive in a tailored cream-colored suit and a vivid aqua silk blouse. In an effort of severity, her golden hair had been arranged in a bun, but a few strands had managed to free themselves, curling down against her shoulders and at her ears. She was exquisite, and Matt caught his breath with sheer pleasure. The doubts of only minutes ago faded in the reality of her lovely presence.

Her expression was far from businesslike, despite her attire. A mischievous sparkle lighted her eyes, and her lips curved into a delightful half smile, half laugh. Her arms were laden with packages.

"What's all this?" Matt asked as he reached out and took the largest one from her. When he'd relieved her of the burden, he leaned forward to give her a kiss.

"Cake and champagne," Shannon said when he finally allowed her to speak.

"What're we celebrating?" he asked with irony as he led the way to the kitchen. "The business going to rack and ruin?"

Her eyes widened as she set the bottle of champagne on the counter beside the other package. "Should we be celebrating that?" she asked with a baffled expression. At his scowl she laughed and said, "Go ahead, look at the cake."

Matt slid the boxed cake from the paper bag. A grin spread across his face. The cake read Happy Anniversary to Us, and nestled within its cluster of sugared flowers was a single candle.

"We're having an anniversary already?" he asked.

"Of course. One day. I thought it deserved celebrating, don't you?"

"I sure do," he said huskily. He drew her into his arms and kissed her with satisfying thoroughness.

Over drinks they discussed their current business anxieties, each assuring the other that soon the black cloud must lift. Over dinner, as though by a silent pact, they abandoned business matters altogether and talked of personal things—their birth dates, their habits, even their most secret dreams. Shannon had once longed to be a ballet dancer, and had even been accepted into a troupe just after high school, but a virus struck her down only two weeks afterward and lingered so long that she couldn't regain the valuable time she had lost, and so she'd dropped out and enrolled in college, instead. Dance was an unfulfilled ambition that still left her wistful whenever she thought about it.

Matt was sympathetic as he listened, and when she asked about his dreams, he told her of his secret yearning to be an adventurer. He'd grown up wishing he could sail around the world, or discover lost tribes in jungles, or scale mountains.

"Foolish ambitions," he said with a shrug, "but when you're a teenage boy, you want the excitement of discovery, not to be shackled to the mundane."

"Of course. It's no more foolish than my desire to be a ballerina." She smiled. "I wasn't nearly as good as I wished, and eventually I became a far better teacher than I could ever have been as a dancer. What kept you from attempting your adventures?"

Matt grinned. "A healthy dose of reality. My father was willing to foot the bill for a college education. He wasn't willing to shell out one penny for a latter-day Tom Sawyer. Not being able to figure out how I could support my habit of eating regularly and afford the costs of adventuring, too, I opted to keep on eating."

Shannon laughed, and they went on exchanging revealing tidbits about themselves.

Finally, Matt told her about his marriage and subsequent divorce, and though he spoke in a straightforward, unemotional manner, Shannon could read between the lines and tell how terribly he'd been wounded.

When dinner was over they carried their cake and champagne into the living room. The lights were dim, and the music on the stereo was soft, romantic.

They sat together on the sofa, and their hearts were in their eyes as they gazed at each other.

Matt raised his glass and said, "To you."

Shannon lifted hers. "And to you," she said huskily.

Their glasses clicked and they drank their toast. Afterward Matt took both their glasses and placed them on the low table in front of them. He clasped Shannon's hands, and not knowing until that moment that he was going to do it, he asked, "Will you marry me?"

Shannon stared at him, apparently as surprised by the question as he was over asking it. Yet Matt knew with sudden, unshakable certainty that it was what he wanted more than anything.

Shannon withdrew her hands from his. "Matt," she whispered unsteadily. "You've taken me by surprise. I didn't expect this."

He managed a tiny smile. "Neither did I," he confessed. "But I mean it. Maybe this isn't the best time to ask you, what with all the uncertainty in the business just now, but I know I love you, Shannon, and that's not going to change. I want you to be my wife, I want us to have a family together. I want to be with you for the rest of my life."

Abruptly Shannon stood up, took a few steps toward the balcony door as though she were compelled to put space between them, and only then did she turn to face him. Matt's heart sank at the stricken expression he saw on her face.

"I can't!" she exclaimed. "Please don't ask this of me."

Matt rose, too, and his jaw was rigid. "Why? Because I couldn't ever measure up to Brad? I don't want to try to take his place, Shannon! I want to take my own place with you."

"No! It's not that!" she cried. "Honestly it's not. Why can't we just leave things the way they are? We were happy last night, today. I don't see why we should change anything. We don't need a marriage certificate to prove that we love each other!"

"Maybe I do," Matt said quietly. "I want to be able to tell the world you belong to me. And I want children. Is that so wrong?"

"I can't!" Shannon choked and vigorously shook her head. "I'm not ready for that. I don't want to be married again, to have more children. It hurts too much later when you lose them! I can't and I won't put myself through all that again!"

"You're letting fear get in the way of living, Shannon!" Matt went to her and caught her by the shoulders. "You can't base the future on what happened in the past. Don't you understand? I love you and I want to be with you forever. If you really loved me you'd feel the same."

Shannon thrust him away. "And what's forever?" she asked stormily. "Another day? A few years? We love each other now, today, and that should be enough. You tempt fate by demanding more. Planning for forever is a futile waste of time. In the end you lose everything that matters."

Something froze inside Matt. "You're a cheat just like my ex-wife. Except instead of cheating with other men, you're cheating us both out of all the things that come with love— real love. People who love each other commit to each other, however long or short that lifetime might be. You're a coward, Shannon. You're afraid of life, of yourself, of what love really stands for."

"You just don't understand," she said wearily.

"I don't? When I was first divorced I swore I'd never love again, never marry again. I wanted a family, but not enough to take a chance on getting hurt again. Then I met you. I thought with you I was finally getting another shot at happiness, that I could get past the fears and doubts and try for it, but now I see how wrong I was. Because you're too selfish to let that happen for us." His voice iced over. "You came into my life, turned it all upside down and made a fool of me once too often. Well, you'd better enjoy the victory while you've got it, because it'll never happen again."

Chapter Thirteen

Your claim is being studied by a review panel, but I don't think you have too much to worry about,'' the insurance agent stated. ''Even though the perpetrator of the fire hasn't been found, your company records are clean. You've always met your debts, and while there seems to have been a cash-flow problem recently, your efforts to minimize its effects have been commendable. No one can claim that you're in dire straits, so it isn't likely the review board can deny you a settlement.''

''That's good news!'' Matt said. Relief was evident in his voice.

''It sure is,'' Shannon seconded. ''How soon do you think they'll make their decision?''

The insurance agent clasped his briefcase shut and stood up. ''Within a week, I'd say. Now it's not a hundred percent certain they'll rule in your favor, so I don't want to get your hopes up too much, but in the absence of any evidence to the contrary, I believe they'll have no choice but to exonerate you and pay the claim. Now I'd better get a move on. I have another client to see this afternoon, and if I don't hurry office hours will be over."

"Thanks for stopping by," Matt said. There were handshakes and cordial goodbyes and then the man was gone.

Once they were alone in their office, Shannon breathed, "Maybe the nightmare's almost over."

Matt shook his head. "I won't feel that way until they catch whoever set that fire. As it is now, I keep waiting for the next blow to strike."

"You're right, of course." They would never be really safe until the arsonist was behind bars. Shannon was thoughtful, but then she brightened. "Kevin's already turning the sales around, and with the good news that the insurance company will probably pay our claim soon, at least things are beginning to look up for us."

"Are they?"

Shannon was distressed at the cold tone of his voice, of the underlying tension between them. For just a moment they'd actually forgotten their differences and talked without constraint like team members pulling together. Now the moment was gone, and the strained atmosphere had returned.

"Don't," she pleaded impulsively. "Matt, please, stop it. If we try to be civil, things will be so much easier for both of us."

Matt quirked one thick eyebrow and asked with excessive politeness, "Was I being uncivil? Pardon me!"

Shannon sighed in defeat. "You know what I mean."

"Sorry, I'm afraid I don't." Matt glanced at his watch. "I promised Kevin I'd meet with him this afternoon to go over some contracts, so I'd better push off." He tossed a few things inside a desk drawer, slammed it shut, then glanced at her impersonally. "Is there anything else you need to discuss with me before I leave?"

"No," she said in a hollow voice.

Matt nodded curtly and, without another word, strode from the room. Shannon gazed miserably at his back until he was out of sight, and then she dropped her face into her hands.

Almost two weeks had gone by since the night Matt had proposed. Since that time they'd been wary and formal around each other. Not that they'd been together often. Matt had resumed his habit of avoiding her as much as possible, and Shannon did her best not to attract his attention any more than was strictly necessary.

She hated the estrangement between them, and yet she told herself that what was done was done, and it was best to leave it alone.

It was easy telling herself everything had worked out for the best. She was very good at it now and repeated it every night until she finally fell asleep. The problem was she hadn't quite convinced herself in spite of her best efforts. Crawling into bed alone every night brought back memories of the night Matt had spent with her. She thought of the tender way he'd smiled at her whenever he was teasing her; the way his browned hand looked against the whiteness of her skin; the glow in his eyes that so clearly had spoken his desire for her. If she could only forget those things, she thought in annoyance, she'd be on the way to complete independence. And that was what she craved—independence from all attachments. She'd already lost too many people she'd loved to risk any more loss. True, she was suffering the loss of Matt's love even now, but if they married, if they had children and she lost all over again, the loss would be a trillion times worse. No one had any right to expect that of her.

Shaking herself out of her brooding thoughts, Shannon decided she might as well call it a day. She began clearing her desk, and was suddenly brought up short by the realization that her presence in the business was entirely superfluous. The ad campaign on which she'd worked so diligently was now in operation, and besides, as it evolved further, Kevin was perfectly capable of handling it. As for overseeing the construction of the resort itself, Matt and the building foreman had that under control. In the office Anne was a whiz—all the records were up-to-date and her accounting procedures were impeccable. When you got right down to it, Shannon thought dismally, there was nothing of importance for her to do here. If she vanished tomorrow, only her physical absence might be noted, but any contributions she made to the well-being of the company itself would not be missed.

It was a depressing insight. On the other hand, maybe that was all to the good. Maybe the time had come to let go and leave everything in Matt's hands. It was what he wanted; it was what he'd always wanted.

For the time being, Shannon decided to get away for just a day. Maybe a break, a change of scenery was what she needed. What she also needed was companionship. Impulsively she picked up the telephone.

At midmorning the July sun was already blazingly hot. Heat waves shimmered up from the parking-lot pavement as the two women emerged from the car and walked toward the shopping-mall entrance.

"I'm glad you came up with this idea," Caroline Avery said. "For the past two weeks I've been thinking about coming to Corpus to buy a few things for our vacation, but I just never seemed to get around to it."

"When are you leaving on your trip?"

"Saturday." Caro wrinkled her nose. "Which means tomorrow I'll spend all day packing. The kids and I are driving to Dallas to spend a few days with my cousin, and next Friday Mike will fly up to join us and then we'll go on together to the Smoky Mountains. I wonder," she said speculatively, "if you can buy sweaters in this weather? It'll probably be chilly at night in the mountains and the kids have outgrown everything from last winter."

"If you can't find them here, you probably will when you get there."

"I suppose you're right."

They entered the mall and soon were totally engrossed in their shopping. Caro was unable to find the sweaters she needed but she did find several short sets on sale, which she bought for her children. She also picked up a couple of shirts for Mike and new shoes for herself. Shannon found a plain, unremarkable white blouse on sale, the kind that goes with anything, and purchased it. After that, her enthusiasm for shopping waned and she was content merely to trail along behind Caro.

When they tired, Shannon suggested an early lunch, but Caroline vetoed the idea. "I need to look for a birthday gift for my cousin. Let's just rest a few minutes and then I'll get busy. After that, I'll be ready to sit over lunch all afternoon."

In the center of the mall, beneath the skylight, they found a vacant bench. They were surrounded by lush greenery and the sound of rushing water could be heard from the spraying fountains located near the benches.

As soon as they were settled, with their packages at their feet, Caro gave Shannon a shrewd look and said, "Okay, out with it. What's bothering you?"

Shannon tried to look surprised. "Why, nothing. I guess I'm just not in the mood to buy out the stores the way I thought I was."

"Is that so?" Caro asked softly. "You wanted to get away from the office on a business day and now you don't feel like shopping when you get here. All this wouldn't have anything to do with a certain partner of yours, would it? Like a lover's tiff?"

Shannon grimaced. "I'm afraid it's a lot more than a simple tiff. How did you know?"

"Matt was at our house a few nights ago and I could see he was really down. Even fires and other assorted business problems wouldn't make a man look quite that discouraged.'' She paused. ''It's the real thing between you two, isn't it? You've actually gone and fallen in love.''

Shannon clasped her hands together and gazed down at them. ''Yes,'' she answered softly. ''It's the real thing.''

''So what's the problem?''

''The problem is the whole thing terrifies me,'' Shannon confessed. ''Maybe it's just happened too fast—I don't know. Matt wants to get married, Caro. He wants children. He wants to go the whole nine yards, you know? And I just can't do it.''

''But honey, if you're sure you really love him—'' Caroline began, but Shannon interrupted impatiently.

''That's just it, don't you see? I am, I am. But marriage! And children! Your whole world revolves around them, and then suddenly one day they're snatched away from you and . . .'' Her voice broke and she had to stop.

Caroline touched her clenched hand and said gently, ''Everybody loses someone they love somewhere down the road, Shannon. Death is as inevitable as life. But loving someone, well, that's a confirmation of life, don't you see? Would you wish that Brad and Timmy had never existed, that you had never had their love just to have avoided the pain you went through when you lost them?''

''Of course not!'' Shannon gasped. ''I could never wish they hadn't lived!''

''But that's what you're saying about Matt. You're saying you won't accept his love because he's only human and might die. You're saying you won't allow yourself to be a mother again because a child is vulnerable, and that scares you.''

''Am I?'' Shannon asked in astonishment. ''Yes, maybe I am.''

She glanced away, acknowledging the truth in Caro's words. She'd been demanding the impossible, asking for guarantees against loss, privation, pain. No one could grant such an outrageous demand.

And no one who ever truly loved could lose completely, she suddenly realized. What had Matt told her that day on the beach? That she had to stop spoiling the good memories she had of Brad and Timmy. He'd been right. She had lost the physical presence of her husband and son, but no power on earth could take away from her the loving mental pictures that lingered with her, forever fresh and beautiful whenever she recalled them. Matt had been trying to tell her that by getting to the good memories, her life would be enriched because she had known that past love. He had seen what she had not . . . that the love of her family had shaped her and molded her into the woman he found worthy of love today.

Odd, the way things worked out. Matt had been involved in a terrible, humiliating, destructive marriage and it had left him bitter. She'd felt his bitterness when she'd become his business partner. Yet Matt had moved beyond all that and opened himself up to be vulnerable again, by loving her and wanting to share his life with her. She, who'd had the happy marriage, was paralyzed by the fear of being close to another human being.

Shannon didn't go to the office on Friday. She called Anne and said she had something important to do. And she did. She had a lot of thinking to do and she didn't want to be distracted. She also didn't want to see Matt in a business atmosphere where he would be distant and cold to her.

Carrying a glass of tea with her, she went downstairs to sit in a wooden swing beneath the shade of a live oak tree, and she allowed herself to reminisce.

Her father had never remarried after her mother's death when Shannon had been just a baby. For the first time she wondered about it. Was it because he had feared another loss, or was it simply because he'd never been fortunate enough to find a woman who could mean as much to him as his wife had? Shannon knew he'd gone out with woman friends—he'd never made any secret of that. But never once had the subject come up about the possibility of his marrying a second time.

It was a question that would never be answered.

She thought about Brad again. They'd been such opposites. His steadfastness had kept her feet on the ground many times, and she knew that her lighthearted touch had been good for him, as well, keeping him from taking himself too seriously. Taken as a whole, they'd had a successful, happy marriage because they'd been best friends as well as lovers.

And they'd had their share of quarrels, just like any other couple. Though she'd grieved because of the unresolved argument that last night together, she saw now that had he lived they'd have gone on quarreling and making up, because that was just a part of married life. Their last quarrel had been more heated than most and they'd both said and done things to regret, but the argument had cleared the air between them. She'd gotten her point across that he needed to spend more time with her; he'd gotten her message, because he'd offered to take her away.

It would be the same with Matt. If they married there would be a lot of loving, but there would also be some quarreling and making up, whether they both lived one day more or fifty years more.

If she and Matt had children, she couldn't be so overprotective that she never allowed them out of the house. If she were permitted the extraordinary privilege of watching them grow up, she would have to be strong enough to let them venture out, to learn and experience, to make mistakes of their own. She realized that she couldn't keep people she loved from the world. It would stifle and suffocate them. She saw now that she hadn't been a bad mother because she'd left Timmy at her mother-in-law's that day. It had happened many times, not just for her convenience, but because Mrs. Edwards had taken great pleasure in spending time with her grandson. No, Shannon thought with quiet certainty, she would never have denied Mrs. Edwards that joy. Loving *was* sharing, even when you took chances.

That was when Shannon knew that at last she really was ready to take a chance again. She loved Matt and she wanted them to spend the rest of their lives together, however long it might be. She wanted the fullness that came with linking their days and nights together. She wanted to be sheltered in the center of his embrace at night, to be his companion at mealtimes. She wanted to be his friend when he was troubled and his playmate when he was happy.

And she wanted his children—her children. One child could never replace another, but a different child could be loved for its own special self. A heart had space for many different loves.

Tonight, she decided with happiness flooding through her. Tonight she would go to Matt and tell him.

But that evening when she went to his apartment, he did not answer the doorbell; nor did he answer the telephone later, when she repeatedly tried to call him.

What had she expected, she demanded of herself angrily as she finally gave up and prepared for bed. That Matt would sit home patiently waiting for her to come to her senses?

Because he couldn't face the loneliness of an empty apartment that night, Matt went home after work only long enough to shower and change. Then he went out to grab some dinner before going to a nightclub where he could be around people.

There he ran into a few casual friends, and he spent the evening with them. It was what he needed—to get out and forget his problems—and he tried to relegate the thought of Shannon to a small, dark corner of his mind.

As he danced, Matt told himself how lucky he was to be free, to be tied to no one. He'd gone off the deep end over Shannon, it was true. But it was never too late to swim to safety. He'd only been kidding himself about the possibility of spending the rest of his life with her. Hell, she was the smart one for turning him down! She'd known better than he that nothing was forever in this world, so why try to pretend it was? Sooner or later they'd have come to the end of the road, anyway, so it was just as well that it had happened now. The trick to survival in this old world, he thought cynically, was to hang loose and care for no one but *numero uno.* That way, you didn't get hurt and you didn't hurt anybody else.

"You know something, Matt?" his partner said as they danced. "You've never taken me out on that boat of yours."

Her name was Linda and she was a bank teller. "Haven't I?" he said.

"No. And you promised me months ago that you would."

Linda was flirting with him, and damned if it didn't feel good. It was soothing to his ego. Linda was nice enough and Matt liked her fine, but he'd never been interested enough to ask her for a date. Now he thought, *why not?*

"How about tomorrow?" he heard himself suggest. "We'll get some of the others and see if they want to go along, too, and we'll spend the day on the boat."

In the end there were six of them—Matt and Linda and two other couples, Tom and Karen, Lori and Jim. It was a relaxing day, with a little fishing and a lot of sunbathing. There was a generous amount of good-natured joking and plenty of food and drink.

Matt was pleased. Having a party aboard the *Lady June* was the perfect way to banish the specter of Shannon and that day they'd shared on the cruiser.

Since everything seemed to work so well with the boat, he decided to carry the outing to the next natural step. No one seemed in any mood to break up the party when they got back to the dock late Saturday afternoon, so Matt suggested they all stay at his apartment for dinner. The invitation was accepted, and once his guests were inside, very shortly the haunting images of the evening there with Shannon, of her turning him down flat, were replaced by lively new ones.

Everyone wanted baths first thing, so the bathroom adjacent to Matt's bedroom was appropriated by the women, while the hall bath turned into the "boys' locker room." While waiting his turn, Matt lighted a fire in the grill on the balcony, and when Tom came out, freshly showered, Matt was waiting with a grocery list for Tom to go out and fill.

When Tom returned from the store with the supplies, everyone got busy amid much laughter and chatter. Karen was toweling her hair dry while she supervised how much garlic she would allow Matt to crush into melted butter for the French bread; Jim took on the job of seasoning the chicken and sausage while Lori concocted a salad.

When the doorbell rang, Matt felt more annoyance than anything else. He wiped his hands on a towel, excused himself and left the kitchen.

He opened the front door and froze with surprise.

Shannon's heart thudded. She'd rehearsed since yesterday what she would say to him, but now, as their eyes met, the words were forgotten. She wanted to throw herself into his arms, but in the next second she was glad she'd restrained the impulse.

Matt was not alone. She could hear music, and a woman's laughter in the background, followed by other voices.

"What can I do for you?" he asked after a moment.

The tone of his voice was not welcoming. Shannon knew at once that she'd chosen the wrong time to come. Now she felt foolish and ill at ease.

When she didn't speak, Matt asked again. "Did you want something? I presume you *are* here about business, aren't you?"

"Yes, I—" Shannon's voice was thick with embarrassment. "I came to discuss something with you, but I can see this isn't a convenient time."

"No," he agreed, "it isn't, but if it's important I can spare a few minutes."

"No!" she said hastily. "It can wait. It's not that important." *Liar! Liar!* But what else could she say when all he offered her was a few minutes away from his guests, from another woman; when she'd come to discuss their entire lives! The irony was too much. Shannon stepped backwards, eager now to escape before he saw too much in her eyes. "We . . . we can talk some other time."

Matt shrugged. "Suit yourself. Good night, then."

Shannon heard him close the door as she walked away. It sounded as though he had closed the door to her future.

Chapter Fourteen

For the remainder of the weekend, Matt wondered why Shannon had come to him Saturday evening, and then he was furious at himself for even wondering. He had to get it through his head once and for all that she wasn't for him, and he'd been convinced he was doing a great job of it until he'd seen her.

Luckily, though, his resolve had been bolstered by the presence of his guests. Shannon had looked startled and somewhat dismayed when she'd heard voices in the kitchen and realized he wasn't alone, and as rejected hearts will, Matt's had rejoiced. It had done his pride good for her to know that he wasn't sitting around alone, moping over her.

But by Monday morning he'd realized the absurdity of it all. When Shannon walked into the office, his heart lurched at the sight of her and he knew that he was light-years away from getting over her.

As always, he thought she looked ravishingly beautiful. She wore neat white slacks and an antique gold blouse that

accentuated her overall golden look. Her hair waved sauci-
ly against her shoulders and her gold-flecked eyes glowed
like fine jewelry. Matt found his gaze traveling longingly
from her face down to her throat, over her exquisitely
shaped breasts to her narrow waist and shapely hips. *Damn!*
he thought angrily. *She's so lovely.*

If she was disturbed by their brief encounter at his door
Saturday, she didn't show it. Shannon gave him a cool, level
look and inclined her head in a casual greeting. "Good
morning."

"Morning." Matt had been lounging in his chair with his
feet crossed on his desk while he nursed a cup of coffee.
Now he shifted and put his feet on the floor as he swiveled
his chair so that he was facing Shannon's desk. "What was
it you wanted to talk to me about Saturday?" he asked casually, as though the question hadn't consumed him with
curiosity ever since.

Shannon bent to put her purse in the bottom desk drawer.
She straightened before she answered. "I told you—it wasn't
important. I hope you had a nice evening with your
friends," she added politely.

"It was fine," Matt said shortly, "but let's not stray from
the subject. Whatever you wanted to see me about must
have had some importance for you to come to my home."

"It was nothing. Forget it." Shannon pulled out her chair
and sat down.

Stubbornly Matt pursued the matter. "You're being
childish," he told her. "If there was something you had to
say to me, say it."

"If anyone's behaving childishly," Shannon said calmly,
"you are. What I had on my mind then doesn't matter anymore, so there's no point wasting time talking about it."

Matt exhaled loudly. "You are without a doubt the most
exasperating woman I've ever known."

Shannon shrugged indifferently and studied her desk
calendar. A moment later she picked up her phone, buzzed

Anne and reminded her to check with a local supply company on an order of window frames. That done, she asked Matt, "Have you heard from Kevin today?"

"Not yet. He should be—" He was interrupted by his telephone ringing. He sighed. The business of the day had begun. Whatever he'd been hoping to pry out of Shannon was shoved to the background.

A few minutes later he was grinning as he hung up the phone. Shannon, who'd been listening avidly to his end of the conversation, clasped her hands almost as though in prayer and demanded, "Tell me! I'm going crazy here!"

Matt laughed at her impatience. "The insurance company's coming through with the money!"

"Fantastic!" Her eyes sparkled and her voice had a musical sound.

"A relief, anyway." Matt's mood changed abruptly. His smile vanished and he got to his feet. He couldn't bear to be around Shannon any longer. The lure of her was a torture and the urge to touch her was too strong. "If anyone needs me, I'll be at Spinnaker's Run."

Not, he told himself morosely as he went outside and climbed into the truck, that Shannon was ever likely to need him. She didn't need anyone, least of all him.

When he was gone, Shannon closed her suddenly stinging eyes. For one single moment Matt had shown a natural warmth, and they had shared their jubilation over the good news. But the very next instant he had withdrawn, freezing her out again.

He was still angry with her for turning down his proposal, but Shannon realized now that it had only to do with his bruised ego. Otherwise he couldn't possibly have found consolation with another woman so quickly. She could still hear that melodious feminine laughter floating from Matt's kitchen, followed by other voices. Forlornly she wondered who the woman had been and whether she now had competition for Matt's heart.

Not that there was any question of competing. Matt had made his choice plain enough Saturday evening. Shannon had already lost. She hadn't been actually jealous, nor was she now, because she realized that by her own actions she'd paved the way for another, more amenable woman to step into Matt's life. She felt sick at heart to realize that all she'd ever brought Matt was despair and pain at every turn. It was hard facing the fact that Matt was better off without her, but it was true. All she'd ever achieved was a stormy upheaval in both their lives.

If she had a more generous nature, Shannon told herself with harsh condemnation, she'd be glad Matt had found someone else. If she didn't want him herself, she should be pleased for him. The trouble was that she did want him—terribly—but she'd realized it too late. By the time she'd gone to tell him she'd made a mistake, that she did want to marry him more than anything else in the world, Matt plainly didn't care anymore.

What hurt most of all was that she knew Matt really hadn't been as serious about her as he'd claimed. He still might be furious with her, even hurt to some extent, but he hadn't really loved her. People just didn't recover from one love and find another that fast. She ought to know.

At least Matt had spared her from humiliating herself Saturday evening. If he'd been more receptive, seemed glad to see her, been eager to listen to her, she might have spilled her heart to him. Thank goodness that hadn't happened. Her pride was intact and she could face him here at the office with a certain measure of dignity.

Anne knocked at the door and entered. Grateful for the interruption, Shannon put her unhappy thoughts away and focused her attention on problems of a different nature.

Later that afternoon June Madison called her. "I really hate to ask this of you, especially since it'll mean taking you away from the office while Matt's out of town, but could you keep Jason for me tomorrow afternoon? I have a doctor's appointment in Corpus and there's just nobody else I can ask. My mother-in-law's under the weather, Caro's away and so are a couple of other good friends I usually can depend on. I can't even count on Harry because he's going to Houston with Matt.''

"I don't mind," Shannon said readily. "It'll be a pleasure. But what's this about Matt's being in Houston tomorrow?''

June laughed. "You mean he hasn't told you yet? I guess he hasn't had the chance. I just found out myself. Harry and Matt both have some business there, so they're flying up in the morning in my father-in-law's Cessna.''

"I see." Shannon frowned, glad June couldn't see her face. "What time do you need me?''

June told her and Shannon promised to be at her house by then.

"I really appreciate this," June said fervently. "I was at my wit's end.''

They hung up, and for some minutes Shannon speculated on the reason Matt was taking a trip he hadn't so much as mentioned to her. Did it concern Anchor Development, or was it about something entirely different? She recalled his mentioning that he had other business interests in Houston. Maybe the trip concerned that. She hoped so.

Matt returned to the office shortly after four, and as soon as he was settled behind his desk Shannon said conversationally, "I hear you're going to Houston tomorrow.''

Matt looked at her in mild surprise. "How'd you know?''

"Your sister called and happened to mention it. Do you mind telling me if you're going on company business?''

Matt nodded. "Kevin's going, too. We've got an appointment with the bankers. If I can negotiate a more favorable rate of repayment on our outstanding loan and borrow a little more, we'll be able to get started on the clubhouse right away. The sooner it's finished, the sooner we'll be able to have that introductory party. If we get the extra loan, we'll be able to do it all without having to tighten our belts too much more.''

"I see." Shannon concealed her mounting anger. She managed to ask in a calm voice, "Why do you need Kevin to go with you?"

"He's drawn up a presentation showing the bankers our new advertising promotions. His ideas for the party are pretty interesting, although I'll be the first to admit they're expensive. He thinks we should charter a plane to bring in the guests from Dallas and Houston, and have a golf tournament for the men and a fashion show luncheon for the wives, with maybe even a top-name designer to appear as an added draw. Or another route might be—"

Shannon trembled with an overwhelming fury as she cut off his flow of words. "Why did you neglect to discuss any of this with me? Or have you forgotten that I'm also a partner in this company?"

"I'm discussing it with you now," Matt said impatiently.

"We aren't *discussing* it," Shannon snapped. "You're *telling* me, and there's a big difference."

Matt shrugged. "You're making a big deal over nothing."

"Am I? When my father was alive you wouldn't have dreamed of making such a decision without first consulting him. You have no right to commit this company to a new loan or fashion shows or anything else out of the ordinary without my approval! I will not be pushed aside, Matt, and you'd better think twice about the consequences before you try it!"

Matt's face darkened with matching anger. "You're overreacting. What's needed in business is calm and logic."

"Logic?" Shannon lashed out. "Calm? Is it logical that the minority stockholder in a company should run roughshod over the majority? You're crazy if you think I'm going to put up with that!"

Matt's eyes glinted like hard stones. "I knew it was only a matter of time before you went in for the kill. Just like my ex did. Only," he added bitterly, "in this case you didn't have to bother marrying me to do it!" With lightning speed he got to his feet and went to the door. With his hand on the knob he swung around, and his dark eyes glittered ominously. "You can take me to court if you like, Shannon, but let's get one thing straight. Until a judge hands you this company lock, stock and barrel, I'll go on doing what I think is in the best interests of the business."

Shannon enjoyed the afternoon she spent with June Madison's son. The boy was lively and bright, and his infectious laughter and uninhibited delight in almost everything cheered her immensely. She took him for a swim and, with a strong effort, kept her mind off the time she'd been at the beach for an early-morning breakfast with his uncle.

While she watched Jason playing at the water's edge, for the first time she was able to think of her own child without pain. Only the bittersweet warmth of love remained. Healing had come at long last, and she felt at peace about both Brad and Timmy. With the discovery, Shannon wondered if perhaps the time had also finally come to return to teaching.

The idea took root as Jason showed quick curiosity in a seashell, intense concentration in sand-sculpting a cat's face, keen intelligence when he easily memorized a short children's song she sang for him. In teaching children, Shannon was on firm ground; in business, she was merely adequate. It came to her that she had missed this very much—the deep joy of watching the spark of knowledge come to a child's eyes, the satisfaction in knowing that you've helped that child develop an interest in his world and, perhaps most important of all, given him a sense of worth and confidence in himself. She could do that for children—other people's children, if not her own. Maybe it was indeed time to return to the classroom, where her life could once again have real purpose.

She was neither needed nor wanted in Anchor Development. If she stayed, the way things were between them, she could only envision endless confrontations ahead with Matt. Why keep on subjecting herself to such misery and continuing unhappiness? She'd be far better off not having to see Matt every day. Yet Shannon was reluctant to leave. Matt's stubbornness made her stubborn, too. If she left, Matt would feel he'd won, that he had the upper hand and that he owed her no accountability. She wasn't prepared to concede him that. Things couldn't go on the way they were now, but for the life of her, Shannon couldn't see an easy or satisfactory resolution to the situation.

Just past five o'clock Shannon drove Jason home, and her timing was perfect. June was getting out of her car when they arrived, and Shannon pulled into the driveway and parked behind her.

Jason's dog ran out from beneath the shade of a tree to greet him, and while boy and dog cavorted on the front lawn, the two women met at the edge of the driveway.

"Thanks a million for watching Jason," June said. "I don't know what I'd have done without you. Why don't you come inside and I'll make us some iced tea."

As much as Shannon liked June, she had an instinctive feeling that since her break with Matt it was better not to cultivate too close a friendship with his sister.

"Thanks, but I'd better not," she said lightly. "I need to stop by the store before I go home, and you'll probably need to be starting dinner soon, anyway."

June accepted her excuse without protest. "Did my young hurricane exhaust you?" she asked.

Shannon laughed. "He kept me on my toes, but I enjoyed every minute of it. How was your visit with the doctor?"

June grinned. "I shouldn't tell you before Harry, but he won't be back from Houston for a few more hours and I'm dying to tell someone." She lowered her voice conspiratorially. "Jason's going to have a baby brother or sister around Valentine's Day."

"Congratulations!" Shannon smiled warmly. "I'm really glad for you. It's wonderful news."

"Yes, it is. We've been wanting another child for ages and..."

Shannon was no longer listening. She happened to be facing the street while June's back was to it. In the flash of an instant, Shannon saw it happening. Jason's dog had scampered into the street and the boy was dashing after it.

Bearing down upon them both was a car.

Afterward Shannon had no clear idea how she'd managed it. Somehow the taste of fear had galvanized her body to action. Without thought, she darted into the street herself, lifted the child and tossed him toward the lawn, all in the split second before the car, with brakes squealing, hit her and knocked her to the pavement.

A hubbub immediately ensued. The driver was kneeling beside her with an agonized expression on his face; June was white and shrill voiced, asking how she was; Jason, ignored but safe as he sprawled on the grass, was crying. Even the dog, now nuzzling Shannon's throat, was whimpering as though somehow he knew he'd been responsible for the accident.

"Call an ambulance," the man told June.

Obediently she turned toward the house, but Shannon's voice stopped her. "No. I'm all right. Honest, I am. Just help me up."

Although her leg was bloody and bruised, in the end Shannon was able to convince both the shaken driver and June that they were only surface wounds. Relief slowly crept into their faces.

"You saved Jason's life!" June exclaimed in a choked voice. "You saved my son's life!"

"Thank God you're both all right!" the driver declared fervently. "I started to swerve as soon as I saw the little boy, but he was too close. It happened so suddenly. He just ran right in front of me! Right in front of me! I couldn't help it."

"I know," Shannon said kindly. "It wasn't your fault, and if you hadn't reacted so quickly, one of us might have been really hurt."

"Or dead!" June moaned. "Oh, Shannon, how can I ever thank you enough?" Jason came to her side, and she hugged him against her hip, rocking him to and fro and clasping him as though she would never let him go.

Both June and the driver of the car insisted on driving Shannon to see a doctor, but she was determined not to make a big deal of the accident. At last she convinced them that she really felt fine and that she would seek medical help later if she found she needed it. At last, over June's protests, still blood-streaked and dirty, she got into her car and drove home, where she could soak in a warm bath.

Shortly before dusk Matt walked toward the stairs of the summerhouse, but as he was about to mount them, something light caught his eye. He glanced toward the darkening waters in the distance and saw Shannon sitting on a beach towel on the back lawn. Her back was to him and her golden hair rippled over her shoulders like ripe wheat swaying in the breeze. She wore shorts and a white shirt that hung loosely about her hips. Nestled in the grass beside her was a ceramic mug.

Tenderness and longing rose inside him. He gazed at her with all the love in his eyes that he fought so hard to conceal from her. He wanted to much to have the right to show her that love, to hold her close to him, to take care of her, to share day and night with her. He wanted her forever, but

Shannon didn't want any more forevers in her life. She ran from love the way other people ran from hurricanes or floods, tornadoes or war.

Matt sighed for what was beyond his reach and slowly began to walk toward her. The sound of his approach was cushioned by the grass, and he had almost reached her before she sensed his presence.

Abruptly she twisted around, her eyes large and startled. When she saw him, her gaze became shuttered and not particularly welcoming. Matt didn't blame her for being wary. He hadn't been exactly agreeable lately and now he was intruding upon what was, after all, her own private turf.

He dropped to the ground beside her, and for a time they stared at each other in silence. Then Matt's gaze fell on her left thigh, and when he saw the huge, ugly bruise he gasped aloud.

"You *were* hurt!" he exclaimed accusingly. Gently his fingers touched the area. "June said you wouldn't see a doctor. I think you should—just to make sure you're all right."

Shannon shifted, moving out of his reach as though she hated his touch. "I'm fine," she said shortly.

Matt's gaze was probing now, noting the long jagged scrape along the calf of that same leg, another on her right arm. But when he looked at her face again, her eyes dared him to comment.

After a moment she asked in a cold, ice-hard voice, "How did your business go in Houston?"

Matt didn't miss the scorn or the slight emphasis on the word "your." He had it coming, of course. Yesterday he'd been a bullheaded clod.

"Fair," he said, shrugging. "We got the new loan at a better rate, but they didn't give much on the old one. Even so, what with the recent sales since Kevin came, we should be able to reinstate your profit shares within the next couple of months. Things really are looking up."

"That's nice." Her voice was flat.

"It wouldn't be against the law if you displayed a little more enthusiasm," Matt said softly.

Shannon shrugged. "Why should I?"

"I'm sorry about getting so high-handed yesterday," Matt said contritely. "It was wrong of me, and it won't happen again."

"Sure," she retorted sarcastically. "I've heard that line before, and frankly, it's grown a little stale."

"I mean it," Matt insisted. He sighed, then said in a different tone, "I've got some other news that may interest you more than the results of my trip. Just before I came I got a call from the sheriff's department. They've got a couple of men in custody who confessed to setting that fire, vandalizing the other house and stealing those supplies."

Curiosity overcame Shannon's resentment. "Who are they? Do you know them?"

"No, but I know why they did it. Get ready for a shock." He paused and tilted his head. "Jack Waring hired them to do it."

"Hired them?" Shannon was stunned, and her face reflected her shock in the waning light. "But why? What did he have to gain?"

"He wanted that piece of land he'd been badgering us to sell. He not only wanted it, Shannon, he really needed it. He simply didn't have enough land to go forward with his plans. That land meant the difference between building or not building his project."

Shannon shook her head. "But how does arson or vandalism tie in with getting what he wanted?"

"He was trying to drive us into a bargaining position. If we got into a financial bind, we'd be more inclined to let him have it for some quick cash."

"But arson!" Shannon exclaimed. "And assaulting the guard!"

Matt shrugged. "Well, the thugs he'd hired wouldn't be too squeamish about clobbering a man over the head. They both have criminal records a mile long."

"What happens now? With Jack, I mean?"

"They're booking him now. He'll face trial, but—" Matt grimaced "—you know how the system works. He'll probably get off. His father can afford the best lawyers in the state."

"It's hard to take in," Shannon said thoughtfully. "I didn't like him, but I didn't think he was a criminal. Yet now I remember something from the night he tried to break into my house."

"What's that?"

"He'd called me earlier, supposedly to express sympathy about the fire. He brought up the subject of arson himself. He pointed out that the insurance company wouldn't pay the claim if they suspected we might have set the fire ourselves because we needed the money. Then he offered again to buy that property. He was hoping the insurance wouldn't pay off and that in desperation we'd sell him the land!"

"Yes." Matt's face was grim. "Well, it didn't happen, thank goodness. Anyway, he shouldn't be bothering us anymore." The tone of his voice changed, becoming softly gruff. "Shannon, about what you did today—saving Jason. I'll be forever grateful to you."

Shannon shrugged and looked away quickly. "Anyone else would have done the same. I was just lucky I saw him in time."

"No," Matt corrected gently. "He was lucky you were there." He took her hand in his, concentrating intently on it as he spoke. "I know it doesn't make up for losing your own child, but for Jason's sake, for all of us who love him, I thank you from the bottom of my heart."

"There's no need." Shannon's voice took on a strange huskiness of its own. "I'm glad, too. And oddly enough, it does help just a little—about Timmy, I mean. I can't have him back, but June and Harry still have Jason and that makes me feel absolutely terrific.''

''That's because *you're* so terrific,'' Matt said tenderly.

He drew her into his arms, and though Shannon stiffened and tried to free herself, his embrace tightened. Her face was patterned by silvery light and blue-black shadows in the swiftly falling darkness as his mouth closed over hers.

His lips moved gently over her mouth, but there was no response. Passively Shannon resisted. She no longer sought to escape, but neither did she react in any way.

At last Matt lifted his head and his dark eyes searched hers. The anger he'd expected to find was not there. Yet there was no pleasure, either. There was merely indifference.

''You don't have to make a show of interest in me out of gratitude,'' she told him. ''In fact, I'd hoped you'd have more integrity than that.''

''Integrity!'' Matt snapped harshly. Anger suffused him; forgotten were the tender emotions of a moment ago. ''You talk about integrity, yet you're cheating both of us by denying yourself the right to love again. You may cheat me out of my business, and cheat me out of your love, but I'll be damned if tonight you're going to cheat us out of what we both want!'' She gave a muffled cry as his mouth met hers. Shannon froze for an instant as his hand found the full swell of her breast. Then she shoved his hand away, to free herself.

''There's no use fighting me,'' Matt rasped as he withdrew his mouth from hers. ''You want me, too.''

''No, I don't!''

Matt's hand slid down her hips to her inner thigh. Her flesh was warm to his touch, warm and soft as the summer night itself. She began to quiver as he stroked the sensitive area, and he smiled with irony. ''Tell me again,'' he murmured, ''how you don't want me. I know you don't love me, but that doesn't mean you don't love us—together—like this. You know you do."

It was true. Treacherously her body was betraying her. Since the night Matt had reawakened her to her own womanly being, her flesh refused to let her find peace again in nothingness. She had but to think of Matt and her body began to grow warm, clamoring for fulfillment. Now, at his intimate touch, tremors of barely concealed passion shuddered through her, and her resistance was ebbing away.

But her mind refused to accept her body's decree. She tried to think, to focus on why this shouldn't be happening, but before she could frame words of protest Matt was kissing her once more, and she knew she was doomed. Her lips became flower soft as warm, sweet desire radiated through her like sunshine, stilling all efforts to repel the very food of life.

Matt was instantly attuned to the change in her. His mouth softened, too, and he was able to sip and savor the taste of her. His arms slid up her back until one hand cradled her head, and then gently, he carried her down until they were both reclining on the beach towel.

When he began to unbutton her shirt she didn't object, but lay quietly with her eyes closed. Matt was gentle in his task of undressing her, acutely mindful of the bruises and scrapes on her arms and legs. When he had finished, he hastily shed his own clothes and stretched out next to her.

Soft evening darkness enveloped them. Only a few stars dusted the sky above, and though there was a crescent moon, it was partially obscured by a cloud. Yet their bodies gleamed in the pale silvery light and the breeze sensuously caressed their skin with featherlight coolness.

Matt reached for Shannon, and to his intense satisfaction, she readily opened her arms to him. She made no more pretense of not desiring him, and that gratified him. At least now she was being honest about that. He pressed her to him. Her tender, smooth breasts were touching his bare chest, sending an erotic thrill shuddering through him. Her silken curls tickled his chin, and tenderly Matt tucked them behind her ear. His gaze met hers and he was suddenly shocked and dismayed to see that her eyes were glistening brightly like wet stones.

"You're crying!" he exclaimed incredulously. Anxiety tensed his muscles, and he muttered a self-loathing curse and started to pull away. "I've hurt you! Your bruises! God, I ought to be shot!"

"No! No, I'm all right!" Shannon's hands clasped his shoulders with unexpected strength, fiercely holding him to her. "Don't leave me, Matt. Not now!"

"Then why are you crying?"

"I'm not!" she denied, even while she dashed away a teardrop with the back of her hand. "It's just that I'm glad you're here and that—"

Exultation shuddered through Matt. His arms tightened about her once more. "I told you I was right about this," he said in a low voice.

"Yes," she acknowledged. "You were right." She quivered and then allowed one delicate hand to travel down his shoulder to his hip. "You were right," she repeated with soft urgency.

In that instant they became locked into their own special universe. The world around them, the sky, the stars, the bay waters lapping at the nearby shore, the trees, even the ground beneath them, no longer existed. Nothing else existed except the wondrous world of each other.

Shannon became immersed in the pleasurable sensations that came, one by one, each impossibly better than the last. It was like birthday and Christmas gifts lavishly bestowed all at once. With overwhelming delight she ran her hands over rippling muscles, through the thick mat of wiry hair on his chest, to the tender velvet softness of his hips to the powerful hardened strength of his thighs. The musky male scent

of him enticed her and his warm breath caressing her skin
sent tingles through her.

Her soft, pliant body sent Matt's senses spiraling. She
gave and received with equal fervor, slowly driving him
mad. He heard her purr with satisfaction like a kitten as he
kissed her taut, straining nipples; when he caressed her hips
she moaned; when he stroked her thighs again she arched
her body toward him with demanding, urgent insistence. It
pleased him greatly that he could give her such pleasure. He
wanted her satisfaction above his own, and yet as her excitement raced higher, he was rewarded as it heightened his
tenfold.

White-hot flames leaped within Shannon, and she moistened her lips with her tongue. Matt instinctively knew just
where to touch her to extract the maximum response from
her. Never in all her life had she felt quite like
this . . . throbbingly alive, with her blood singing, her heart
tap-dancing, all her senses acutely attuned to the subtle
pressure of flesh against flesh. It was at once blissful and
shattering.

Her fingertips dug into his back as though she were
clutching to hang on for dear life. She had reached the outer
limits of sanity itself, could feel herself sliding over the edge.

Matt knew. He had reached those same limits himself. He
fitted her to him then and she gasped with relief.

And then together they rose, floating above time and
space, and when they reached the plateau where their spirits met as one, they hovered there, overwhelmed by the in-
describable beauty of this newfound dwelling place,
reluctant to return to their world.

"Shannon!" Matt shuddered. "I didn't mean for this to
happen. Forgive me."

"Shhh!" Shannon felt deep tenderness as she stroked his
forehead. "There's nothing to forgive. You said it yourself.
I wanted it to happen, too."

Abruptly Matt withdrew from her. Shannon's body, damp with perspiration, was chilled by the evening breeze as she lost the warmth of him.

"That's just it," she heard him say in a gruff voice. "I didn't want it to happen. I lost control."

Through the now thick shield of darkness, Shannon heard the rustling of clothes. Matt was dressing. Blankly, not understanding this abrupt change, she sat up and began groping for her own clothes.

"Wh-what is it, Matt?" she asked through a throat suddenly parched by dread. "What's wrong?"

Matt gave a short, humorless laugh. "Wrong? Why just about everything to do with you and me. Except maybe what just happened," he conceded.

"It was wonderful," she said in a low voice.

"Yes."

"If you feel like that, then why are you upset? Why are you leaving? Matt, please," Shannon went on swiftly, knowing if she didn't say the things that were in her heart now, she might never again find the courage. "I love you and if... if you'll still have me, I want to marry you."

"I don't want to hear it," Matt said, shocking her by the vehemence in his voice. "I don't believe it, anyway. You've already made it plain enough you don't want *me* as a husband, don't want to have *my* children. You claimed to be afraid of a lifetime commitment because you might lose another loved one. But what really scared the hell out of you was the idea that you might have to spend the rest of your life with me. So don't give me the line that you love me, because I won't buy it anymore. All you've ever really been interested in is the business."

"Matt!" Shannon choked. "You're wrong. I—"

Relentlessly he went on, his voice harsh with condemnation. "You're not satisfied being top dog with your fifty-one percent, are you? Even that's not enough control to suit you. You demonstrated that yesterday when you objected to my making any decisions at all independently of you. You won't be content until you've got the whole damn pie, and marrying me is the only way you can figure to do it, so you've decided to 'sacrifice' yourself for your objective. Well, think again, lady. I've already been a sucker once with my ex-wife and I almost was again with you, but I've come to my senses now. I may never stop loving you or wanting you, but I'd be crazy to marry you just so you could have the pleasure of going after the rest of the business!''

"None of that is true!" Shannon cried. "Please believe me, Matt—I want you, nothing else."

Matt turned swiftly and his dark silhouette loomed menacingly over her. "I don't want to hear any more, Shannon! You came here with the intention of pushing me out of my own business and you won't be happy until you do. As for our personal relationship, you balked every step of the way. If I'd been seeing clearly, I'd have realized from the first how little you cared. Well, I can live with that if I have to, but I'm warning you, I'll fight you to the bitter end before I let you walk away with my company!" He sucked in a deep, ragged breath. "The only thing in the world that would make me really happy right now is if I never had to see you again as long as I live."

Chapter Fifteen

Matt stood in the doorway of the sales office, watching the cold, winter rain. Some of it lashed at him from time to time, stinging his face, spraying his heavy jacket with moisture. He didn't care. Such discomforts made little impression upon him these days.

It was the same with things that once would have filled him with great satisfaction. Ahead of him through the curtain of rain he could see the completed condominium and, a short distance from it, the attractive new clubhouse. Nearby was the beautifully landscaped golf course.

A month ago they'd finally thrown the big promotional bash Kevin had worked so hard to make a success, and it *had* been an unqualified success. Several sales had resulted from it, in addition to ongoing sales Kevin and his team had closed in the preceding months. Almost three-quarters of the homes and condominium units in Spinnaker's Run had now been sold. Anchor Development Company was solidly on its feet once again, and just last week Matt had purchased a large parcel of land near Ingleside. With the Navy Homeport coming to the area, it offered a prime opportunity for development. At the beginning of the new year he would go into the planning stage with the architects.

But it all meant little, because Shannon was not there to share the success with him. He'd hoped against hope that she might relent and return for the promotional party, but of course she hadn't come, and now Matt wondered why he'd ever thought she might.

"Here's a copy of those contracts, Matt," Kevin said from behind him.

Matt turned and accepted the large manila envelope the other man offered him. "Thanks," Matt said briefly. "I'll be shoving off now."

Kevin peered at the rain past his shoulder. "Looks like it's set in to stay. I sure hope it clears up by Saturday."

Kevin and his family were leaving Saturday to drive to Dallas, where they would visit with relatives over the Christmas holidays. Matt had gladly given the man extra time off. Kevin had earned that and more.

Christmas for Matt would not be so cheery, however, even though he would be included in the Madison family's celebrations as usual.

Matt tucked the envelope beneath his coat, nodded at Kevin and dashed through the icy drizzle toward his truck.

When he left the development, on an impulse, he turned in the direction of the Main summer house instead of toward town. It wasn't the first time he'd done so since Shannon had left.

The For Sale sign was still standing beside the road. He went past it and pulled into the driveway. The house itself was shuttered, looking lonely and abandoned, but Matt could tell that Sam Bole had been there recently. The fall leaves had been raked since he'd last come and the shrubbery beds around the house had been mulched. A pile of brush was stacked at one side of the yard, as though the caretaker meant to come back for it.

A familiar sense of helplessness came over Matt as he sat in the truck, gazing at the silent, empty house. It was all his fault. He'd driven her away. And he'd never regretted anything more bitterly in his life.

Ignoring the rain, he climbed out of the truck and walked beyond the house to the back lawn. Today the waters of the bay were churning and angry beneath the dreary, moisture-laden sky.

Matt walked slowly until he reached the spot where he and Shannon had made love that last night together. The night he'd wrecked both their lives by rash anger and foolish pride.

She'd tried to tell him then that she loved him, that she'd changed her mind and wanted to marry him, but he'd been too hotheaded to believe it was because she really loved him. He couldn't see past the argument they'd had the day before, when he'd made a business decision without consulting her. He'd convinced himself that Shannon really was another Vicky, ready to choke him out of his own company. Because of that, he'd wanted only to hurt her as much as she'd hurt him.

Well, he'd succeeded; he'd also succeeded in driving a knife into his own heart, because after that night, when he'd told her he never wanted to see her again, she'd granted him his wish.

He hadn't known it then, but when she didn't show up at the office the following day it was because she was busy signing papers at Mike Avery's law office and packing. As a result he, Matt, was now legal owner of an extra two percent of shares in Anchor Development, the crucial two percent; the summer house was up for sale, and cunningly Shannon had dropped out of his life.

Mike Avery knew where she was, of course. Matt had done practically everything short of bodily harm to get the man to tell him Shannon's address, but Mike would not be budged. To reveal what she didn't want revealed would be a violation of the confidentiality between lawyer and client.

Matt's efforts to find her had been stymied at every turn. She wasn't listed in Denver's telephone directory, nor did she have an unlisted number that he could determine. He hadn't been able to locate her former in-laws, either, though he'd called every Edwards in that city. In fact, he wasn't at all certain she had returned to Denver. After all, she'd given up her apartment and sold her father's house before she came to Texas. That was the worst of it—he had no idea where to search.

She was still a partner in the company with her remaining forty-nine-percent stock, but all business communications between them were filtered through Mike Avery. When Matt needed to send her something, it went to Mike's office to be mailed by him; the same was true in reverse. He had, of course, written her a number of personal letters that had been forwarded to her through Mike, but none of them had ever received a reply.

Even the local realtor who was handling the sale of the summer house had been of no help. His communication with Shannon was also conducted through Mike Avery. Shannon had covered her tracks thoroughly.

In desperation Matt had tried another tactic—that of sending her business reports on practically every detail of the business, no matter how minor, and demanding her vote on things from loans to hiring practices right down to office-supply purchases.

He'd hoped that by inundating her almost daily with routine decisions, especially the ridiculously simple ones, that he'd annoy her enough so that she would at least pick up the telephone and call him to protest. Instead she chose to send such letters back to him, via Mike, with neat, red-inked notations in the margins. On most important matters, she'd jot something such as, "Up to you," but the silly items, such as typewriter ribbons or gasoline purchases, she'd write, "Spare me!," or scathingly, "Can't you figure this one out by yourself?"

Now it was almost Christmas and he still didn't know where she was, how she was, or what she was doing, other than answering his constant deluge of mail. He was wild with frustration and consumed by a desperate longing.

Matt stared unhappily at the bay, and all at once a new, fiercer resolve swelled in his chest. He swung around and strode purposefully toward the truck.

Twenty minutes later he was in Mike Avery's reception room, pacing impatiently as he waited for Mike to finish up with another client. Matt's shoulders were straight and powerful beneath his heavy winter jacket and his jaw was rigid. His entire bearing was clear evidence that he was geared for battle.

Mike noticed Matt's determination at once when Matt was finally shown into his office, but he pretended he thought this was just a routine visit. "How's it going, Matt?" he asked casually. He glanced at his watch and added, "You have time for lunch today?"

Matt ignored the invitation and went straight to the point. "I want Shannon's address and I want it now."

Mike sighed. They'd had this argument many times before. "You know I can't do that, Matt." He waved a hand toward the chair on the opposite side of his desk. "Stop standing there glaring at me and sit down."

Matt didn't sit. Instead he braced his hands on the edge of the desk and leaned forward. "I want that address today and if I have to, I'll tear this office apart to get it."

"Threatening me isn't going to do either of us any good," Mike said. "You know I'd be violating a professional trust if I gave it to you. Believe me, Matt, I'd be happy to help you if I could, but my hands are tied. This is the way she wants it and I have to honor that."

Matt lost his belligerence and dropped wearily into the vacant chair. He nursed his forehead with his hand and gazed at his friend with stricken eyes. "Mike, what if it were Caro?" he asked softly. "What if you said some things that hurt her so badly that she ran away and hid from you? What would you do?"

Mike sighed again. "That's not fair, Matt."

"Isn't it?" Matt leaned forward, hands propped against his knees. "I love her, Mike, and I know as well as I'm sitting here that she loves me, too. Or that she did once," he added grimly. "I'm only asking for a break. If I can just see her once more, talk to her, if she doesn't want to see me again after that, I swear I'll leave her alone from then on."

Mike was silent for a long moment, his mouth puckered as he considered what Matt had said. Then abruptly he began flipping through the card index on his desk. When he reached a particular card he remained still for a time, forefinger wedged in front of it as he met Matt's anxious gaze.

Leaving the index open at that spot, he rose to his feet. "How about some coffee?" he offered casually. "I'll just be gone a minute." With his thumb he gently pushed the card file across the desk toward Matt. "You might look around and see if you can find some interesting reading material while I'm gone."

The bell rang and the excited children, bundled in coats, woolen hats, gloves and snow boots, collected their piles of gifts and candy from their desks, shouted noisy goodbyes to Shannon and straggled from the room. The two roommothers stayed behind to help clean up the inevitable debris that follows any school Christmas party.

When the room had been restored to order and the mothers gone, Shannon began to clear out her belongings from the teacher's desk. Once more, she had become rootless.

After she'd returned to Denver, she'd decided to ease back into teaching by doing substitute work. For the first month she'd rotated from school to school, grade to grade, class to class, going wherever she was needed, but in late October she'd temporarily taken over this third-grade class for a teacher who'd had a baby. Shannon had loved it, working with the age group she enjoyed most and having a sense of permanence with one group of children. But now it was over. Today had been the last day of school before the holidays, and after the new year the regular teacher would be returning to work.

Now Shannon wished she'd signed on for a regular position herself. But at the beginning of the school term she hadn't been sure what she wanted to do with herself, so she'd only signed on to substitute.

Evelyn White, the second-grade teacher, came into the room. "It's been nice having you on the team, Shannon," she said as she watched Shannon toss things into a cardboard box.

"Thanks." Shannon smiled. "I enjoyed it here. I was just thinking how much I hate to leave."

"You'll be back," Evelyn said confidently, "even if it's not to this class. The principal thinks highly of you. She'll be calling you whenever we have a teacher out."

"I hope so." Shannon tossed the last of her personal items into the box and stood up. "What have you got planned for the holidays?"

"Rest." Evelyn laughed. "My shopping is already done and fortunately my mother loves to cook Christmas dinner. What about you?"

Shannon shrugged. "My in-laws recently moved to Florida and they've invited me to visit them, but I need to find another apartment, so I probably won't have the time. I'm subleasing from a friend who went to Europe for a few months. She'll be back in mid-January and I'll be out in the cold."

Evelyn made a face. "Ugh! What a thing to have to do at Christmastime." She glanced at her watch. "I'd better run. We have a party to go to tonight and I've got to pick up my husband's suit from the cleaners. Have a merry one, Shannon!"

"You, too."

But as she drove toward home a few minutes later, through light, drifting snowflakes, Shannon felt far from merry. She'd been invited to a number of holiday parties herself, including one tonight, but she didn't have the slightest desire to attend any of them. She knew she would be a lousy guest, so it was better not to inflict her moody presence on others. Besides, the last thing she wanted just now was to be thrown into the company of unattached men eager to get something going with an unattached woman. She didn't feel like playing that game.

It had been months since that last disastrous evening with Matt. Shame and embarrassment still made Shannon wince whenever she thought of it—which unfortunately was often. First Matt had forced her to display her vulnerability by her unwilling, then eager, sexual response to him. She had lost herself in wild, uninhibited abandonment, giving herself to him totally and completely. And then she'd tried to tell him of her love, of just how much she wanted and needed him, but he had shocked her by his unexpected hostility. Only then had she realized the truth—that he'd deliberately wanted to humiliate her. Once she had capitulated, he was then in the position to crush her spirit by coldly, cruelly rejecting her.

His last words had been the wish never to see her again. Horrified and quivering with pain, she'd been anxious to comply, and the next day she'd made preparations to leave. By that evening she'd been on her way out of town.

Shannon arrived at her apartment and in the mail she found the usual manila envelope from Mike Avery's office and a letter from her mother-in-law. She dropped them both on the breakfast bar while she went to change her clothes.

A few minutes later, comfortably dressed in a warm, dark-blue running suit, she curled up on the sofa with the mail.

She chose to read the letter first. Mrs. Edwards was pressing her invitation for Shannon to visit them, and now she seriously considered it. It *was* depressing to be alone at Christmas, and she had a feeling her in-laws were as lonely facing the holidays as she was herself. Brad had been their only child. Now that Shannon's father was gone, she, like Mr. and Mrs. Edwards, had no one else to call family. Last Christmas the four of them had been together.

Before she'd gone to Texas in the spring, her in-laws had already purchased their new home in Tampa in anticipation of their retirement. When she'd come back a few months later, she'd found them busily packing, their old home sold, the telephone already disconnected. They were winding up the loose ends before setting out to fulfill their lifelong dream of living in the sun.

That last day, Mrs. Edwards and Shannon had stolen off for an hour to pay a last visit to Brad's old childhood bedroom. There, sitting on the floor in the empty room, they had talked.

"We're starting a new life for ourselves with this move," Mrs. Edwards had said. "Lots of memories here, mostly good, but some you just have to get past the hard way and go on." Shannon had nodded and her mother-in-law had advised, "You have to do the same. We'd sort of thought maybe you were doing that for yourself by staying so long in Texas, but now you're back. What did you come back here for?"

Shannon hadn't had a valid answer, and Mrs. Edwards had seen that. She'd also seen that there was something Shannon wasn't telling her, and she'd added thoughtfully, "You're young, honey, and your whole future's ahead of you. Don't waste it pining for what you can't have any-more."

Shannon had suddenly felt the urge to confide in the other woman. "I did that until recently, but someone else showed me how wrong it is to hang on to the past to the point where you're not really living in the present."

Mrs. Edwards had nodded wisely, then astonished Shannon by asking, "Why don't you marry him, then?"

Shannon hadn't bothered to pretend the new relationship hadn't become that serious. Brad's mother could handle the truth. "We had some differences that couldn't be worked out," she'd explained.

"Sure they can," Mrs. Edwards had told her. "If you love each other enough, differences can always be worked out. I hope you do remarry, Shannon," she added as she'd patted Shannon's hand. "It's not good to be alone. We couldn't love you more if you were our own daughter and you'll always be welcome to come to us. But that doesn't mean we don't want you to get on with making yourself a new life. And when the time comes that you do have another family, I hope you'll bring them to visit us."

Well, there was no new family on the horizon, but Shannon still had the Edwards. Suddenly she wanted to see them, to be in the midst of people who loved and cared about her. She wanted Mr. Edwards's gentle teasing; she wanted long chats in the kitchen with Mrs. Edwards.

The search for a new apartment could be postponed until after New Year's. If worse came to worst and she had to move out before she'd found one, she could always move into a hotel for a week or two. There was no reason to stay in Denver and spend a dismal Christmas alone.

Her eyes fell on the manila envelope. That could wait, as well. It probably contained nothing more earthshaking than Matt's seeking her okay on a supply of paper clips or ball-point pens. He'd grown ridiculously petty in his campaign to drive her nuts by consulting her on anything business related. Even if there were some important question in the communication, it would be no big deal. If Matt didn't hear from her, he would simply be forced to make a decision alone, and he was more than capable of doing it without her. There'd been a time when he'd done just that, whether she liked it or not.

Tossing both envelopes to the lamp table, Shannon got to her feet. There were a hundred things to do. First she had to see about flight reservations. Since Christmas was still a week away, she might be able to book a seat as early as tomorrow or the next day, but if she waited any later than that she might be out of luck. Once she had a confirmed seat, she would call the Edwards to let them know when she would be arriving.

She was in the process of dialing the airline, when the doorbell rang. Shannon grimaced with irritation at the interruption, cradled the phone and went to the door.

She flung it open and then gasped, completely unprepared for the shock of seeing Matt.

He wore a dark-brown, fleece-lined coat, and the color intensified the fathomless depths of his eyes. His face was somber, oddly white, and there was a diffidence about him.

"Hello, Shannon," he said quietly.

Color surged into and out of Shannon's face. She was alternately hot, then freezing cold. "How did you find me?" she choked after an endless time. "Did Mike tell you?"

Matt saw the spark of anger shoot through her gold-flecked eyes, and his heart sank. It had been a mistake to come, after all. In all these months she hadn't softened. She still didn't want to see him. "No," he fibbed, trying to absolve Mike of any blame. "He refused to tell me. I saw your address by mistake."

Suspicion lurked in her eyes. He could tell she didn't buy his lame story, and he was thankful when she didn't press it further. When she finally spoke again, it was in a dull, lusterless voice. "Why did you come?"

"I need to talk to you."

Shannon shook her head. "Whatever you have to say to me can be put into a letter. I don't want to talk to you." She stepped backward, as though she were about to close the door in his face.

Dark color surged to Matt's cheeks, and he reached out quickly and braced a hand against the door. "But would you read it?" he demanded. "A personal letter that hasn't been typed by Anne? Did you read the others I wrote, or did you throw them in the trash?"

Shannon lowered her eyes to his jacket. It seemed safer than meeting that burning, accusing gaze. "What if I did?" she said defensively. "On a personal level there's no need for us to communicate. There's nothing to say. We're business partners, nothing more."

"That's not true!" Matt said gruffly. He hesitated, then said humbly, "I've come a long way to see you, Shannon. I'd appreciate it if you'd let me talk to you for a few minutes."

Shannon sighed. She wasn't up to a confrontation with Matt, and she sure wasn't up to laying herself open to fresh pain. But the appeal in his voice undermined her reluctance. She just couldn't send him away as though he'd come no farther than from across the street.

She raised her head and met his eyes. Her gaze was hard, as unyielding as the Rocky Mountains themselves. "A few minutes, then," she said at last. "For whatever it's worth."

The time wasn't much, but at least it was something. Matt stepped inside the living room, and for a long moment they stood gazing at each other. An awkward tension vibrated between them, and nervously Shannon wet her lips and offered, "Coffee?"

Matt nodded. "That would be nice. It's a lot colder here than it is back home."

"I suppose so." She turned away hastily, as though she couldn't bear to look at him. She strode toward the kitchen and said over her shoulder, "Make yourself comfortable."

Matt shrugged out of his coat and hung it on a rack near the door. Then he strode over to the window and looked out. In the distance were the imposing, snow-covered mountains; below were white-frosted rooftops and lawns between wet streets. Snowflakes swirled against a slate-gray sky. Soon it would be dark.

The apartment surprised him as he turned back to survey it. French provincial, silk and gilt, formal and stifling, it didn't seem like Shannon to him. He said as much when she reentered the room bearing an elegant silver tray with two cups of steaming coffee.

For the first time Shannon behaved entirely natural. She gave a little laugh as she bent and placed the tray on the polished table in front of the sofa. "It's not me. I'm only subleasing from a friend." Matt sat down on the sofa and she handed him a cup, adding, "She's coming back in a few weeks and then I'll be moving into a place of my own. My furniture's been in storage since before I went to Texas."

"No wonder I couldn't find any listing of you in Denver if the place is leased under another name. Why didn't you just get an apartment of your own when you came back?"

Shannon shrugged. "I wasn't sure I'd be staying here, so it didn't seem worthwhile at the time." She picked up her cup and chose to sit in a chair instead of on the sofa beside him. Her cue was loud and clear. They would talk, but they would also maintain a distance.

"And now you've decided to stay here?" Matt persisted.

She nodded. "When all's said and done, it's still home, even without any family."

"But what about your in-laws?" Matt asked. "I also tried to find you through them, but the only Edwards I did manage to reach claimed they didn't know you."

"My father-in-law retired and they moved to Florida."

Matt smiled wistfully. "Well, at least that mystery's cleared up." He paused a moment, then added softly, "You must miss them a lot. I know you're very fond of them."

"Yes. I've decided to visit them over the holidays."

"That'll be nice," Matt said mildly. He leaned back against the cushioned sofa. "So...what have you been doing since you've returned here? Are you working?"

"I'm substitute teaching this year," Shannon replied. "It's part-time, but I think I've actually missed only three days of the term. How," she asked conversationally, "is June and her family?"

"They're fine," Matt answered. "June and Harry are busy squabbling about names for the baby, and Jason's busy changing his list for Santa on a daily basis."

So far Shannon had managed to avoid looking directly at Matt. Now she took another sip of her coffee and it scalded her throat. She set the cup down into the saucer with a clatter and said sharply, "You didn't come here for small talk." The tension inside of her was unbearable.

"No, I didn't," he agreed softly. He set his cup and saucer onto the table in front of him, got to his feet and strode to the coat rack by the door. He pulled a long manila envelope from his coat pocket, brought it to her and dropped it into her lap. "I brought you this."

Shannon looked at it with disinterest and tossed it to the lamp table on top of the unopened packet that had arrived in the mail. "What is it this time, Matt?" she asked sarcastically. "Are you wanting my approval for more paper cups for the office water cooler or my opinion on what kind of seeds to plant in the clubhouse flower boxes?"

Matt grinned. "At least I got your attention."

"Yes, but enough's enough, and I'm tired of the joke. The business is making a profit, which shows that you're doing a fine job by yourself. Just do whatever you want from now on and leave me out of it."

"That'll be a little difficult to do," Matt said.

"Why?"

"Open that envelope and you'll see."

She cut her eyes at him questioningly and Matt nodded. Shannon hesitated, then reluctantly reached for the envelope.

It was a legal-sized document and at first she merely skimmed it. All of a sudden she began to get the gist of it, and in shock, with her heart racing, she backed up and began to reread it more thoroughly.

When she'd finished, she dropped the papers to the carpet as though they'd burned her hands. She looked across at Matt, who was watching her somberly, and she saw that this was no joke.

"You can't do that," she said quietly.

"It's legal," Matt said. "And it's done."

"Then undo it."

He shook his head.

"This is crazy! You can't just sign over the whole company to me. Why would you even want to, anyway? You were always so worried I was trying to take it away from you."

Matt rose and came to her. He clasped her hands and drew her up beside him. "Why did you sign over the controlling two shares to me?" he asked huskily.

"Because..." The warm light from his eyes that was suddenly flooding through her was disconcerting. "Because I wanted you to have them," she said simply.

"And *why* did you want me to have them?" he asked with soft insistence.

Shannon tried to pull her hands free from his, but Matt's fingers only tightened around hers. She could no longer meet that melting gaze, so she lowered her eyes to his lips. Which was a terrible mistake, because they were so devastatingly appealing.

"Does it matter?" she asked irritably.

"Yes. Quite a lot."

She shrugged. "It seemed the sensible thing to do since I was leaving town."

"I see." His voice was low and sensual. "And why did you leave like you did? With no word of goodbye and then hiding from me?"

This time Shannon did manage to wrench free. She turned away from him and said in a muffled voice, "Stop playing games with me! You know very well why I left. It was what you wanted."

"No." His hand came down on her shoulder. "It was only what I *said* I wanted, and I have paid dearly for it every single day since you left." His arms encircled her waist, and when she tried to step away, he pulled her tighter against him and murmured brokenly, "I love you, Shannon. Please don't pull away from me anymore."

Shannon went very still, and then slowly she turned within the circle of his arms. Matt's face was very pale and his lips were not quite steady. She had never seen him like this, truly vulnerable just as she was, and it shocked her. Without knowing that she had already capitulated, she raised a trembling finger to his lips and gazed at him through sudden tears.

"Matt?" she said wonderingly.

He tried to smile at her, but failed dismally. Then, as though he couldn't bear to look at her anymore, he pulled her closer and buried his face in her hair.

"I was a fool," he told her huskily. "I was so hurt when you wouldn't marry me that on that last night I just lashed back at you. Even though we'd just made love and you'd proved how much you wanted me, I couldn't really trust that you'd changed your mind and wanted me enough to marry me for myself. I'm so very, very sorry about that, Shannon. I was horrible to you that night. It's just that I'd had so many days of being furious with you, of comparing you to Vicky. When you said you did want to marry me, I was convinced it was merely a ploy to wrest the whole company away from me. It was the crazy reasoning of a man in love and suffering, a man who wants love in return and fears he can never really have it."

"But I told you I loved you," Shannon whispered.

"I know, but I couldn't trust in it. Loving me hadn't been enough for you to accept when I first asked you to marry me."

Shannon lovingly stroked his cheek. "Only because *my* reasoning was insane that time," she said with a tiny laugh. "Because I was so afraid to love and lose again."

Matt drew back so he could gaze at her. "And now?"

She inhaled deeply. "Oh, Matt, these past few months without you have been dreadful. I've already discovered how awful it is to lose you. I never want to have to do that again as long as we both live."

"That's all any of us can ask for, darling," Matt said thickly. "Brad was a lucky man because he had your love that long. If you'll give me the same, I swear you'll never be sorry. So I'm asking you again, Shannon . . . will you marry me?"

Shannon gave him a tremulous smile, and then a twinkle entered her eyes. "Only if you'll take back the company."

"Uh-uh." Matt shook his head. "I'll make a deal with you, though."

"What's that?" she asked dreamily.

"We'll have Mike draw up some new papers making the split fifty-fifty. How's that? That way we'll be full and equal partners."

"I'd rather you took the whole—"

"Nope," Matt said decisively. "It's either equal shares or the marriage deal is off."

She gazed at him with a pretense of consternation. "Well, if you're going to make that a condition, I suppose I'll have to agree, because I want very much to be your wife. But you'll have to run it by yourself. I'll be too busy raising our children to have much time to spare on it."

Matt pulled her closer until their lips were almost touching. Shannon's heart raced at the tender expression on his face.

"We're going to share everything, Shannon," he stated seriously. "The business, our family, the good things and the bad things. And I'll never stop needing you beside me as long as there's a breath remaining in my body."

She was shaken by all the love she saw in his eyes, and her voice was unsteady as she whispered, "I love you, Matt. With all my heart."

Their kiss held the intensity of two people who are desperately starved for each other. It was by turns hard and demanding, gentle and sweet. The mountains outside the window became lost beneath the curtain of darkness, and as snowflakes swirled against the windowpanes, the two people inside the room were warm and secure in a love they would gladly share for a lifetime.

Silhouette Special Edition

COMING NEXT MONTH

THE ARISTOCRAT—Catherine Coulter
An arranged marriage in this day and age? There was no way Lord Brant Asher was going to marry Daphne, the ugly duckling. Until he found that the ugly duckling had grown into a beautiful swan.

A SLICE OF HEAVEN—Carole McElhaney
Lamont Cosmetics *had* to have Dr. Alex Harrison launch their new line. So Cass Mulcahy went to Texas to reason with him—and instead found herself losing all reason.

LINDSEY'S RAINBOW—Curtiss Ann Matlock
The Ingraham heiress suddenly found herself fighting for control of the family business. How dared Michael Garrity try to take it from her! Then Lindsey and Michael came face-to-face—and heart to heart.

FOREVER AND A DAY—Pamela Wallace
Stephen Kramer didn't want novelist Marina Turner to write her own screenplay. But she refused to let him turn her novel into a trashy teen flick. How could she prove to him that a collaboration would be profitable to both of them?

RETURN TO SUMMER—Barbara Faith
Fifteen years earlier Sarah had fled Mexico in shame. Now she was back, and history threatened to repeat itself. Was their future doomed by the past, or would it survive the dark secret she kept hidden from the man she loved?

YESTERDAY'S TOMORROW—Maggi Charles
Just one ride aboard *Alligator Annie* convinced Susan Bannister to stay in the alligator-infested backwater that was Florida State Park. She needed a distraction—and *Annie*'s silver-eyed captain filled the bill.

AVAILABLE NOW:

SOMETHING ABOUT SUMMER
Linda Shaw

EQUAL SHARES
Sondra Stanford

ALMOST FOREVER
Linda Howard

MATCHED PAIR
Carole Halston

SILVER THAW
Natalie Bishop

EMERALD LOVE, SAPPHIRE DREAMS
Monica Barrie

Take 4 Silhouette
Special Edition novels
FREE

and preview future books in your home for 15 days!

When you take advantage of this offer, you get 4 Silhouette Special Edition® novels FREE and without obligation. Then you'll also have the opportunity to preview 6 brand-new books —delivered right to your door for a FREE 15-day examination period—as soon as they are published.

When you decide to keep them, you pay just $1.95 each ($2.50 each in Canada) *with no shipping, handling, or other charges of any kind!*

Romance *is* alive, well and flourishing in the moving love stories of Silhouette Special Edition novels. They'll awaken your desires, enliven your senses, and leave you tingling all over with excitement . . . and the first 4 novels are yours to keep. You can cancel at any time.

As an added bonus, you'll also receive a FREE subscription to the Silhouette Books Newsletter as long as you remain a member. Each issue is filled with news on upcoming books, interviews with your favorite authors, even their favorite recipes.

To get your 4 FREE books, fill out and mail the coupon today!

Silhouette Special Edition®

Silhouette Books, 120 Brighton Rd., P.O. Box 5084, Clifton, NJ 07015-5084

Silhouette Romance

**Enchanting love stories
that warm the hearts
of women everywhere.**

SIL-ROM-1RR

Silhouette Romance

FOUR UNIQUE SERIES
FOR EVERY WOMAN YOU ARE . . .

Silhouette Romance

Heartwarming romances that will make you
laugh and cry as they bring you all the wonder
and magic of falling in love.

6 titles
per month

Silhouette Special Edition

Expanded romances written with emotion and
heightened romantic tension to ensure
powerful stories. A rare blend of passion and
dramatic realism.

6 titles
per month

Silhouette Desire

Believable, sensuous, compelling—and
above all, romantic—these stories deliver
the promise of love, the guarantee
of satisfaction.

6 titles
per month

Silhouette Intimate Moments

Love stories that entice; longer, more
sensuous romances filled with adventure,
suspense, glamour and melodrama.

4 titles
per month

SIL-GEN-1RR